Totally Spies!™

PAPERCUTZ™

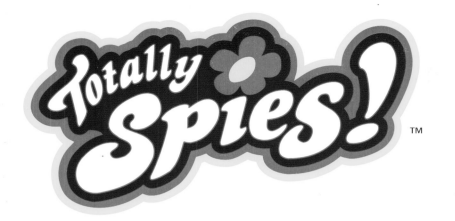

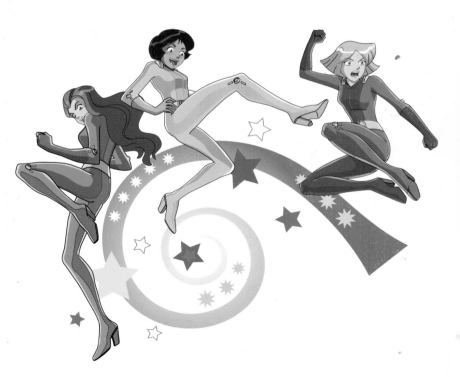

Totally Spies!™

Graphic Novels available from Papercutz
Graphic Novel #1 "The O.P."
Graphic Novel #2 "I Hate the 80s"
Graphic Novel #3 "Evil Jerry"
Graphic Novel #4 "Spies in Space"
Coming in July: Graphic Novel #5 "Mani-Maniac"
$7.95 each in paperback
$12.95 each in hardcover
Please add $3.00 for postage and handling for the first book, add $1.00 for each additional book.
Send for our catalog:
Papercutz
40 Exchange Place, Suite 1308
New York, NY 10005
www.papercutz.com
Please make check payable to NBM Publishing

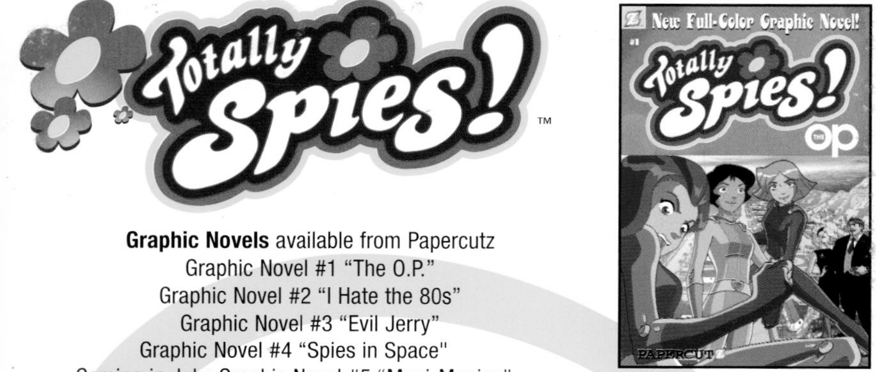
New Full-Color Graphic Novel!
#1
Totally Spies!
The OP
PAPERCUTZ

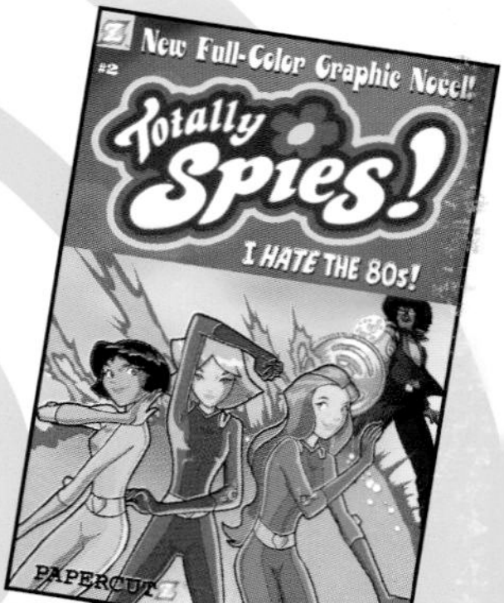
New Full-Color Graphic Novel!
#2
Totally Spies!
I HATE THE 80s!
PAPERCUTZ

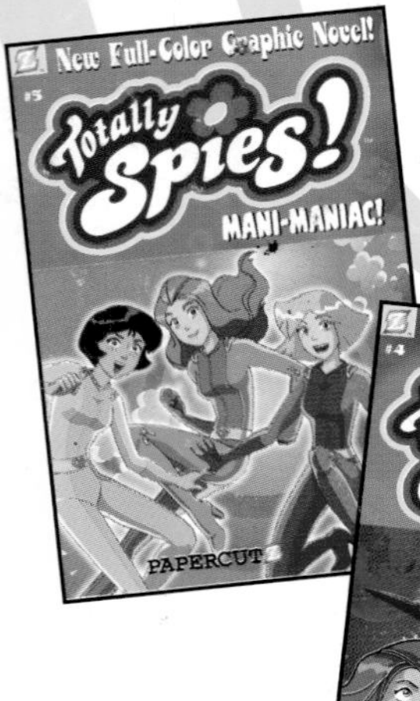
New Full-Color Graphic Novel!
#5
Totally Spies!
MANI-MANIAC!
PAPERCUTZ

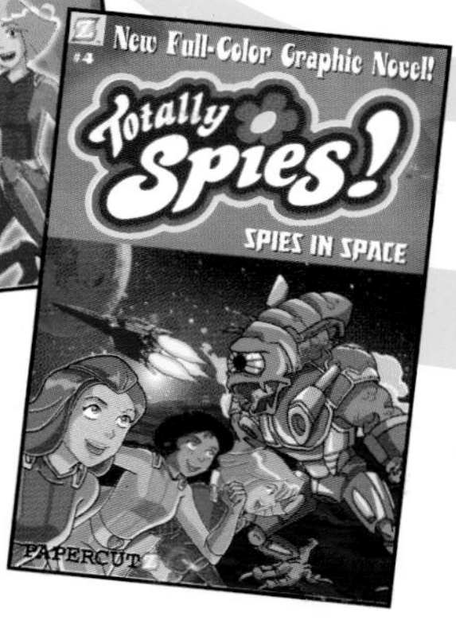
New Full-Color Graphic Novel!
#4
Totally Spies!
SPIES IN SPACE
PAPERCUTZ

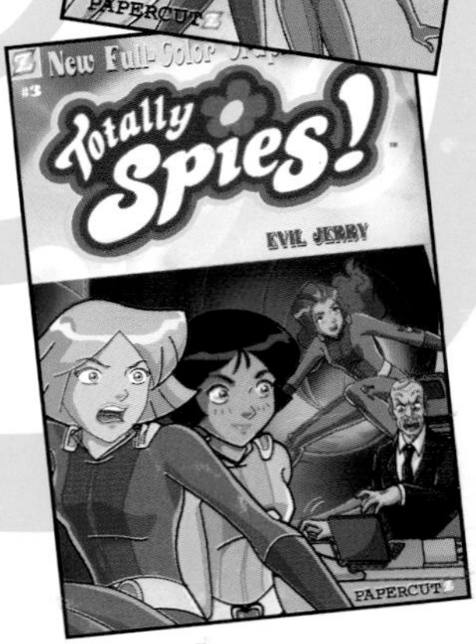
#3
Totally Spies!
EVIL JERRY
PAPERCUTZ

#4

Spies In Space and Spy Soccer

PAPERCUTZ ™

Spies In Space
Spy Soccer
MARK LERER — Letterer
JIM SALICRUP
Editor-in-Chief

ISBN-10: 1-59707-055-6 paperback edition
ISBN-13: 978-1-59707-055-3 paperback edition
ISBN-10: 1-59707-056-4 hardcover edition
ISBN-13: 978-1-59707-056-0 hardcover edition

Printed in China.

Distributed by Holtzbrinck Publishers

10 9 8 7 6 5 4 3 2 1

JUN 2007

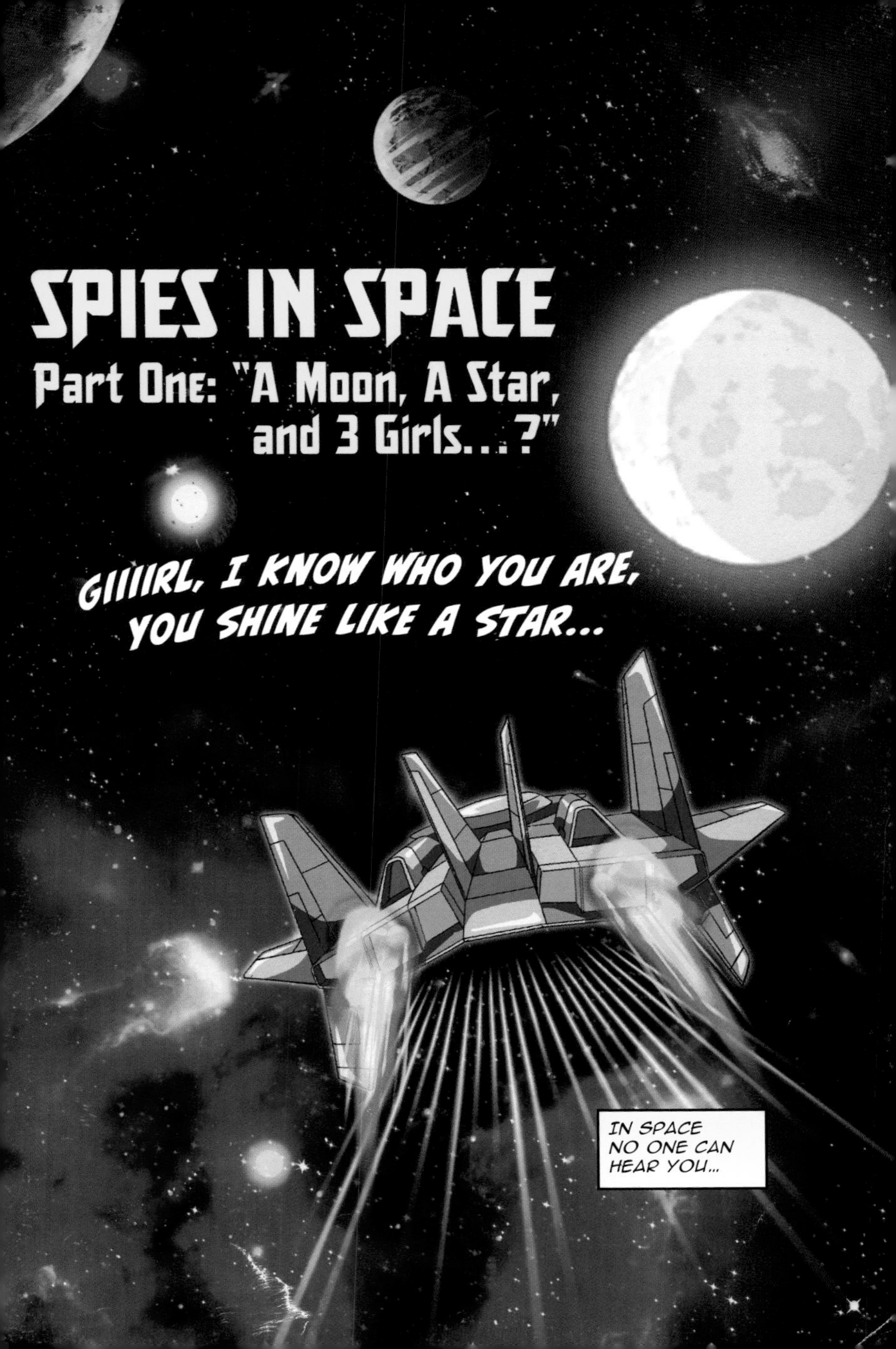
SPIES IN SPACE
Part One: "A Moon, A Star, and 3 Girls...?"
GIIIIRL, I KNOW WHO YOU ARE, YOU SHINE LIKE A STAR...
IN SPACE NO ONE CAN HEAR YOU...

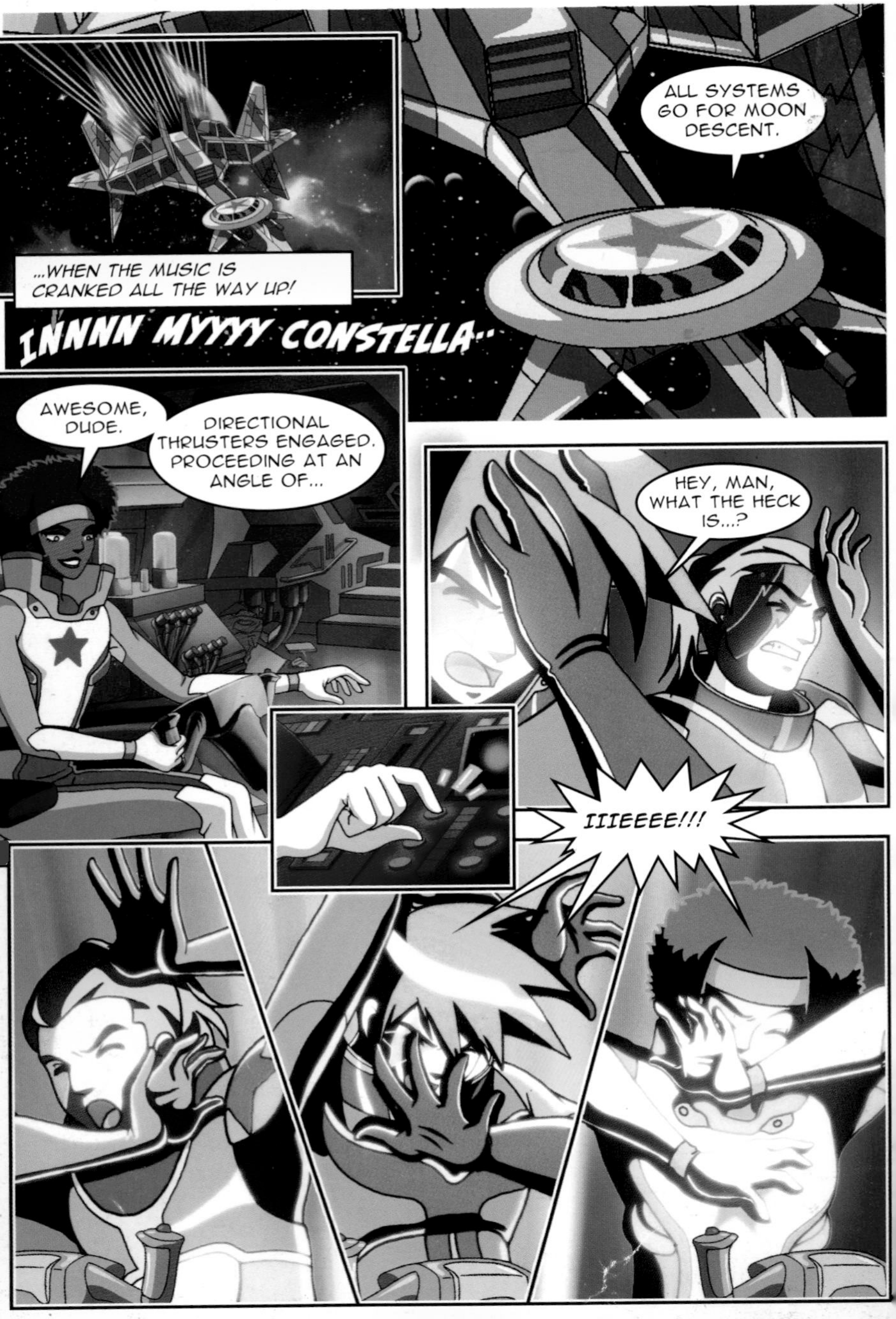
...WHEN THE MUSIC IS CRANKED ALL THE WAY UP!
INNNN MYYYY CONSTELLA..
ALL SYSTEMS GO FOR MOON DESCENT.
AWESOME, DUDE.
DIRECTIONAL THRUSTERS ENGAGED. PROCEEDING AT AN ANGLE OF...
HEY, MAN, WHAT THE HECK IS...?
IIIEEEEE!!!

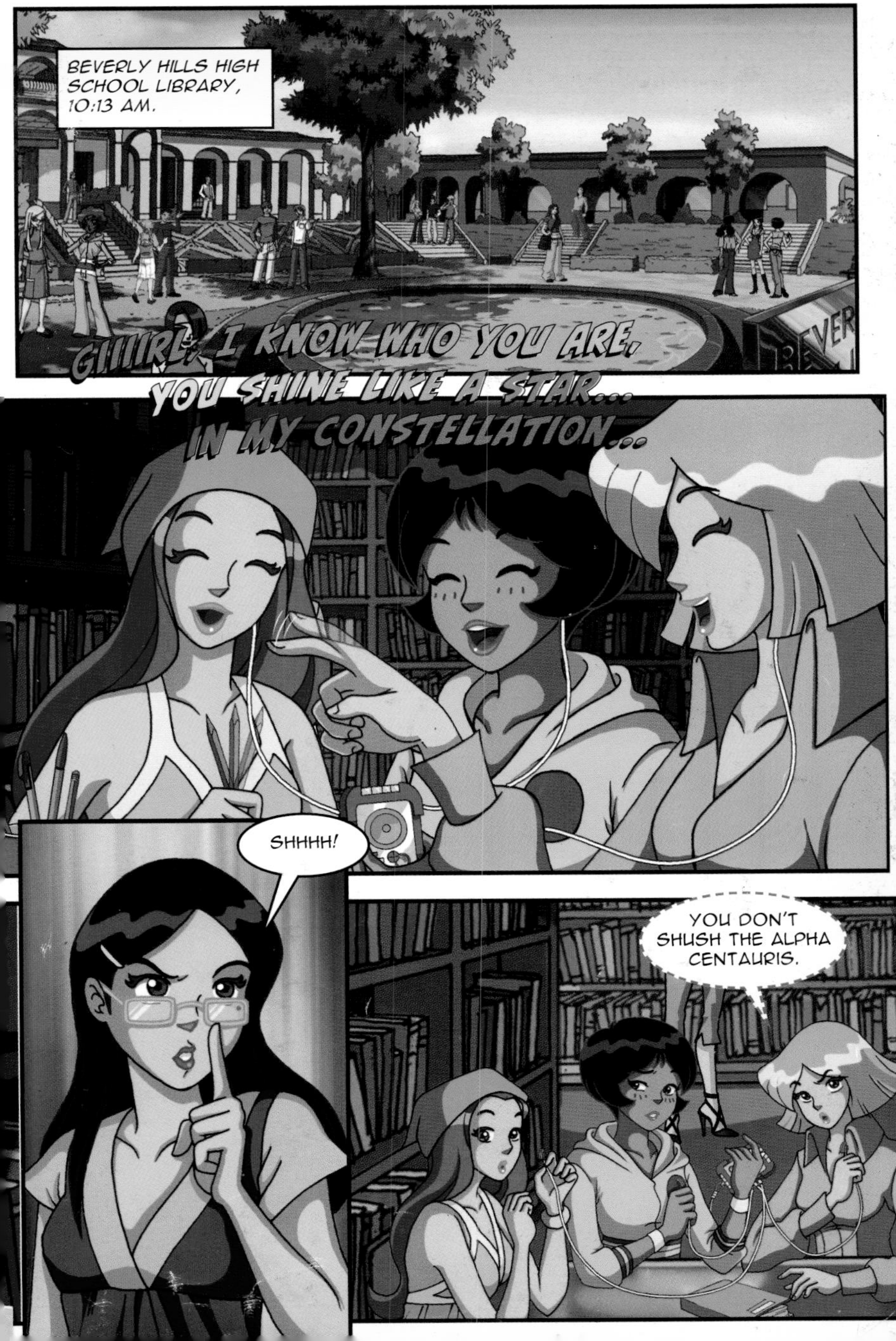
BEVERLY HILLS HIGH SCHOOL LIBRARY, 10:13 AM.
GIIIIRL, I KNOW WHO YOU ARE, YOU SHINE LIKE A STAR... IN MY CONSTELLATION...
SHHHH!
YOU DON'T SHUSH THE ALPHA CENTAURIS.

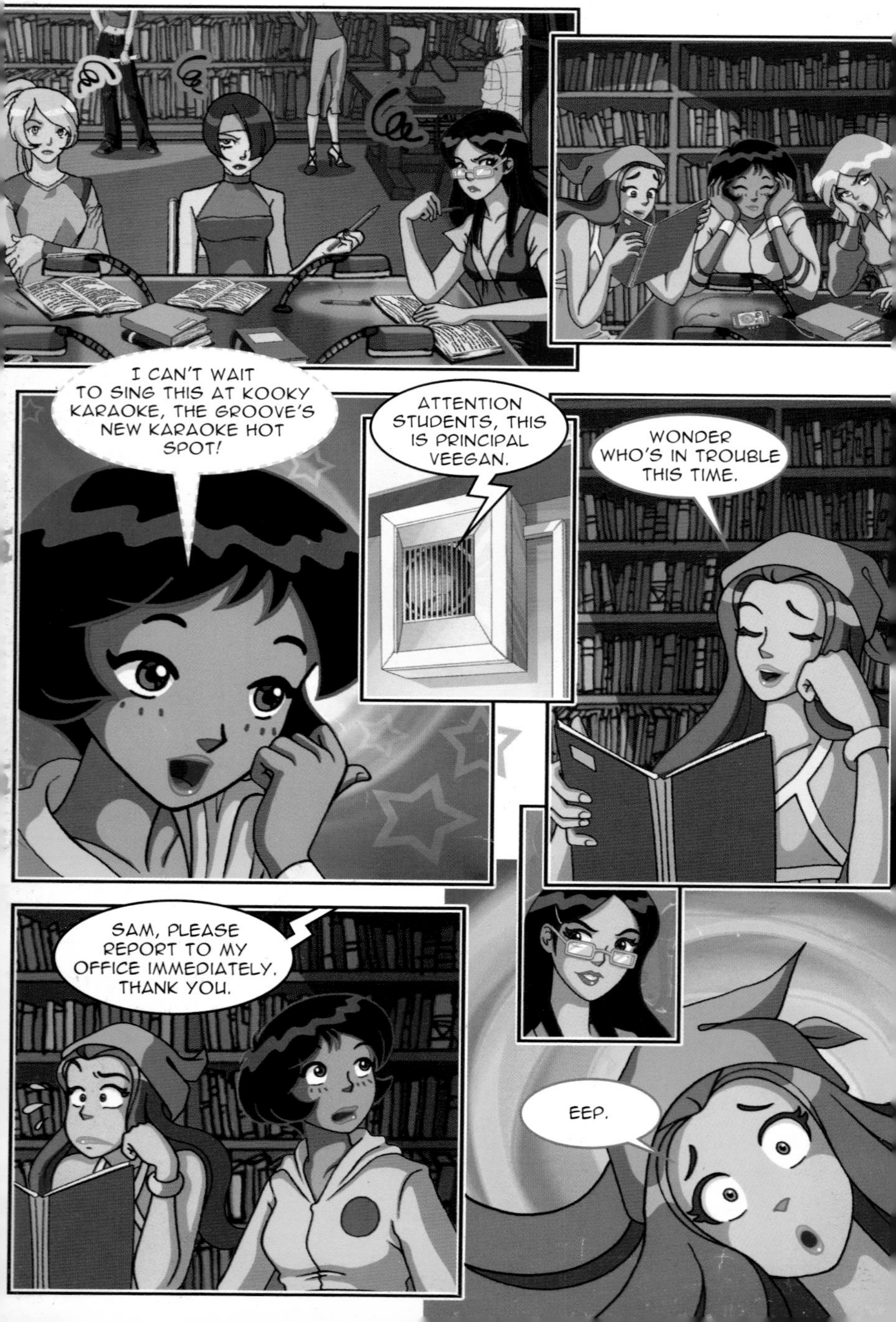
I CAN'T WAIT TO SING THIS AT KOOKY KARAOKE, THE GROOVE'S NEW KARAOKE HOT SPOT!
ATTENTION STUDENTS, THIS IS PRINCIPAL VEEGAN.
WONDER WHO'S IN TROUBLE THIS TIME.
SAM, PLEASE REPORT TO MY OFFICE IMMEDIATELY. THANK YOU.
EEP.

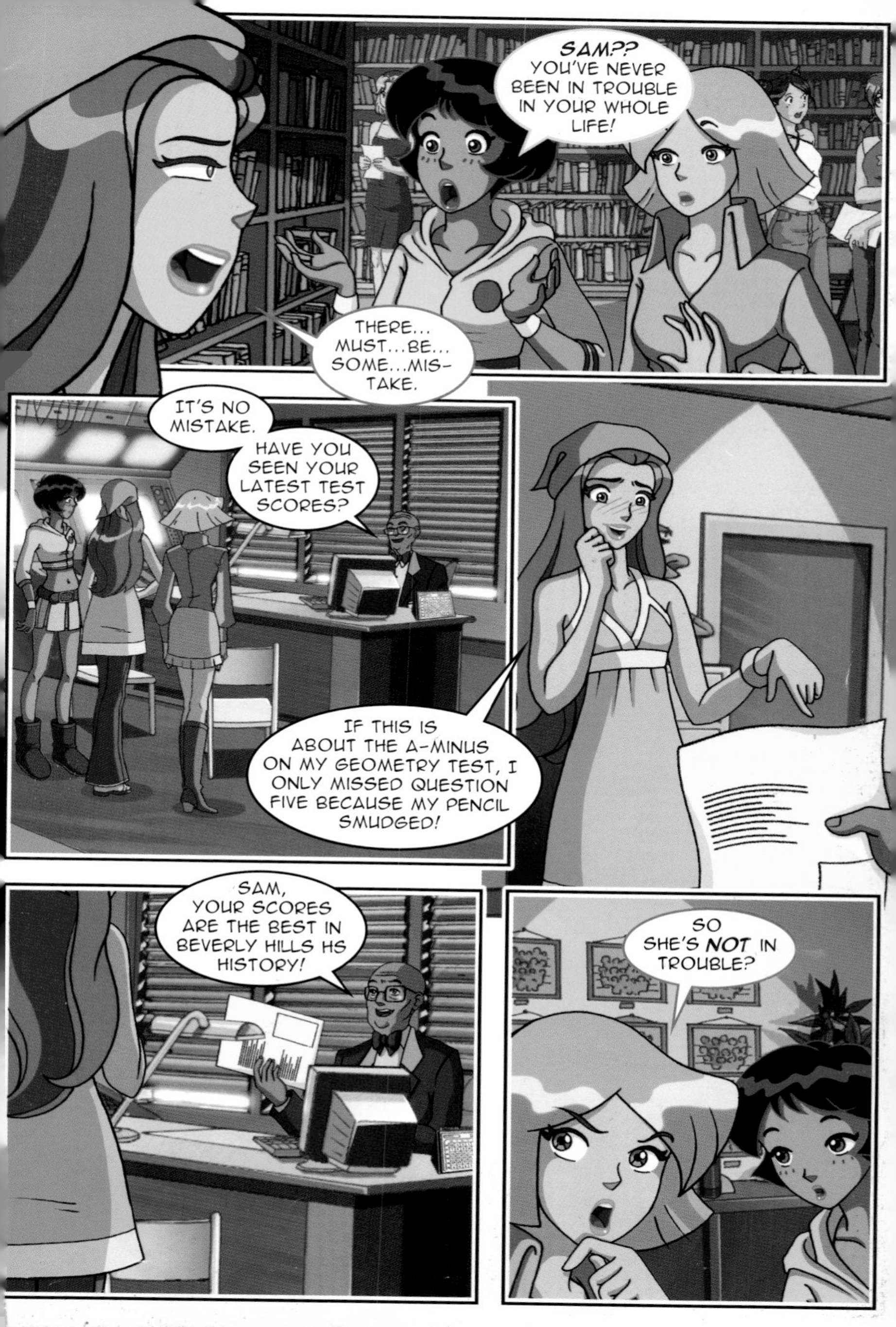
SAM?? YOU'VE NEVER BEEN IN TROUBLE IN YOUR WHOLE LIFE!
THERE... MUST... BE... SOME...MIS-TAKE.
IT'S NO MISTAKE.
HAVE YOU SEEN YOUR LATEST TEST SCORES?
IF THIS IS ABOUT THE A-MINUS ON MY GEOMETRY TEST, I ONLY MISSED QUESTION FIVE BECAUSE MY PENCIL SMUDGED!
SAM, YOUR SCORES ARE THE BEST IN BEVERLY HILLS HS HISTORY!
SO SHE'S NOT IN TROUBLE?

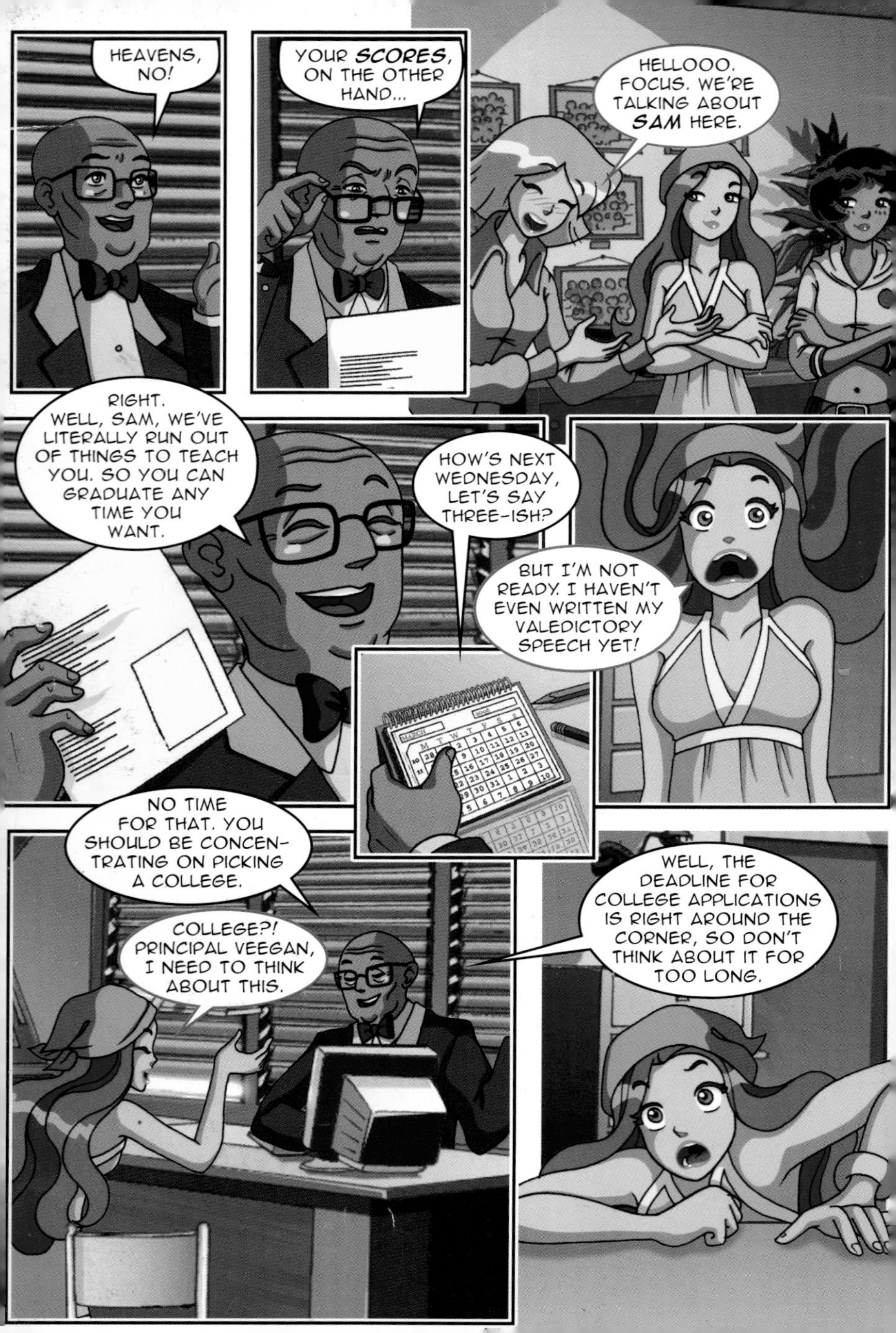
HEAVENS, NO!
YOUR SCORES, ON THE OTHER HAND...
HELLOOO. FOCUS. WE'RE TALKING ABOUT SAM HERE.
RIGHT. WELL, SAM, WE'VE LITERALLY RUN OUT OF THINGS TO TEACH YOU. SO YOU CAN GRADUATE ANY TIME YOU WANT.
HOW'S NEXT WEDNESDAY, LET'S SAY THREE-ISH?
BUT I'M NOT READY. I HAVEN'T EVEN WRITTEN MY VALEDICTORY SPEECH YET!
NO TIME FOR THAT. YOU SHOULD BE CONCEN-TRATING ON PICKING A COLLEGE.
COLLEGE?! PRINCIPAL VEEGAN, I NEED TO THINK ABOUT THIS.
WELL, THE DEADLINE FOR COLLEGE APPLICATIONS IS RIGHT AROUND THE CORNER, SO DON'T THINK ABOUT IT FOR TOO LONG.

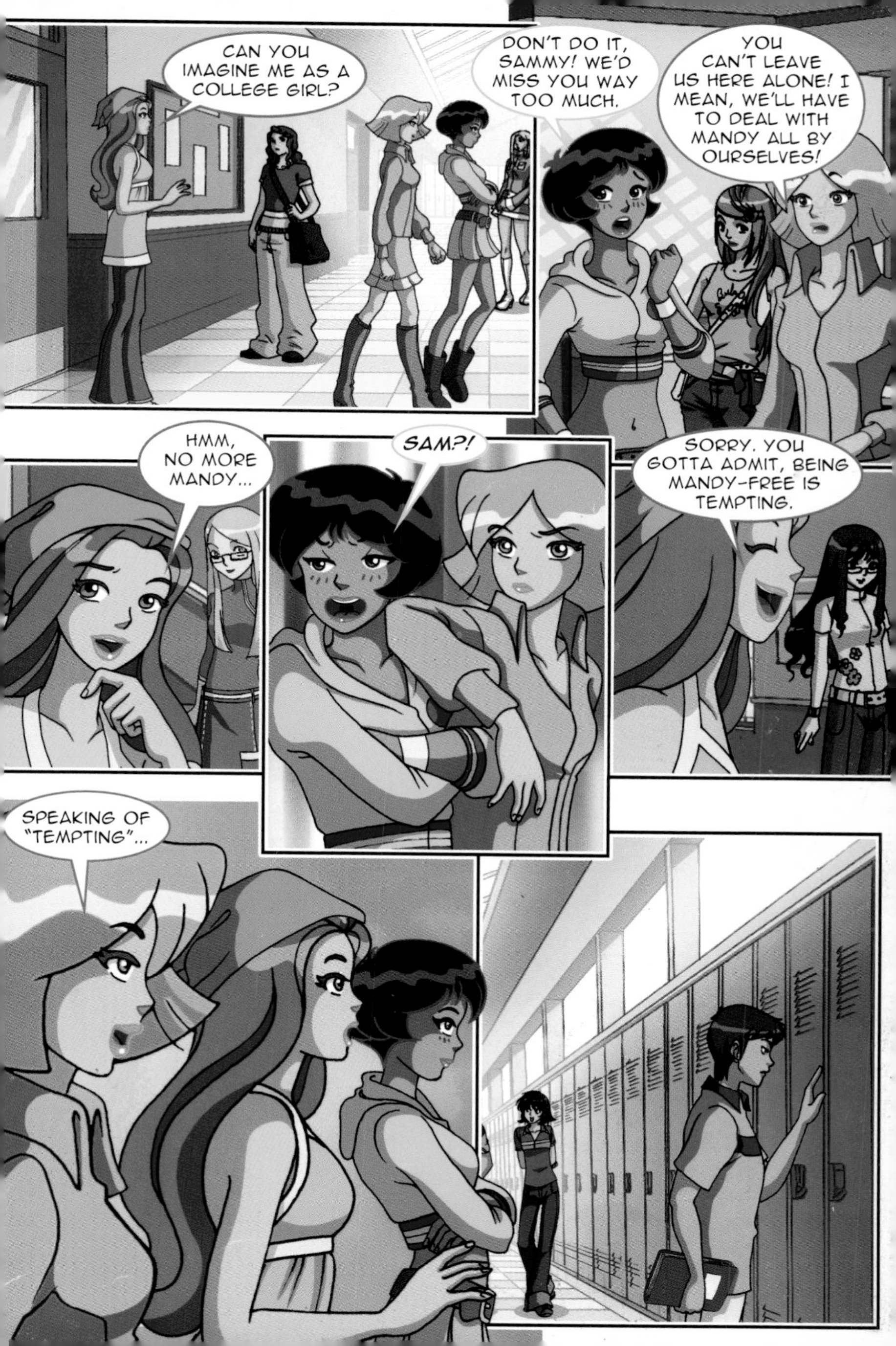
CAN YOU IMAGINE ME AS A COLLEGE GIRL?
DON'T DO IT, SAMMY! WE'D MISS YOU WAY TOO MUCH.
YOU CAN'T LEAVE US HERE ALONE! I MEAN, WE'LL HAVE TO DEAL WITH MANDY ALL BY OURSELVES!
HMM, NO MORE MANDY...
SAM?!
SORRY. YOU GOTTA ADMIT, BEING MANDY-FREE IS TEMPTING.
SPEAKING OF "TEMPTING"...

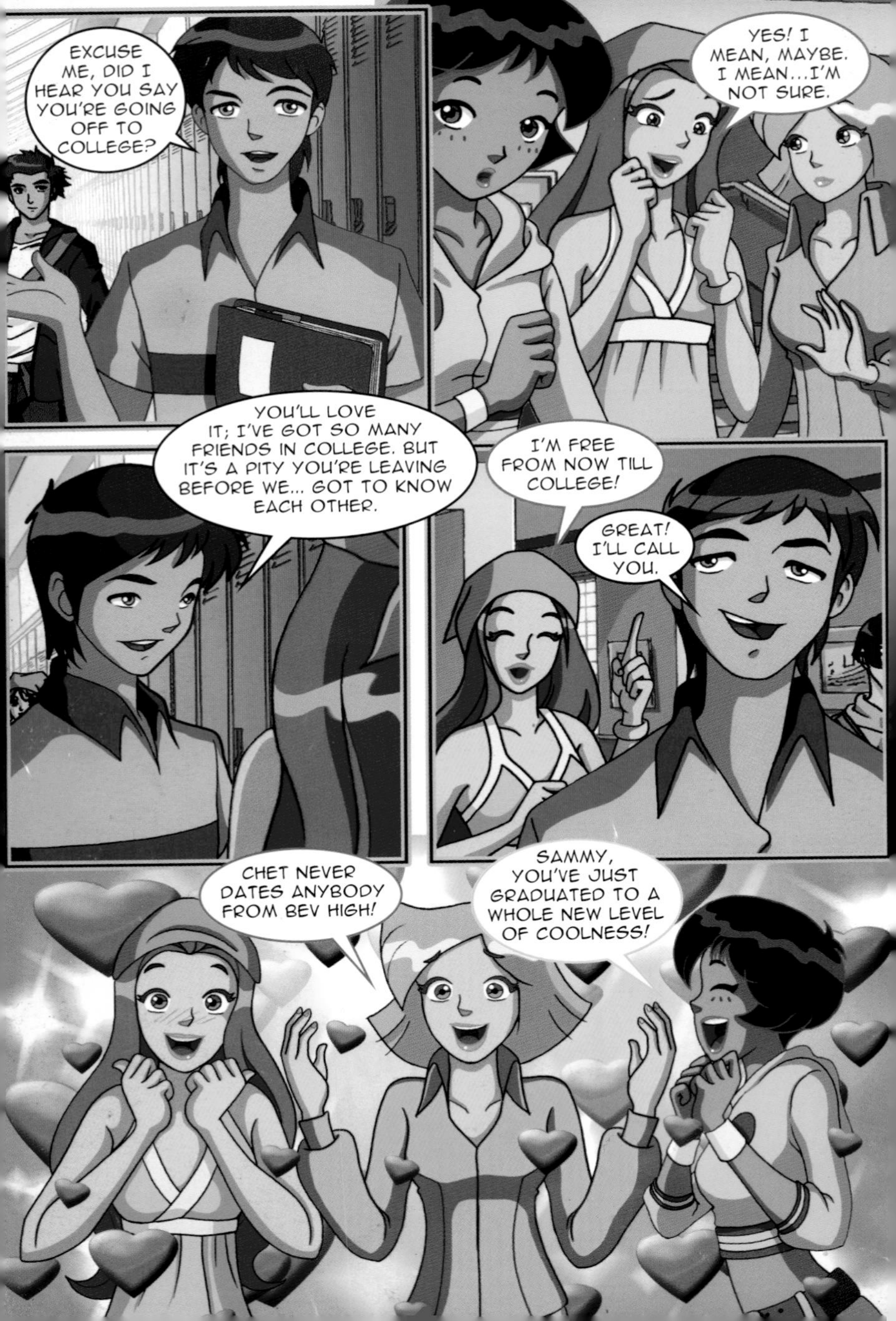
EXCUSE ME, DID I HEAR YOU SAY YOU'RE GOING OFF TO COLLEGE?
YES! I MEAN, MAYBE. I MEAN...I'M NOT SURE.
YOU'LL LOVE IT; I'VE GOT SO MANY FRIENDS IN COLLEGE. BUT IT'S A PITY YOU'RE LEAVING BEFORE WE... GOT TO KNOW EACH OTHER.
I'M FREE FROM NOW TILL COLLEGE!
GREAT! I'LL CALL YOU.
CHET NEVER DATES ANYBODY FROM BEV HIGH!
SAMMY, YOU'VE JUST GRADUATED TO A WHOLE NEW LEVEL OF COOLNESS!

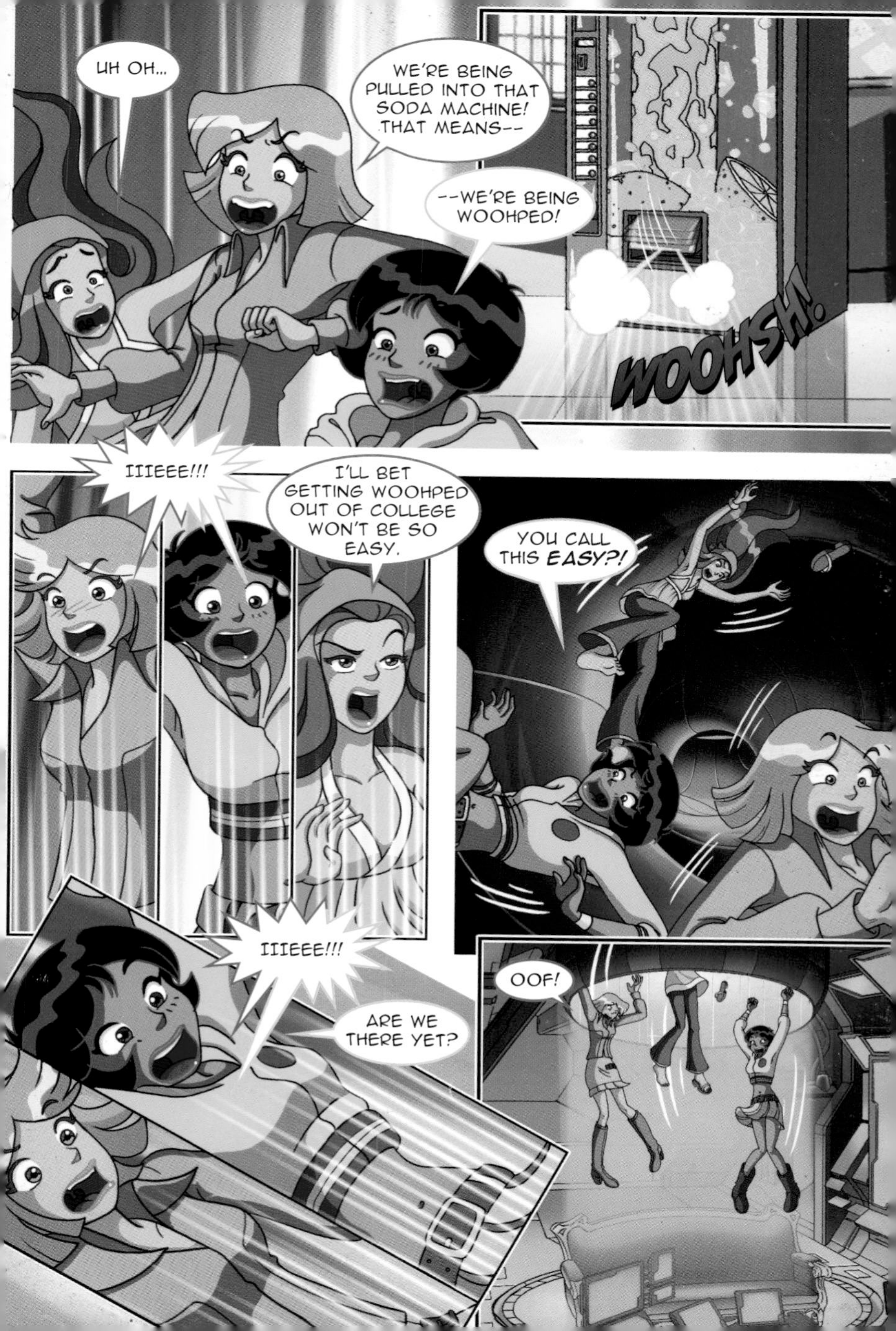
UH OH...
WE'RE BEING PULLED INTO THAT SODA MACHINE! THAT MEANS--
--WE'RE BEING WOOHPED!
WOOHSH!
IIIEEE!!!
I'LL BET GETTING WOOHPED OUT OF COLLEGE WON'T BE SO EASY.
YOU CALL THIS EASY?!
IIIEEE!!!
ARE WE THERE YET?
OOF!

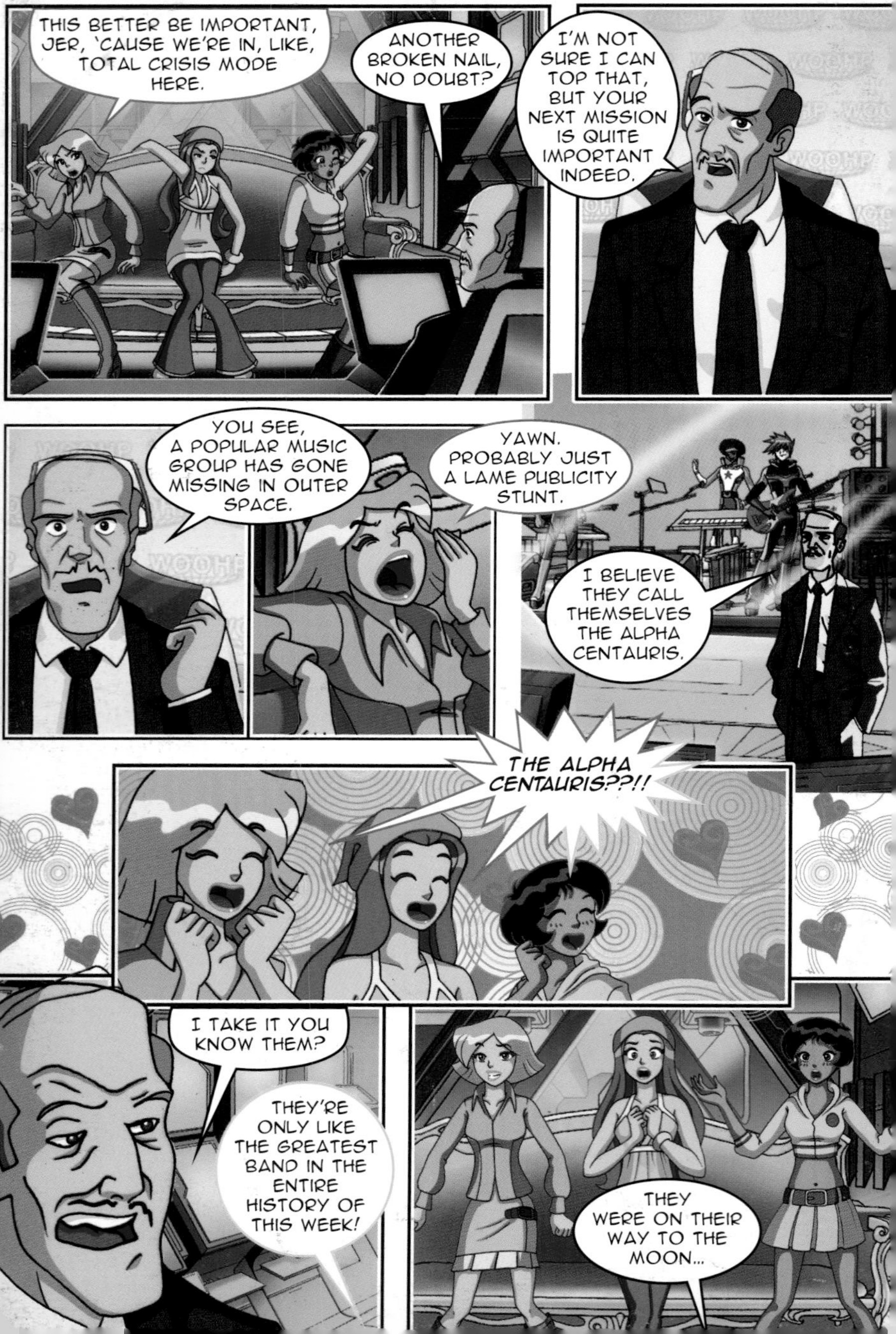

THIS BETTER BE IMPORTANT, JER, 'CAUSE WE'RE IN, LIKE, TOTAL CRISIS MODE HERE.
ANOTHER BROKEN NAIL, NO DOUBT?
I'M NOT SURE I CAN TOP THAT, BUT YOUR NEXT MISSION IS QUITE IMPORTANT INDEED.
YOU SEE, A POPULAR MUSIC GROUP HAS GONE MISSING IN OUTER SPACE.
YAWN. PROBABLY JUST A LAME PUBLICITY STUNT.
I BELIEVE THEY CALL THEMSELVES THE ALPHA CENTAURIS.
THE ALPHA CENTAURIS??!!
I TAKE IT YOU KNOW THEM?
THEY'RE ONLY LIKE THE GREATEST BAND IN THE ENTIRE HISTORY OF THIS WEEK!
THEY WERE ON THEIR WAY TO THE MOON...

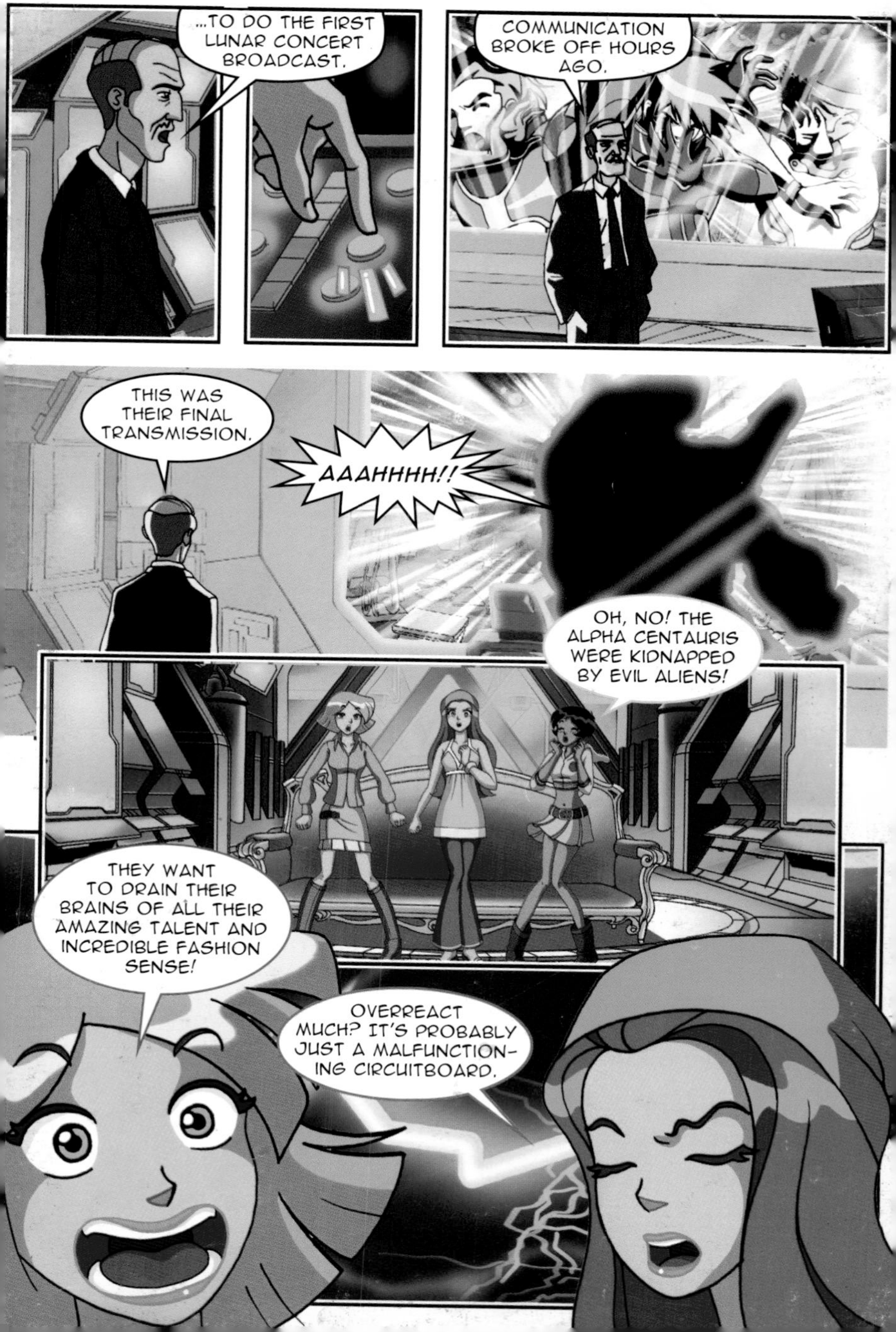

...TO DO THE FIRST LUNAR CONCERT BROADCAST.
COMMUNICATION BROKE OFF HOURS AGO.
THIS WAS THEIR FINAL TRANSMISSION.
AAAHHHH!!
OH, NO! THE ALPHA CENTAURIS WERE KIDNAPPED BY EVIL ALIENS!
THEY WANT TO DRAIN THEIR BRAINS OF ALL THEIR AMAZING TALENT AND INCREDIBLE FASHION SENSE!
OVERREACT MUCH? IT'S PROBABLY JUST A MALFUNCTION-ING CIRCUITBOARD.

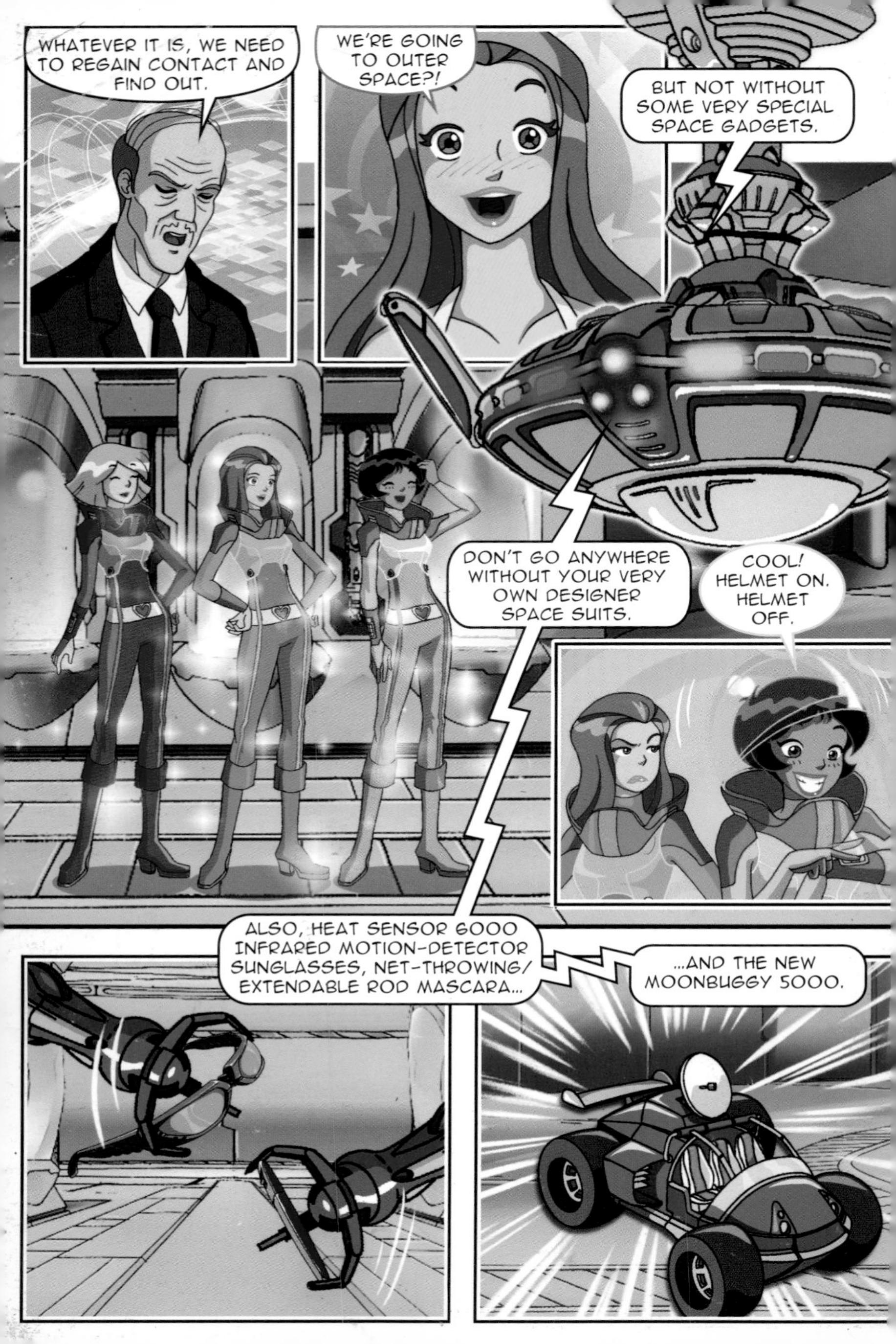
WHATEVER IT IS, WE NEED TO REGAIN CONTACT AND FIND OUT.
WE'RE GOING TO OUTER SPACE?!
BUT NOT WITHOUT SOME VERY SPECIAL SPACE GADGETS.
DON'T GO ANYWHERE WITHOUT YOUR VERY OWN DESIGNER SPACE SUITS.
COOL! HELMET ON. HELMET OFF.
ALSO, HEAT SENSOR 6000 INFRARED MOTION-DETECTOR SUNGLASSES, NET-THROWING/ EXTENDABLE ROD MASCARA...
...AND THE NEW MOONBUGGY 5000.

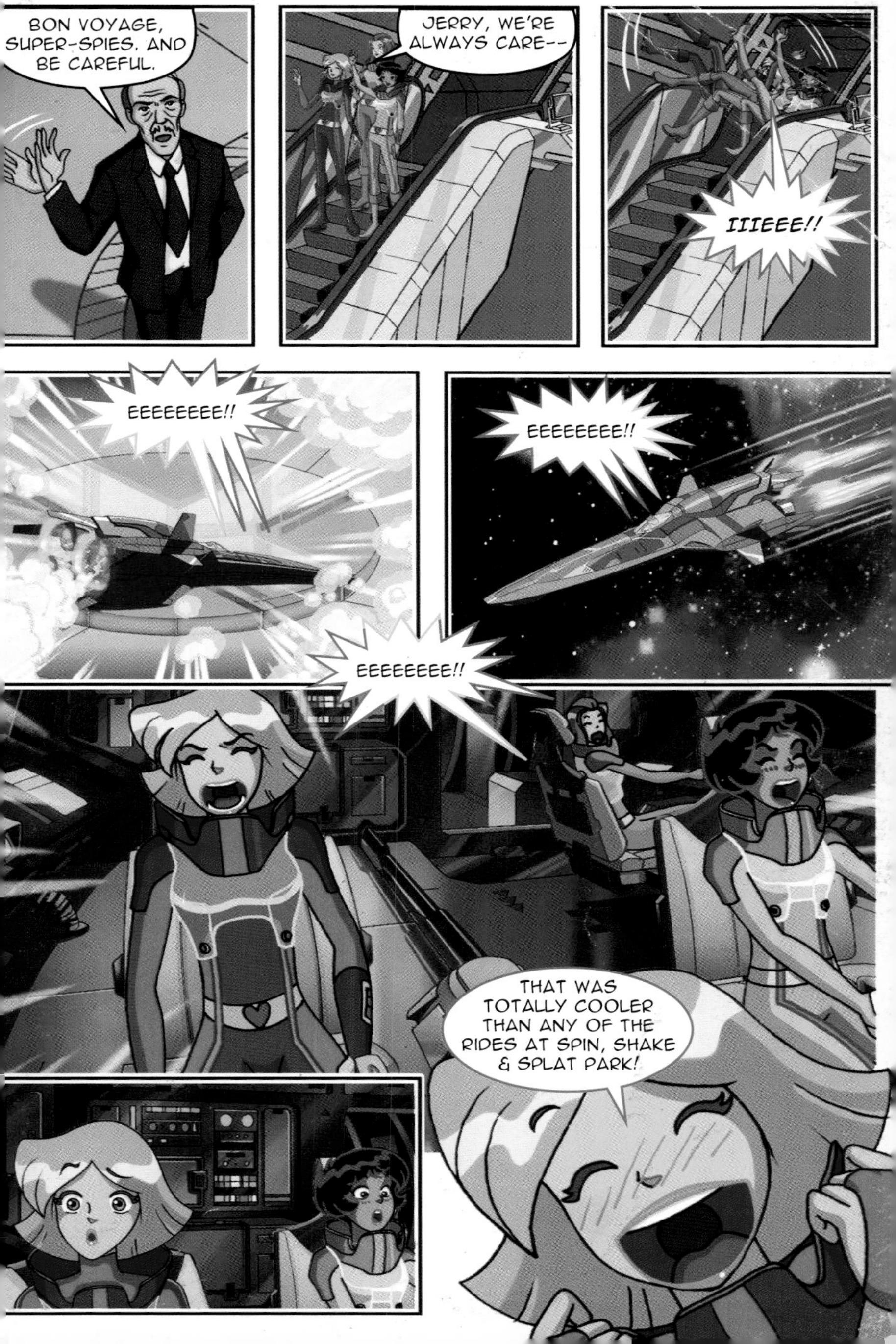
BON VOYAGE, SUPER-SPIES. AND BE CAREFUL.
JERRY, WE'RE ALWAYS CARE--
IIIEEE!!
EEEEEEEE!!
EEEEEEEE!!
EEEEEEEE!!
THAT WAS TOTALLY COOLER THAN ANY OF THE RIDES AT SPIN, SHAKE & SPLAT PARK!

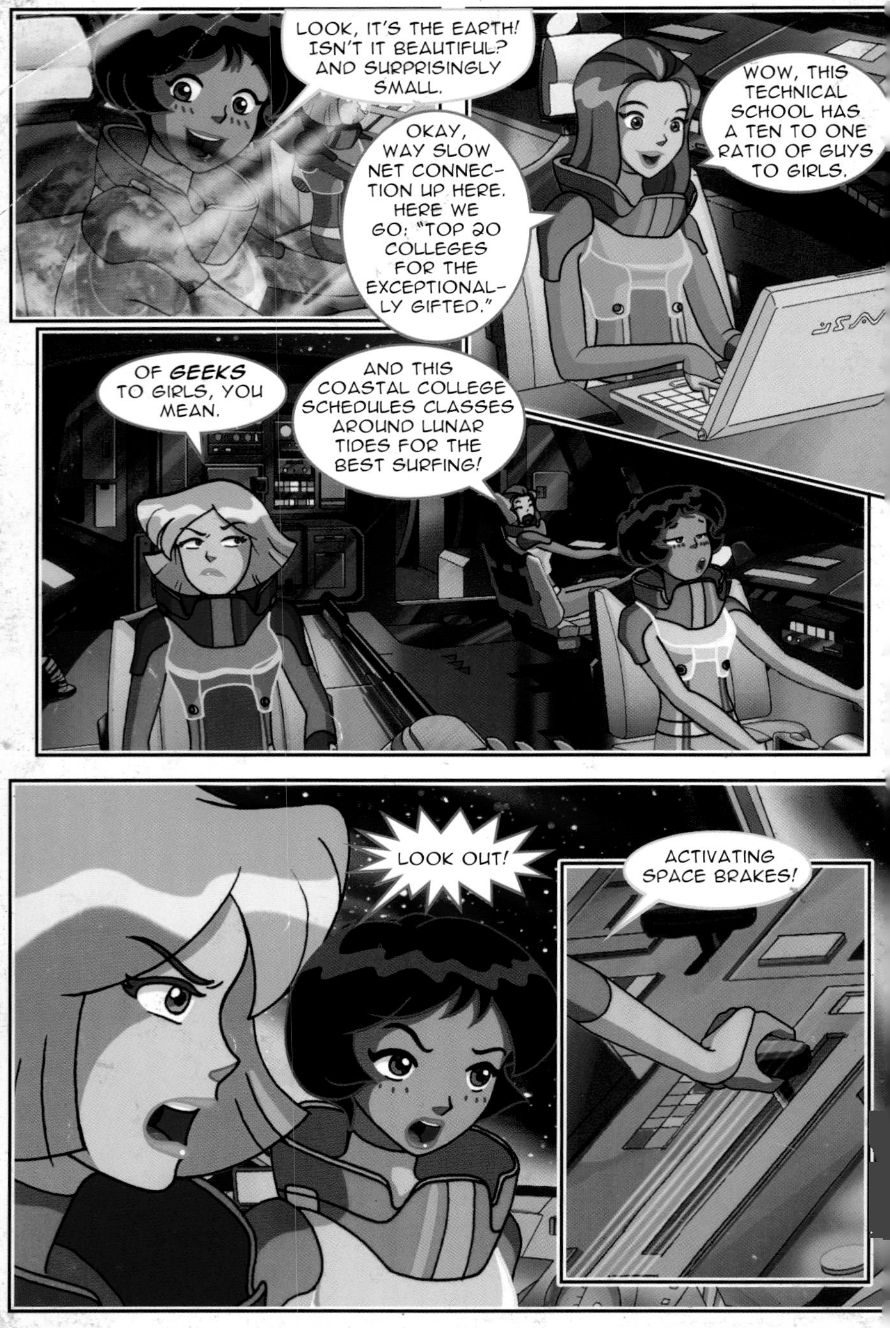
LOOK, IT'S THE EARTH! ISN'T IT BEAUTIFUL? AND SURPRISINGLY SMALL.
WOW, THIS TECHNICAL SCHOOL HAS A TEN TO ONE RATIO OF GUYS TO GIRLS.
OKAY, WAY SLOW NET CONNECTION UP HERE. HERE WE GO: "TOP 20 COLLEGES FOR THE EXCEPTIONALLY GIFTED."
OF **GEEKS** TO GIRLS, YOU MEAN.
AND THIS COASTAL COLLEGE SCHEDULES CLASSES AROUND LUNAR TIDES FOR THE BEST SURFING!
LOOK OUT!
ACTIVATING SPACE BRAKES!

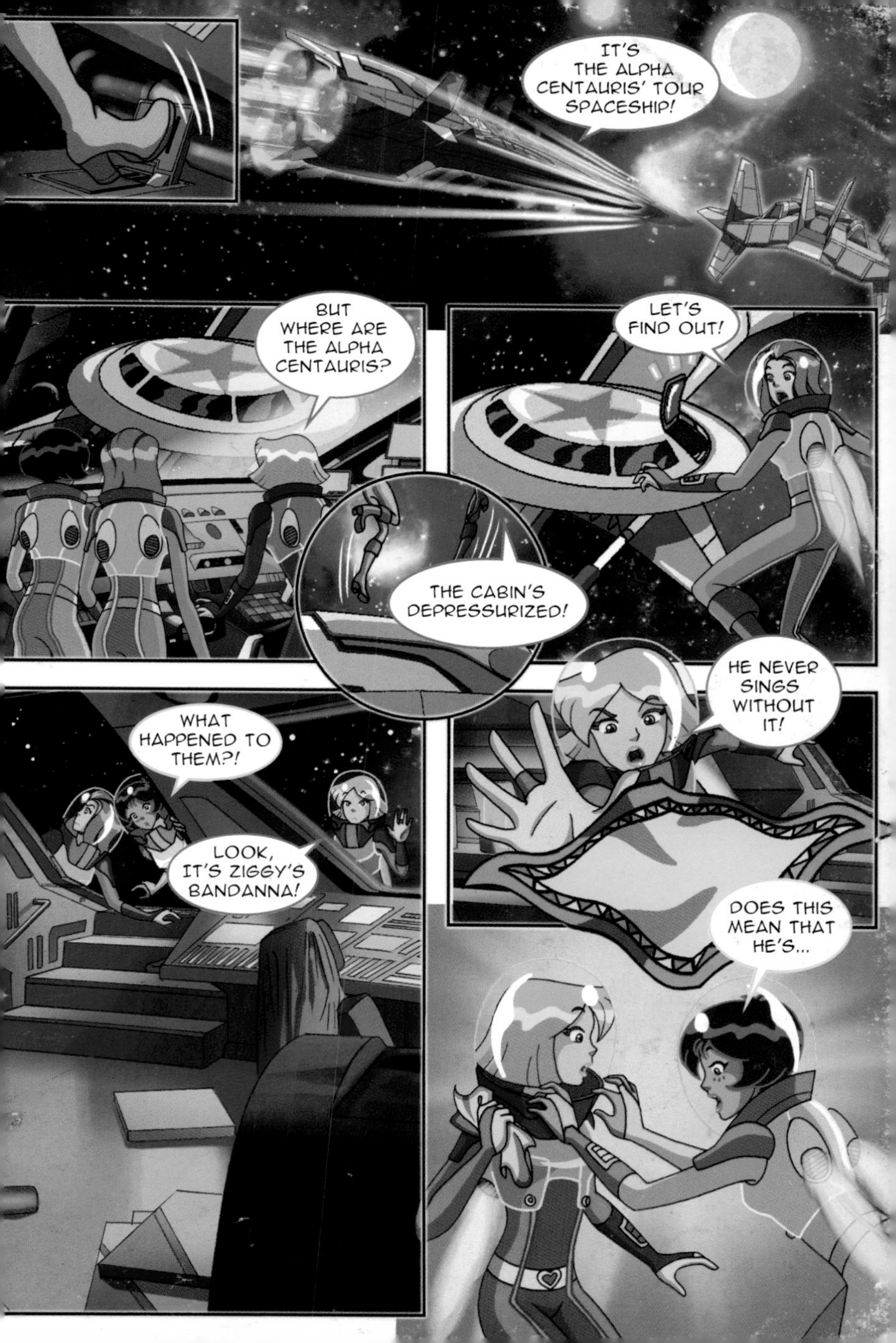
IT'S THE ALPHA CENTAURIS' TOUR SPACESHIP!
BUT WHERE ARE THE ALPHA CENTAURIS?
LET'S FIND OUT!
THE CABIN'S DEPRESSURIZED!
WHAT HAPPENED TO THEM?!
LOOK, IT'S ZIGGY'S BANDANNA!
HE NEVER SINGS WITHOUT IT!
DOES THIS MEAN THAT HE'S...

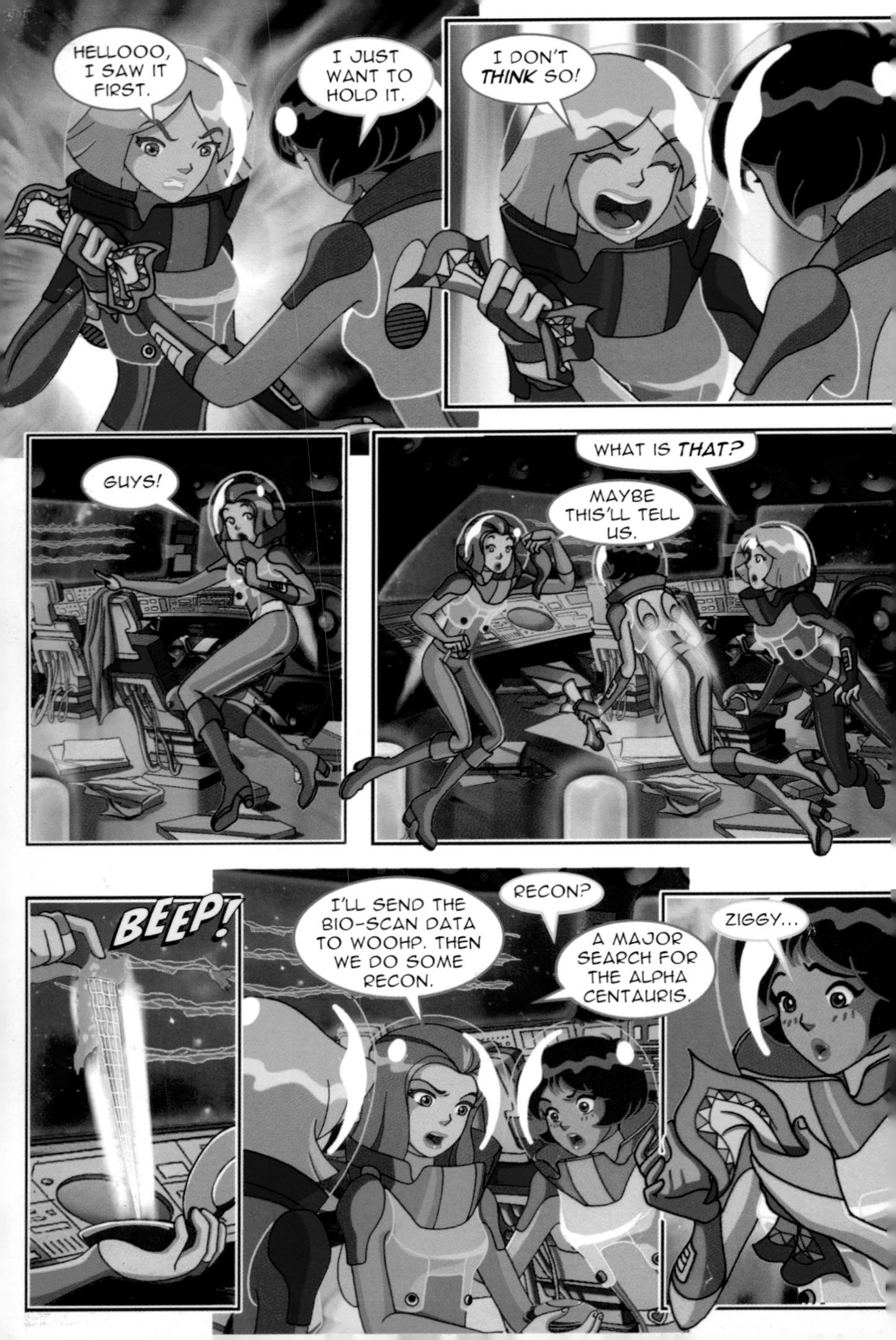
HELLOOO, I SAW IT FIRST.
I JUST WANT TO HOLD IT.
I DON'T *THINK* SO!
GUYS!
WHAT IS *THAT?*
MAYBE THIS'LL TELL US.
BEEP!
I'LL SEND THE BIO-SCAN DATA TO WOOHP. THEN WE DO SOME RECON.
RECON?
A MAJOR SEARCH FOR THE ALPHA CENTAURIS.
ZIGGY...

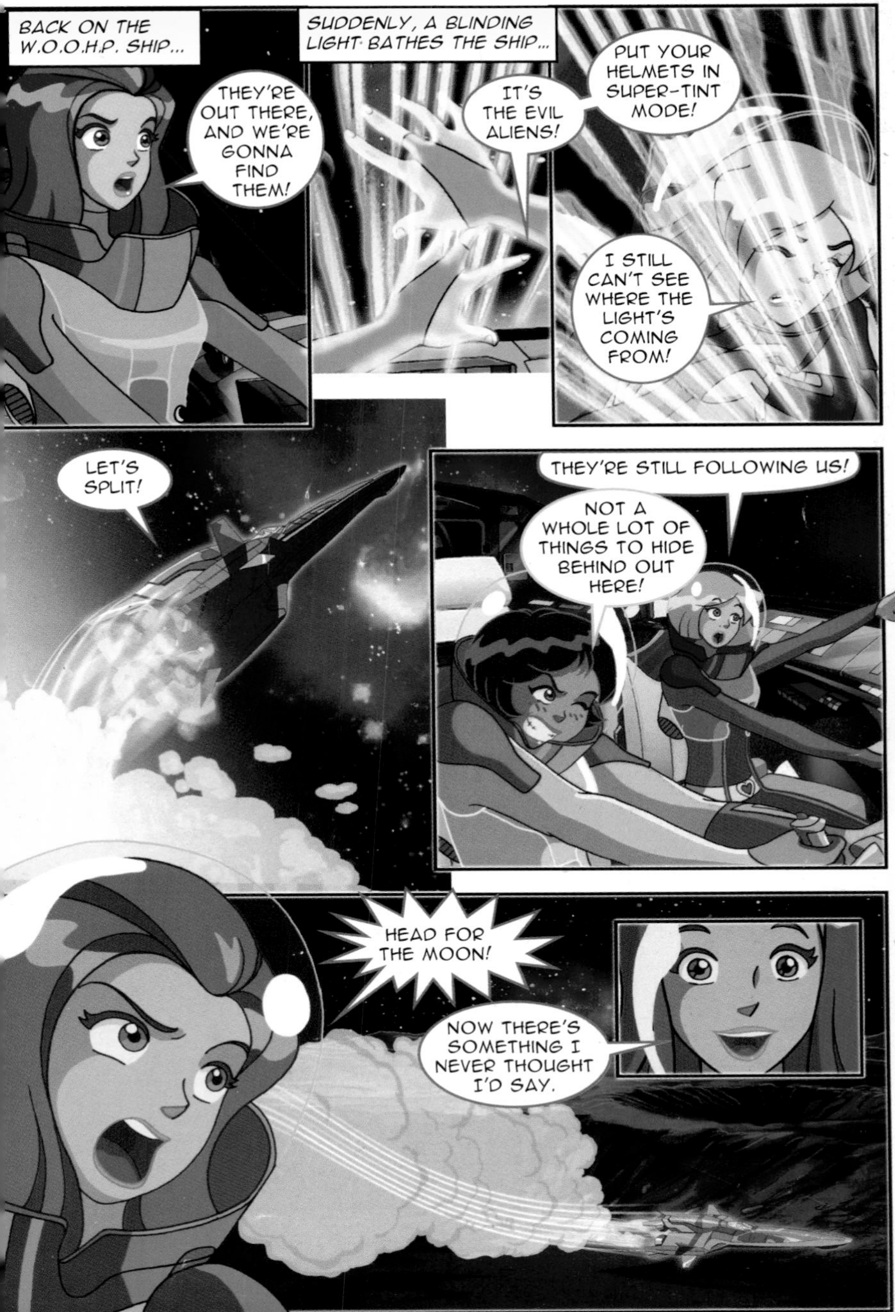
BACK ON THE W.O.O.H.P. SHIP...
THEY'RE OUT THERE, AND WE'RE GONNA FIND THEM!
SUDDENLY, A BLINDING LIGHT BATHES THE SHIP...
IT'S THE EVIL ALIENS!
PUT YOUR HELMETS IN SUPER-TINT MODE!
I STILL CAN'T SEE WHERE THE LIGHT'S COMING FROM!
LET'S SPLIT!
THEY'RE STILL FOLLOWING US!
NOT A WHOLE LOT OF THINGS TO HIDE BEHIND OUT HERE!
HEAD FOR THE MOON!
NOW THERE'S SOMETHING I NEVER THOUGHT I'D SAY.

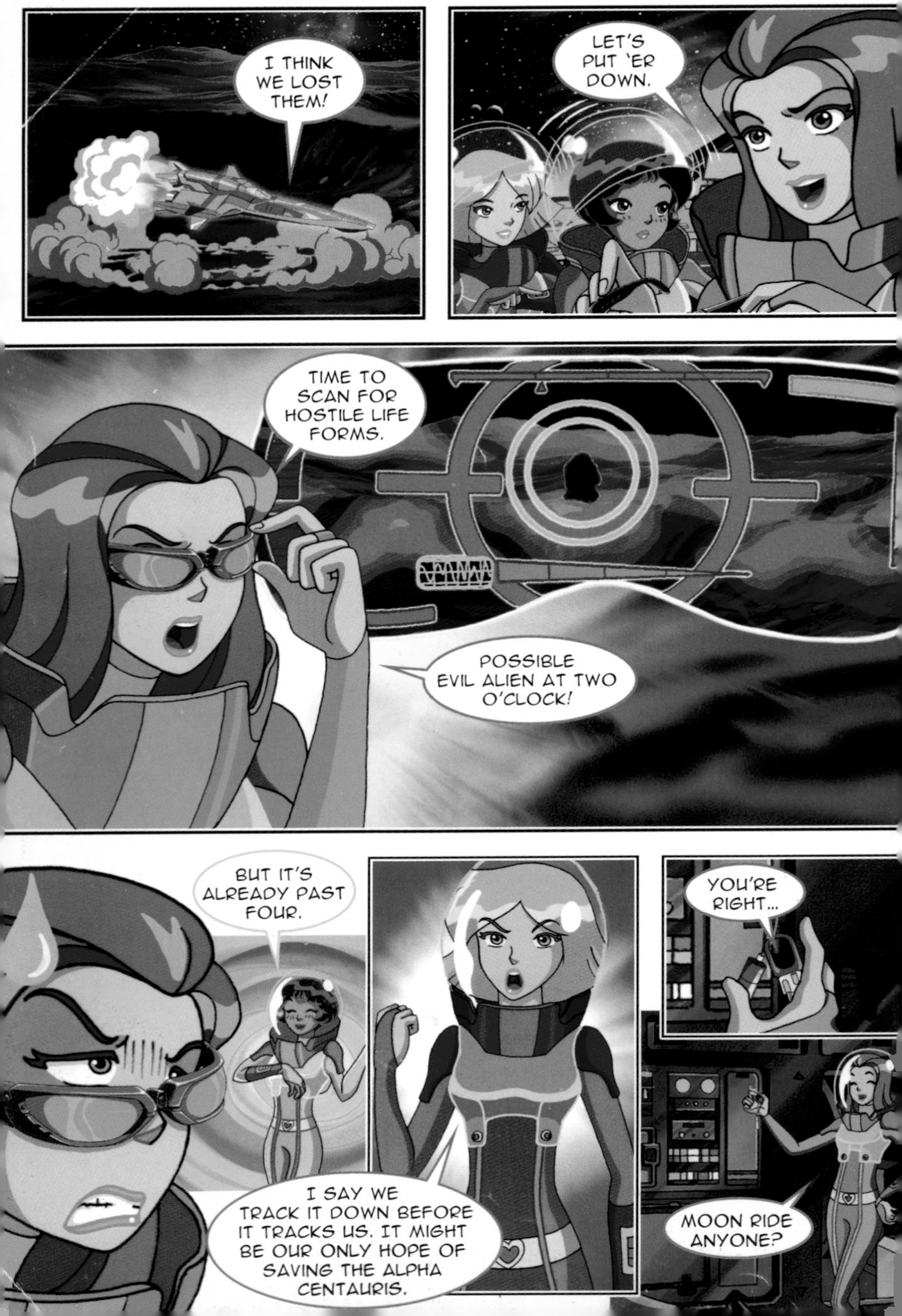
I THINK WE LOST THEM!
LET'S PUT 'ER DOWN.
TIME TO SCAN FOR HOSTILE LIFE FORMS.
POSSIBLE EVIL ALIEN AT TWO O'CLOCK!
BUT IT'S ALREADY PAST FOUR.
I SAY WE TRACK IT DOWN BEFORE IT TRACKS US. IT MIGHT BE OUR ONLY HOPE OF SAVING THE ALPHA CENTAURIS.
YOU'RE RIGHT...
MOON RIDE ANYONE?

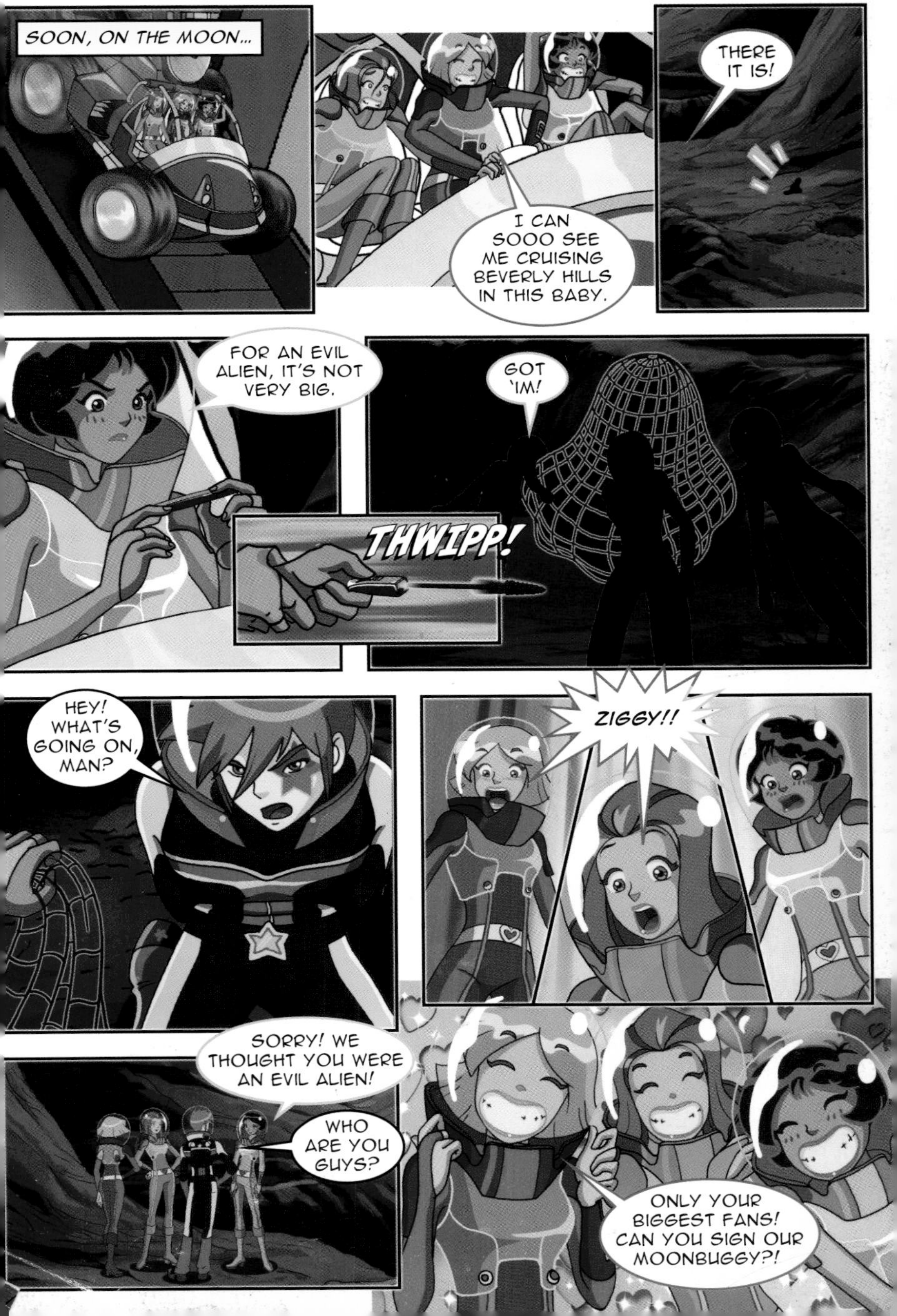
SOON, ON THE MOON...
I CAN SOOO SEE ME CRUISING BEVERLY HILLS IN THIS BABY.
THERE IT IS!
FOR AN EVIL ALIEN, IT'S NOT VERY BIG.
GOT 'IM!
THWIPP!
HEY! WHAT'S GOING ON, MAN?
ZIGGY!!
SORRY! WE THOUGHT YOU WERE AN EVIL ALIEN!
WHO ARE YOU GUYS?
ONLY YOUR BIGGEST FANS! CAN YOU SIGN OUR MOONBUGGY?!

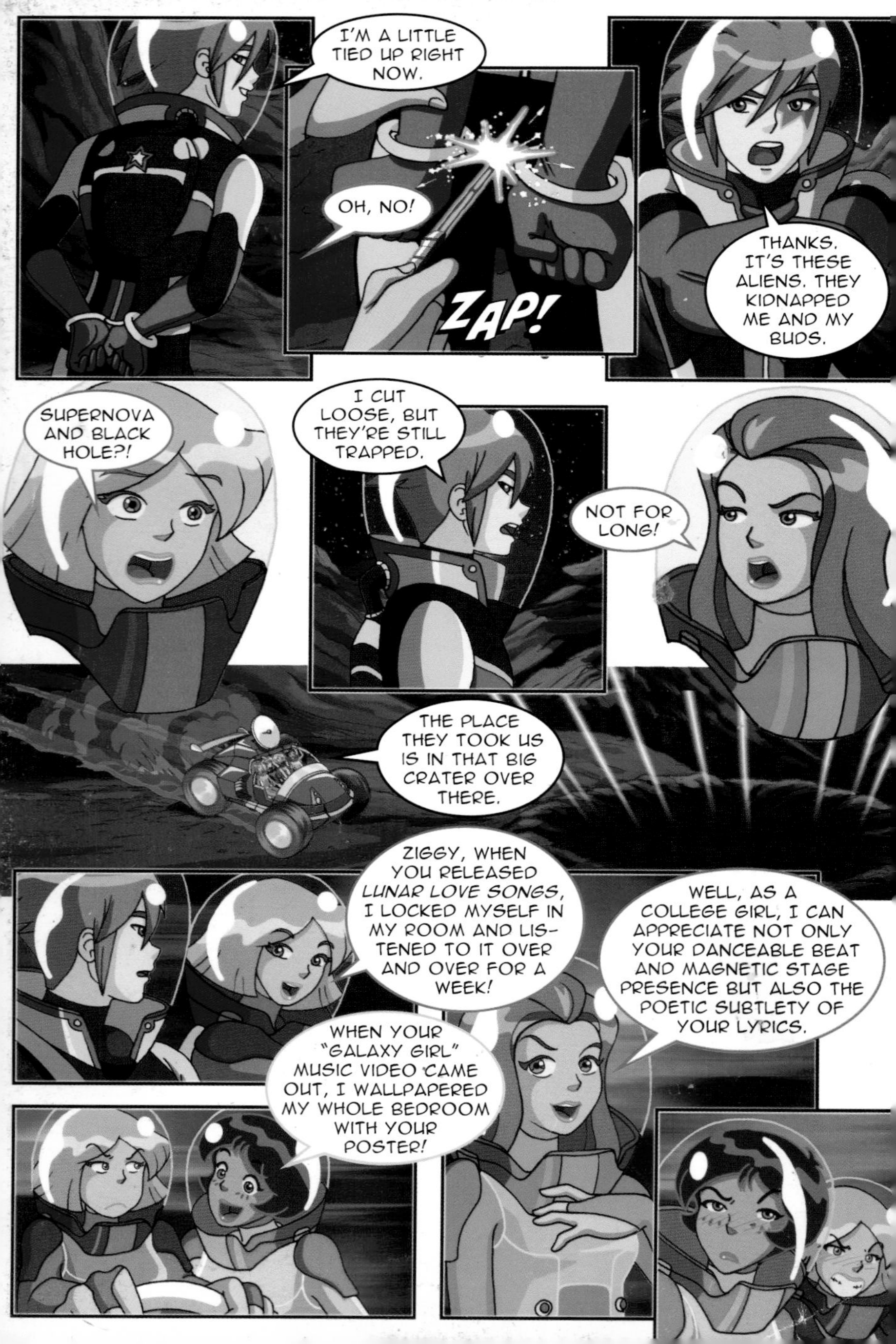
I'M A LITTLE TIED UP RIGHT NOW.
OH, NO!
ZAP!
THANKS. IT'S THESE ALIENS. THEY KIDNAPPED ME AND MY BUDS.
SUPERNOVA AND BLACK HOLE?!
I CUT LOOSE, BUT THEY'RE STILL TRAPPED.
NOT FOR LONG!
THE PLACE THEY TOOK US IS IN THAT BIG CRATER OVER THERE.
ZIGGY, WHEN YOU RELEASED *LUNAR LOVE SONGS*, I LOCKED MYSELF IN MY ROOM AND LIS-TENED TO IT OVER AND OVER FOR A WEEK!
WELL, AS A COLLEGE GIRL, I CAN APPRECIATE NOT ONLY YOUR DANCEABLE BEAT AND MAGNETIC STAGE PRESENCE BUT ALSO THE POETIC SUBTLETY OF YOUR LYRICS.
WHEN YOUR "GALAXY GIRL" MUSIC VIDEO CAME OUT, I WALLPAPERED MY WHOLE BEDROOM WITH YOUR POSTER!

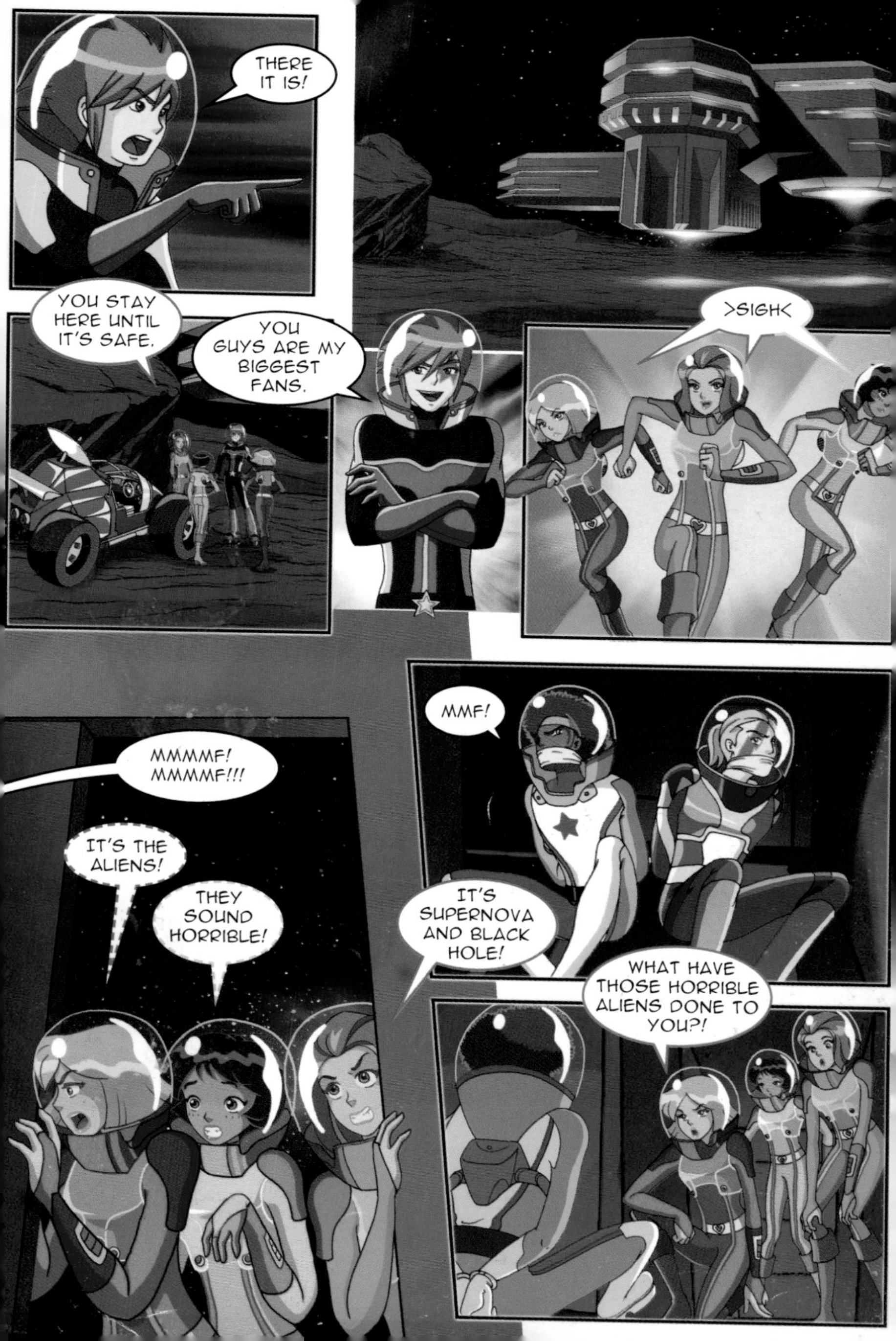
THERE IT IS!
YOU STAY HERE UNTIL IT'S SAFE.
YOU GUYS ARE MY BIGGEST FANS.
>SIGH<
MMMMF! MMMMF!!!
IT'S THE ALIENS!
THEY SOUND HORRIBLE!
MMF!
IT'S SUPERNOVA AND BLACK HOLE!
WHAT HAVE THOSE HORRIBLE ALIENS DONE TO YOU?!

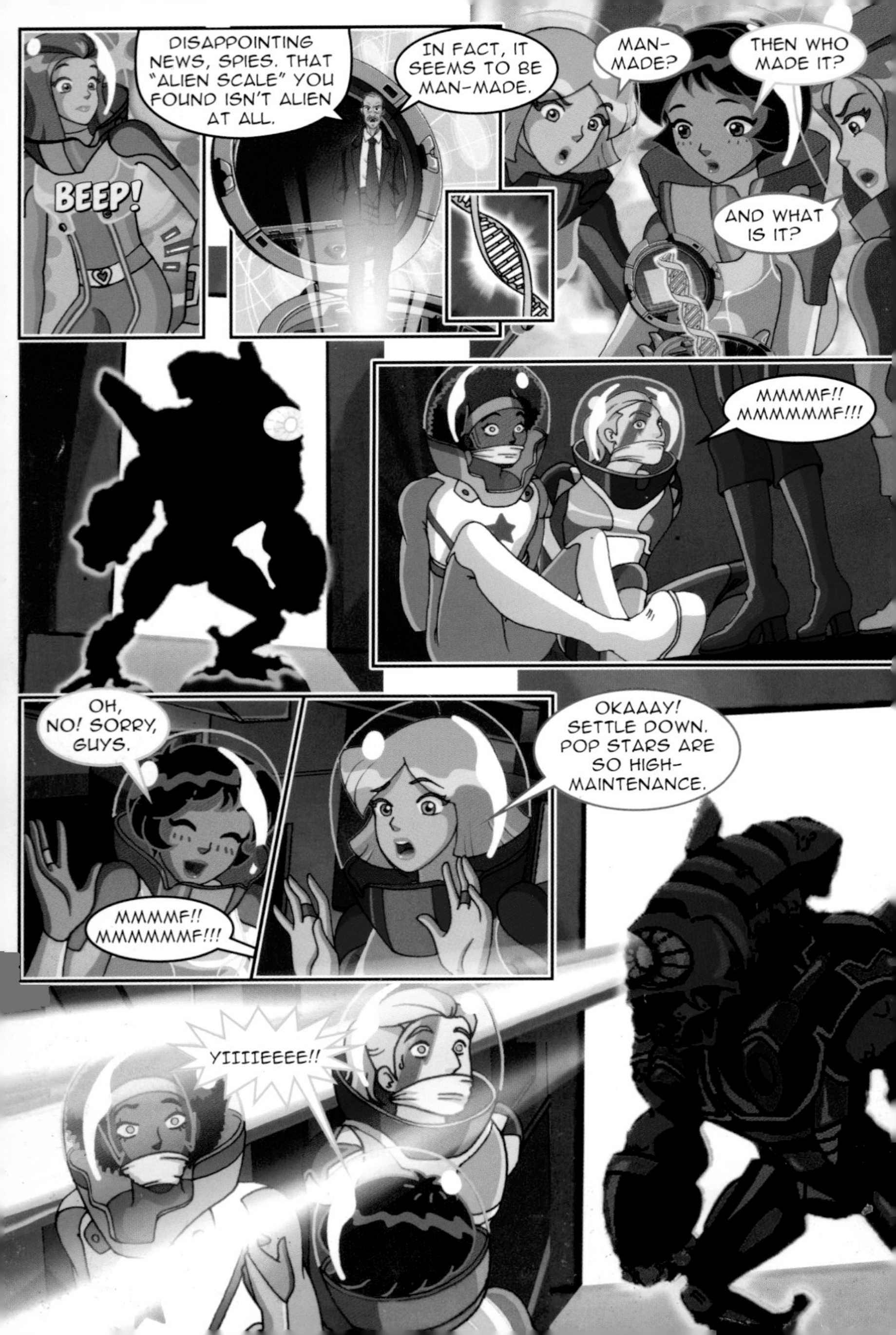
BEEP!
DISAPPOINTING NEWS, SPIES. THAT "ALIEN SCALE" YOU FOUND ISN'T ALIEN AT ALL.
IN FACT, IT SEEMS TO BE MAN-MADE.
MAN-MADE?
THEN WHO MADE IT?
AND WHAT IS IT?
MMMMF!! MMMMMMF!!!
OH, NO! SORRY, GUYS.
MMMMF!! MMMMMMF!!!
OKAAAY! SETTLE DOWN. POP STARS ARE SO HIGH-MAINTENANCE.
YIIIIEEEE!!

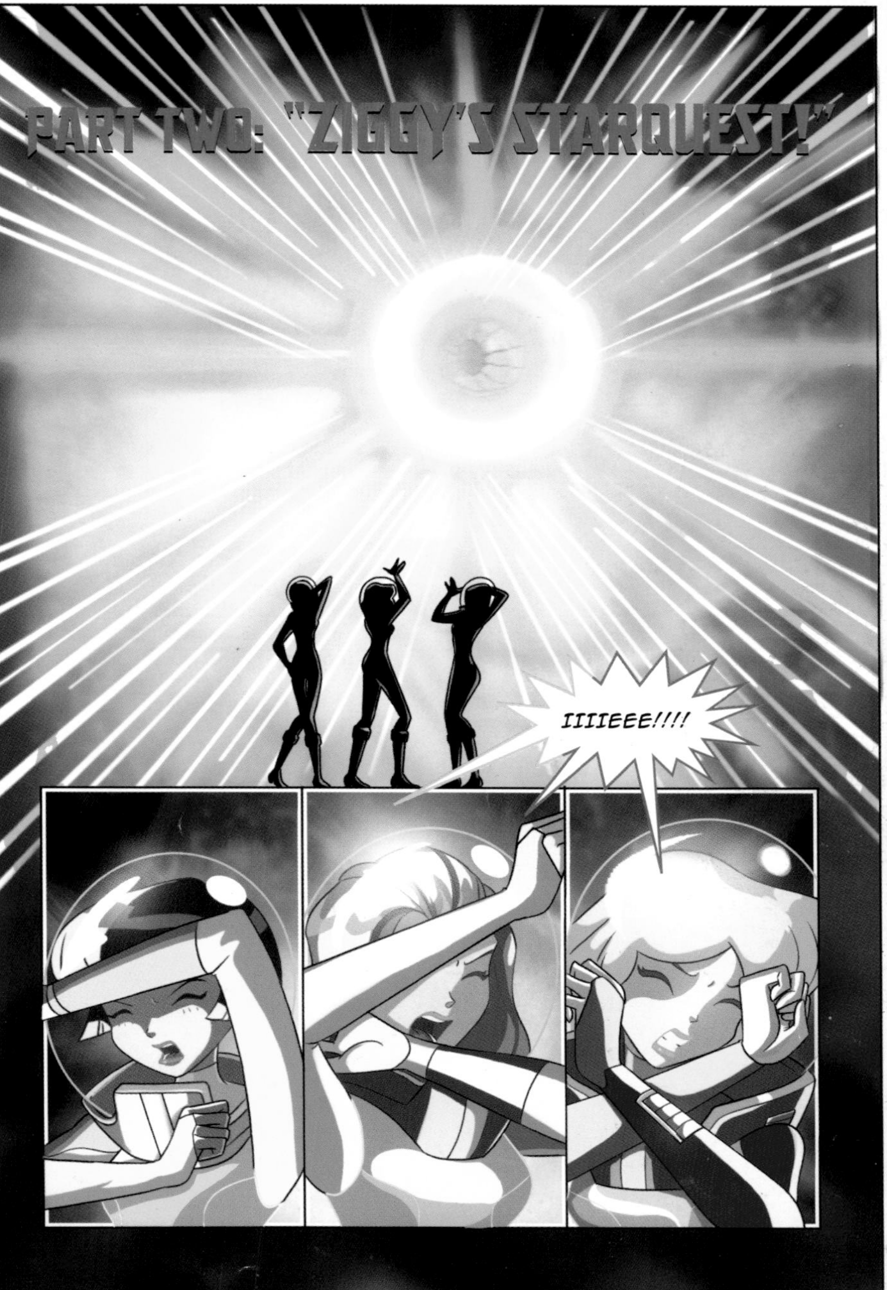
PART TWO: "ZIGGY'S STARQUEST!"
IIIIEEE!!!!

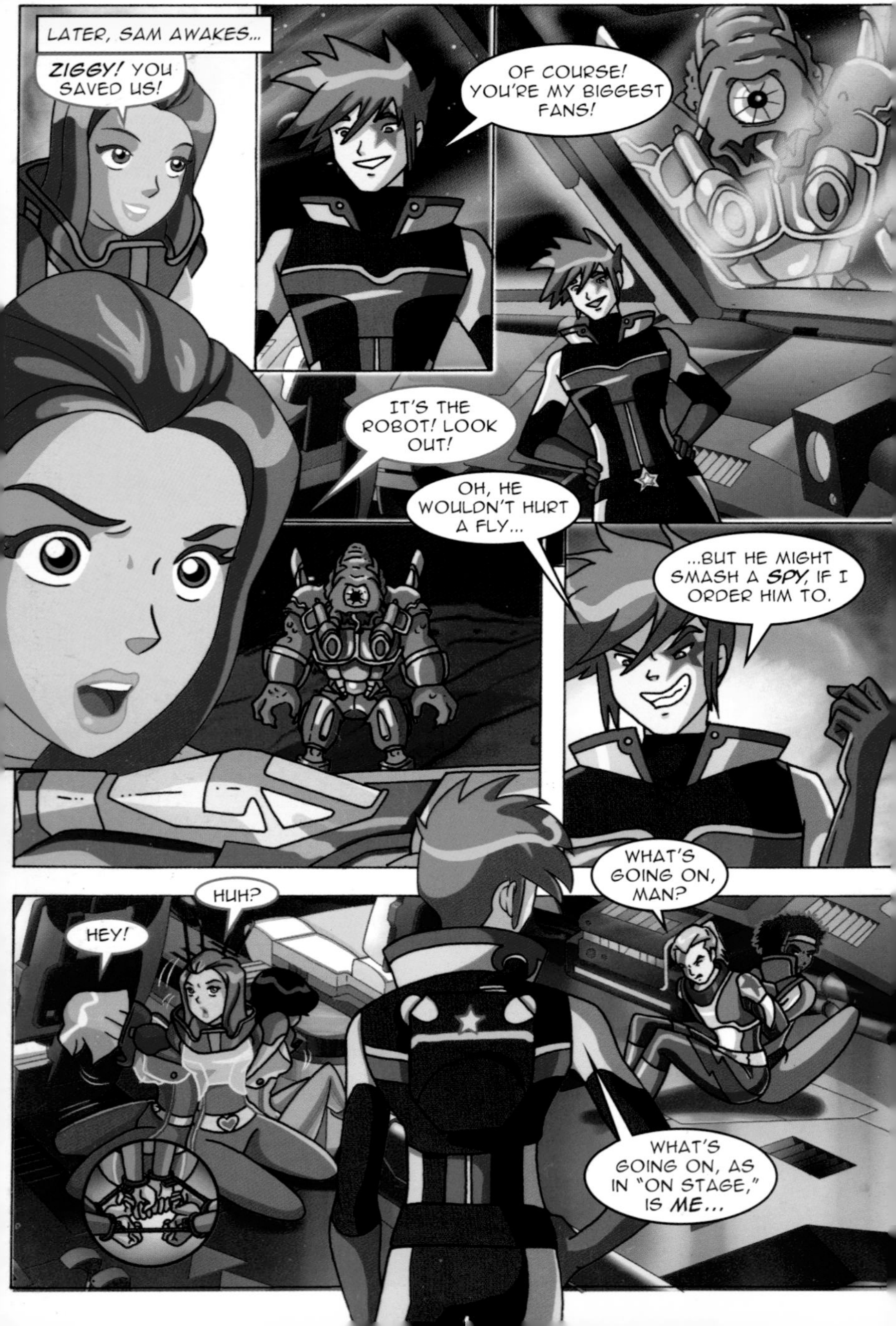

LATER, SAM AWAKES...
ZIGGY! YOU SAVED US!
OF COURSE! YOU'RE MY BIGGEST FANS!
IT'S THE ROBOT! LOOK OUT!
OH, HE WOULDN'T HURT A FLY...
...BUT HE MIGHT SMASH A SPY, IF I ORDER HIM TO.
HEY!
HUH?
WHAT'S GOING ON, MAN?
WHAT'S GOING ON, AS IN "ON STAGE," IS ME...

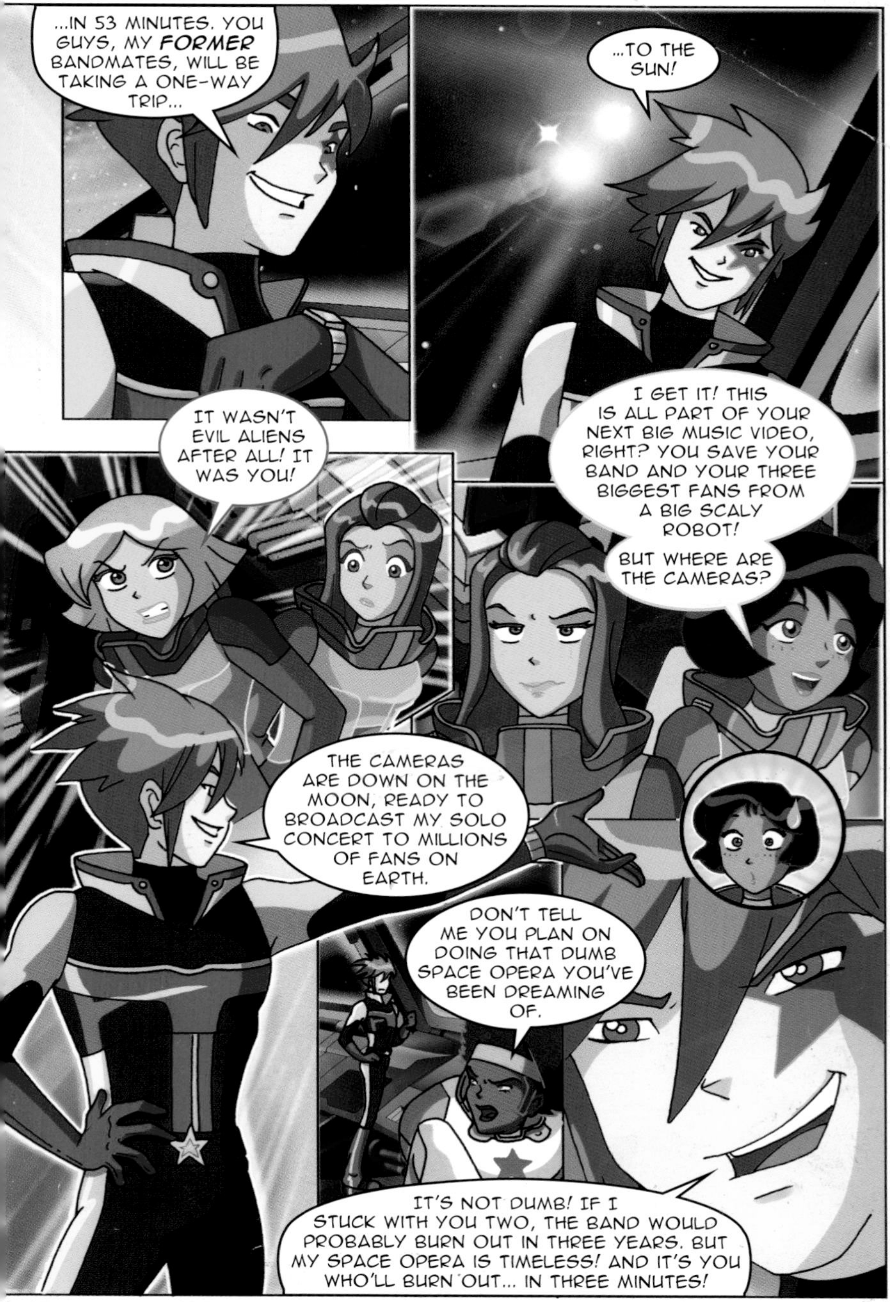

...IN 53 MINUTES, YOU GUYS, MY **FORMER** BANDMATES, WILL BE TAKING A ONE-WAY TRIP...
...TO THE SUN!
IT WASN'T EVIL ALIENS AFTER ALL! IT WAS YOU!
I GET IT! THIS IS ALL PART OF YOUR NEXT BIG MUSIC VIDEO, RIGHT? YOU SAVE YOUR BAND AND YOUR THREE BIGGEST FANS FROM A BIG SCALY ROBOT!
BUT WHERE ARE THE CAMERAS?
THE CAMERAS ARE DOWN ON THE MOON, READY TO BROADCAST MY SOLO CONCERT TO MILLIONS OF FANS ON EARTH.
DON'T TELL ME YOU PLAN ON DOING THAT DUMB SPACE OPERA YOU'VE BEEN DREAMING OF.
IT'S NOT DUMB! IF I STUCK WITH YOU TWO, THE BAND WOULD PROBABLY BURN OUT IN THREE YEARS. BUT MY SPACE OPERA IS TIMELESS! AND IT'S YOU WHO'LL BURN OUT... IN THREE MINUTES!

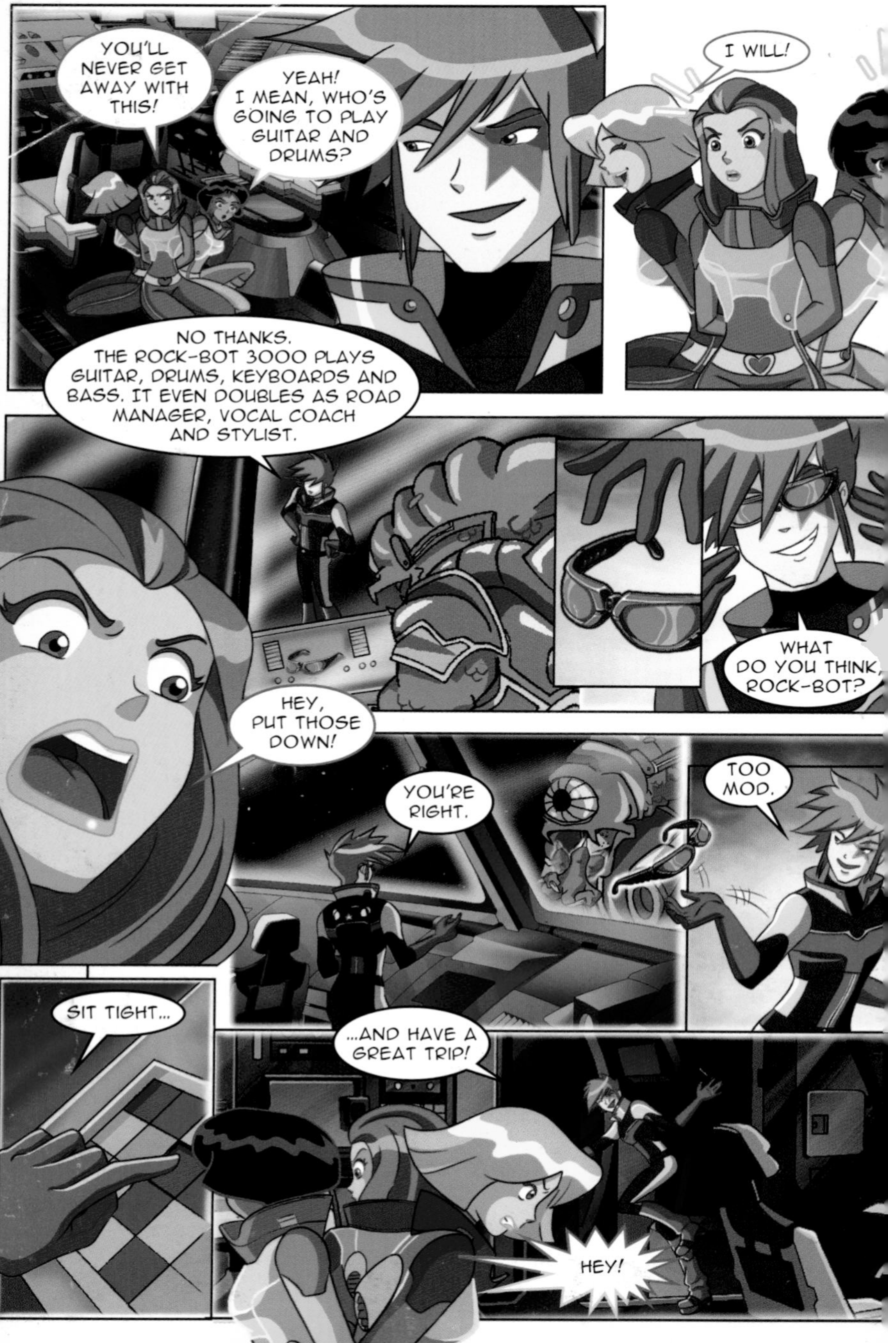
YOU'LL NEVER GET AWAY WITH THIS!
YEAH! I MEAN, WHO'S GOING TO PLAY GUITAR AND DRUMS?
I WILL!
NO THANKS. THE ROCK-BOT 3000 PLAYS GUITAR, DRUMS, KEYBOARDS AND BASS. IT EVEN DOUBLES AS ROAD MANAGER, VOCAL COACH AND STYLIST.
WHAT DO YOU THINK, ROCK-BOT?
HEY, PUT THOSE DOWN!
YOU'RE RIGHT.
TOO MOD.
SIT TIGHT...
...AND HAVE A GREAT TRIP!
HEY!

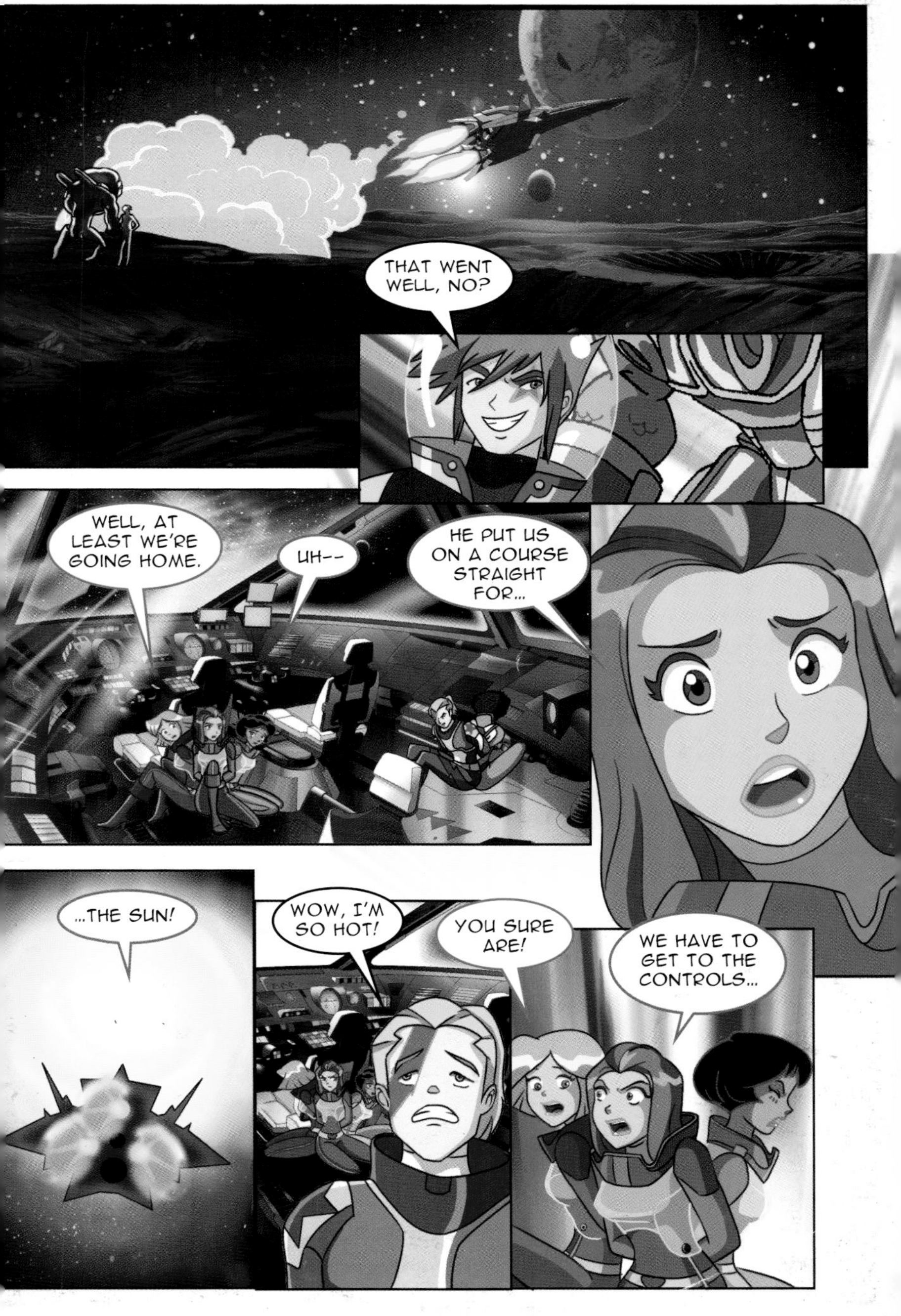
THAT WENT WELL, NO?
WELL, AT LEAST WE'RE GOING HOME.
UH--
HE PUT US ON A COURSE STRAIGHT FOR...
...THE SUN!
WOW, I'M SO HOT!
YOU SURE ARE!
WE HAVE TO GET TO THE CONTROLS...

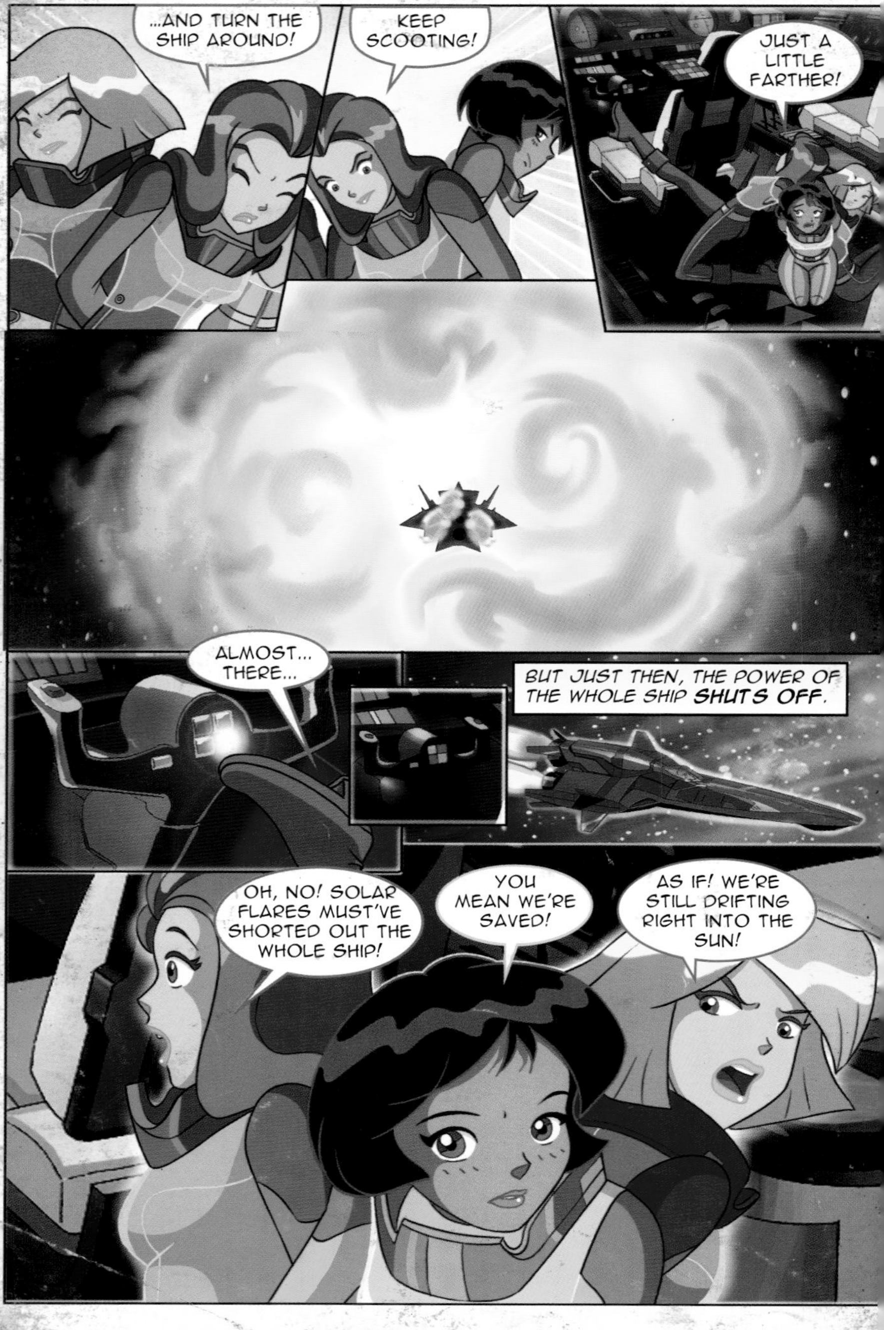
...AND TURN THE SHIP AROUND!
KEEP SCOOTING!
JUST A LITTLE FARTHER!
ALMOST... THERE...
BUT JUST THEN, THE POWER OF THE WHOLE SHIP SHUTS OFF.
OH, NO! SOLAR FLARES MUST'VE SHORTED OUT THE WHOLE SHIP!
YOU MEAN WE'RE SAVED!
AS IF! WE'RE STILL DRIFTING RIGHT INTO THE SUN!

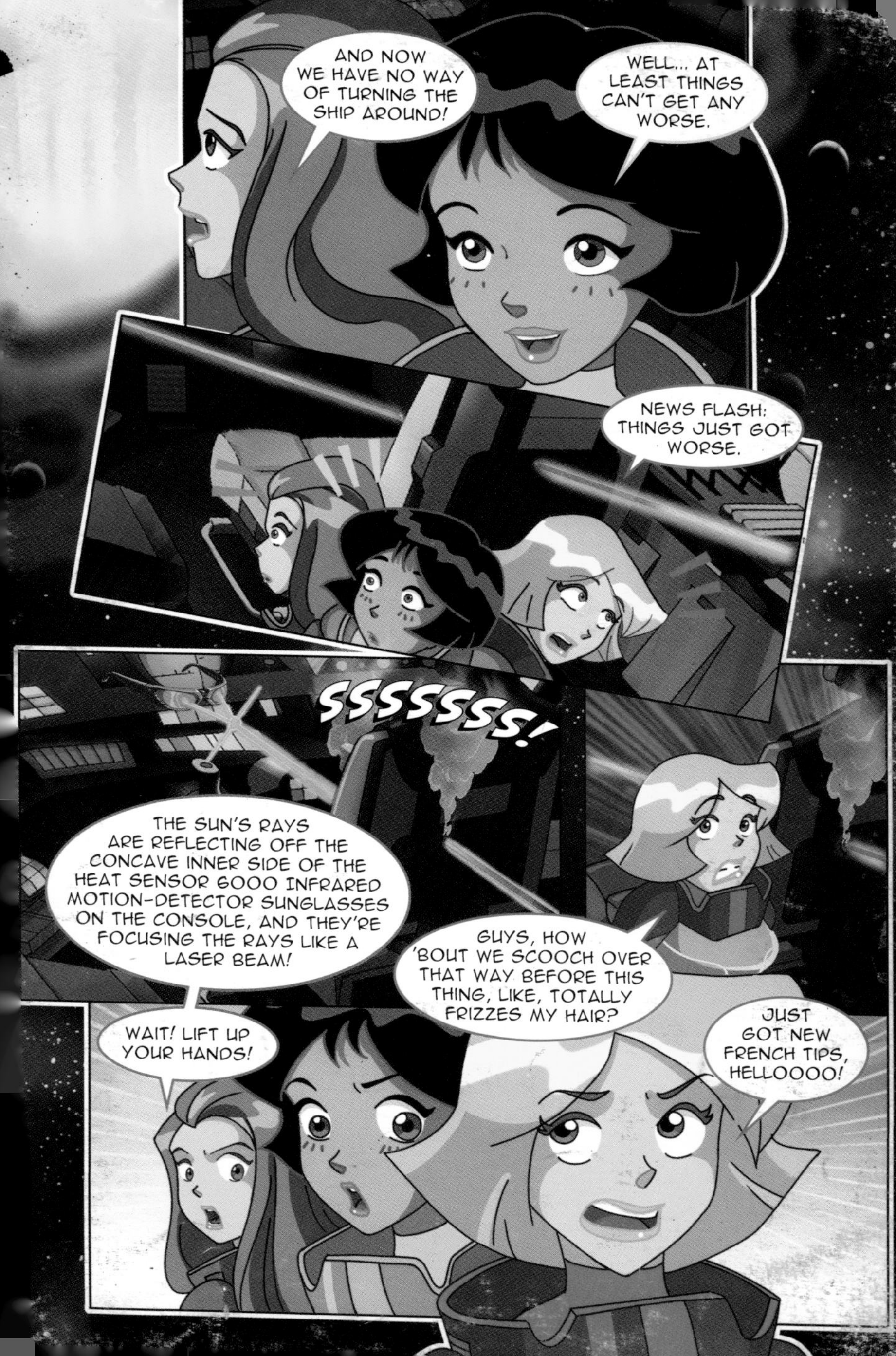
AND NOW WE HAVE NO WAY OF TURNING THE SHIP AROUND!
WELL... AT LEAST THINGS CAN'T GET ANY WORSE.
NEWS FLASH: THINGS JUST GOT WORSE.
SSSSSSS!
THE SUN'S RAYS ARE REFLECTING OFF THE CONCAVE INNER SIDE OF THE HEAT SENSOR 6000 INFRARED MOTION-DETECTOR SUNGLASSES ON THE CONSOLE, AND THEY'RE FOCUSING THE RAYS LIKE A LASER BEAM!
GUYS, HOW 'BOUT WE SCOOCH OVER THAT WAY BEFORE THIS THING, LIKE, TOTALLY FRIZZES MY HAIR?
WAIT! LIFT UP YOUR HANDS!
JUST GOT NEW FRENCH TIPS, HELLOOOO!

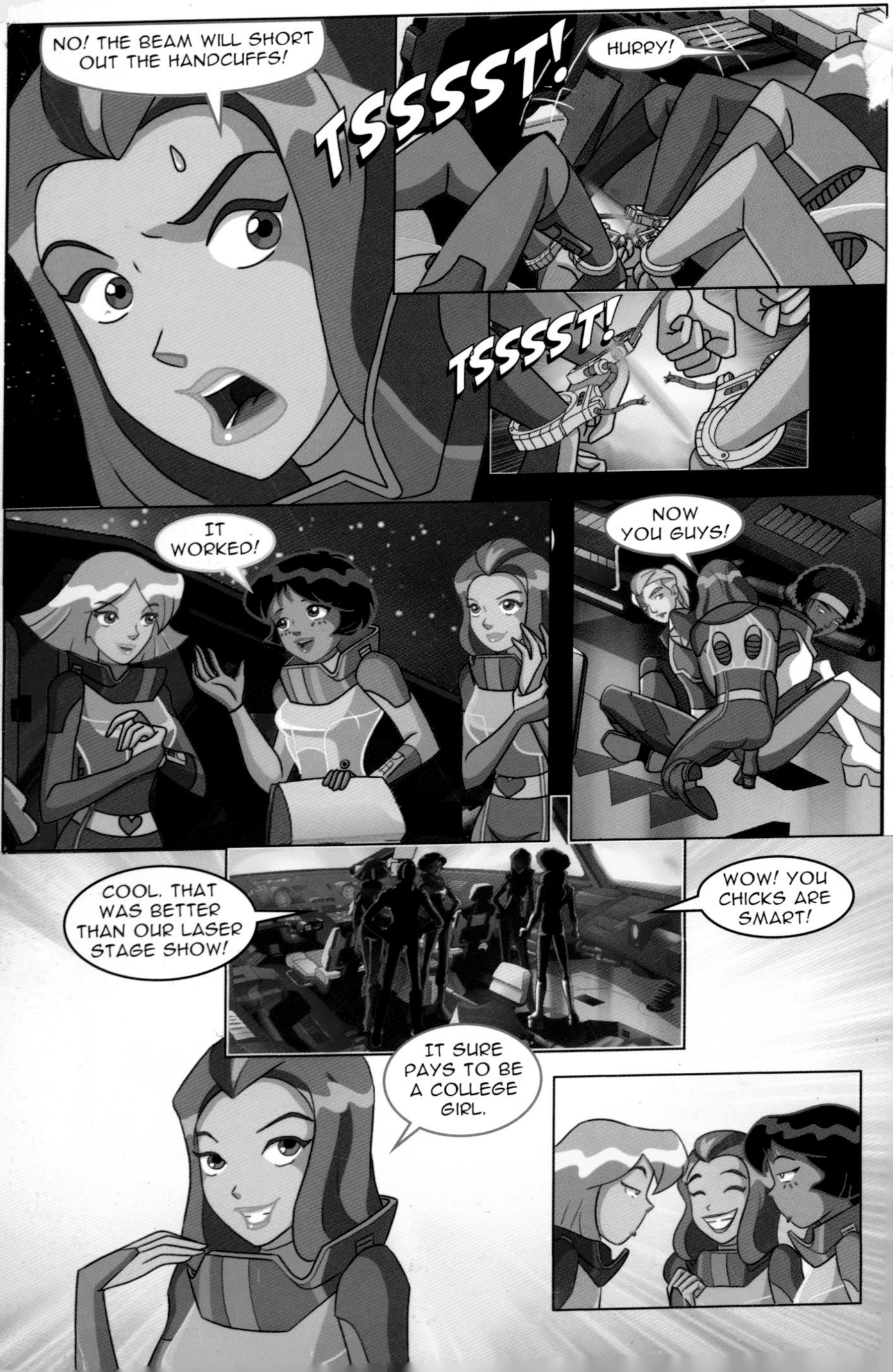
NO! THE BEAM WILL SHORT OUT THE HANDCUFFS!
TSSSST!
HURRY!
TSSSST!
IT WORKED!
NOW YOU GUYS!
COOL. THAT WAS BETTER THAN OUR LASER STAGE SHOW!
WOW! YOU CHICKS ARE SMART!
IT SURE PAYS TO BE A COLLEGE GIRL.

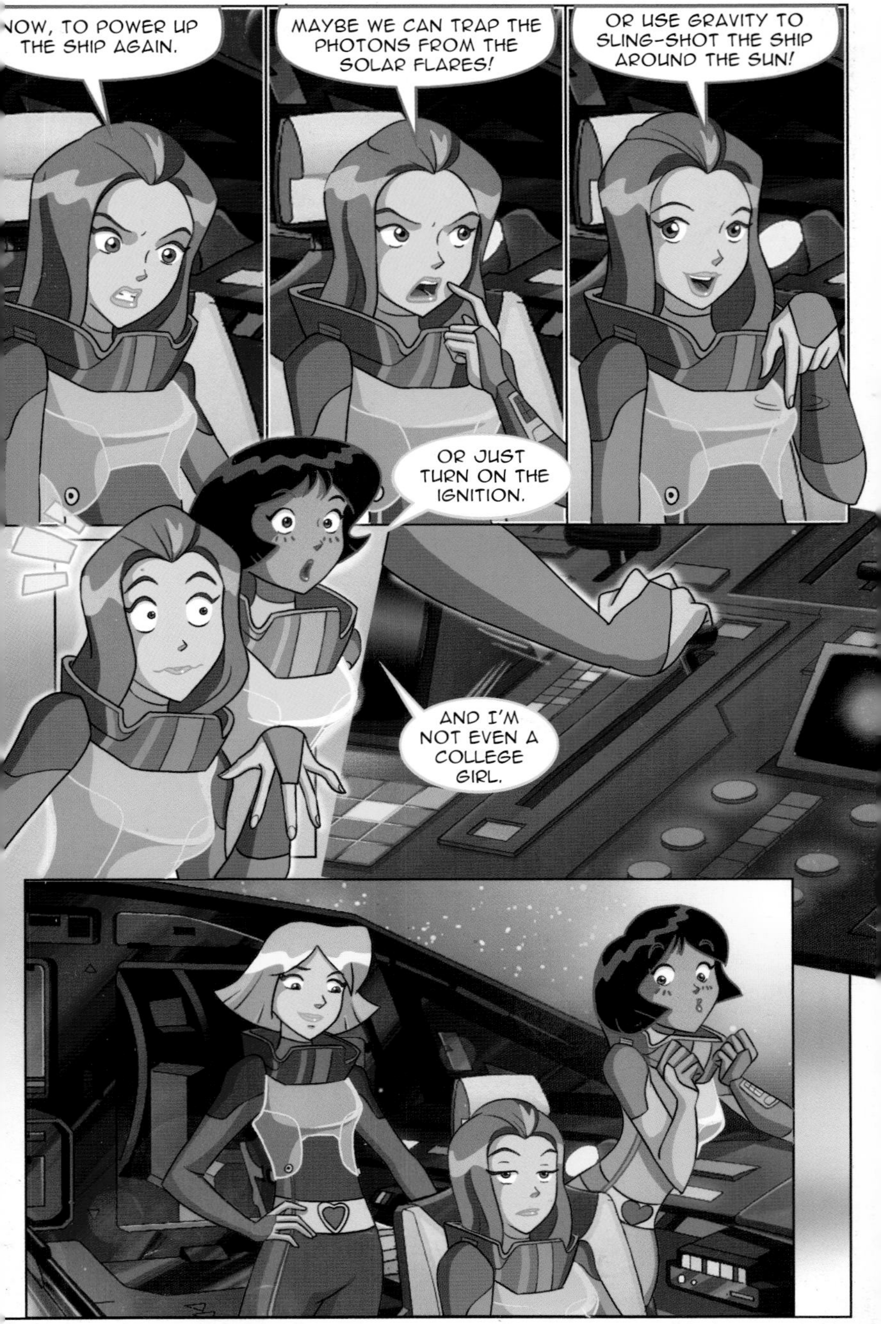
NOW, TO POWER UP THE SHIP AGAIN.
MAYBE WE CAN TRAP THE PHOTONS FROM THE SOLAR FLARES!
OR USE GRAVITY TO SLING-SHOT THE SHIP AROUND THE SUN!
OR JUST TURN ON THE IGNITION.
AND I'M NOT EVEN A COLLEGE GIRL.

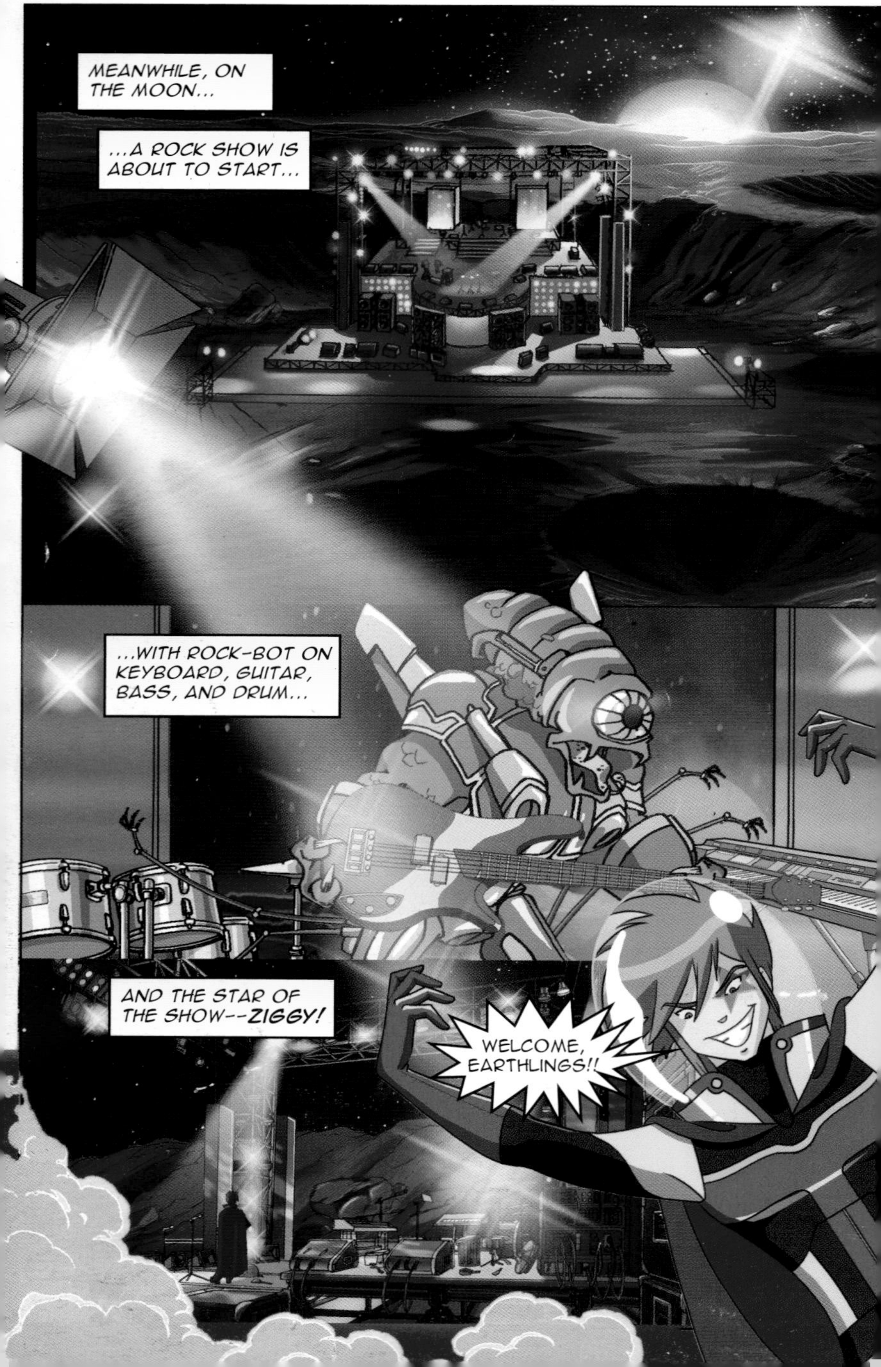
MEANWHILE, ON THE MOON...
...A ROCK SHOW IS ABOUT TO START...
...WITH ROCK-BOT ON KEYBOARD, GUITAR, BASS, AND DRUM...
AND THE STAR OF THE SHOW--ZIGGY!
WELCOME, EARTHLINGS!!

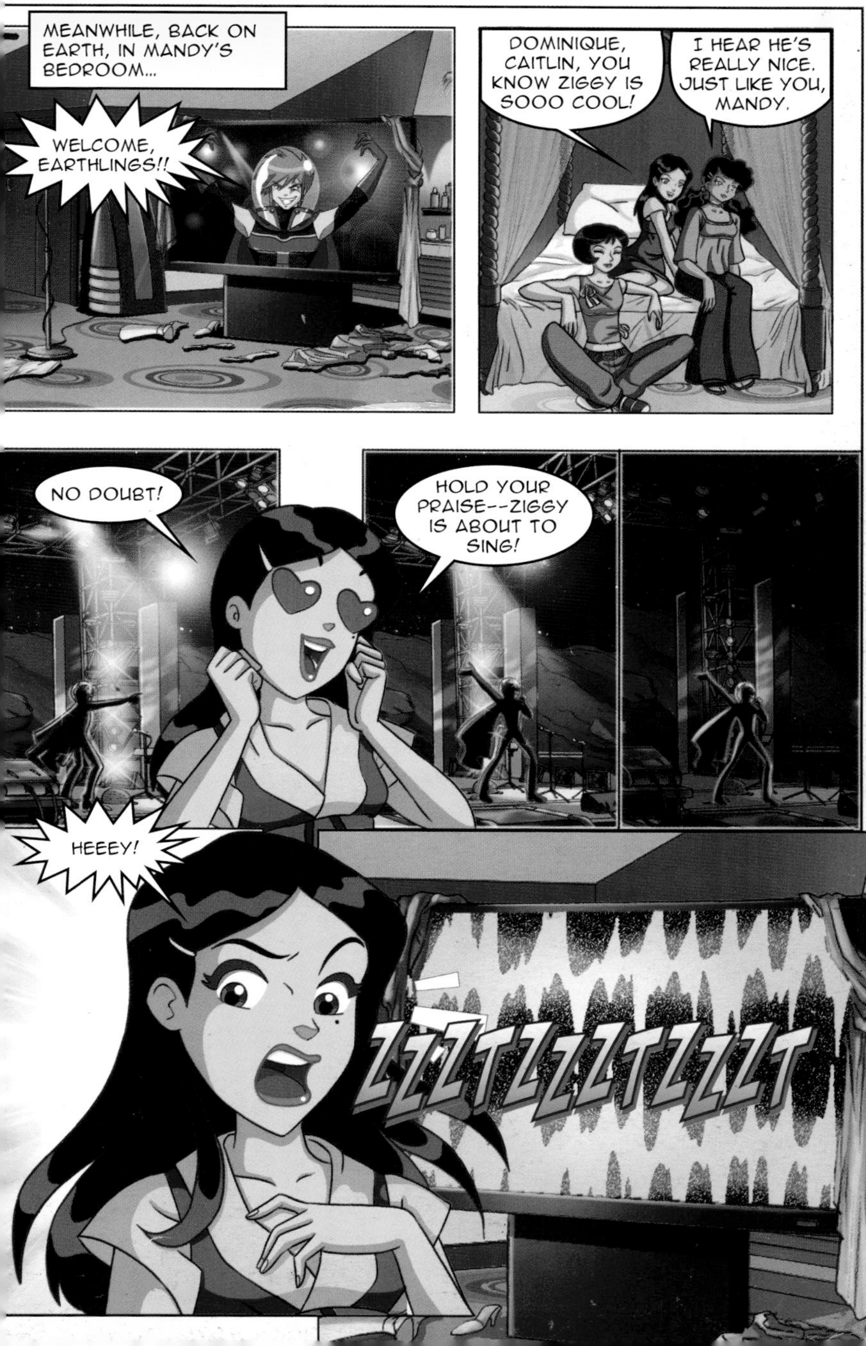
MEANWHILE, BACK ON EARTH, IN MANDY'S BEDROOM...
WELCOME, EARTHLINGS!!
DOMINIQUE, CAITLIN, YOU KNOW ZIGGY IS SOOO COOL!
I HEAR HE'S REALLY NICE. JUST LIKE YOU, MANDY.
NO DOUBT!
HOLD YOUR PRAISE--ZIGGY IS ABOUT TO SING!
HEEEY!
ZZZTZZZZTZZZZT

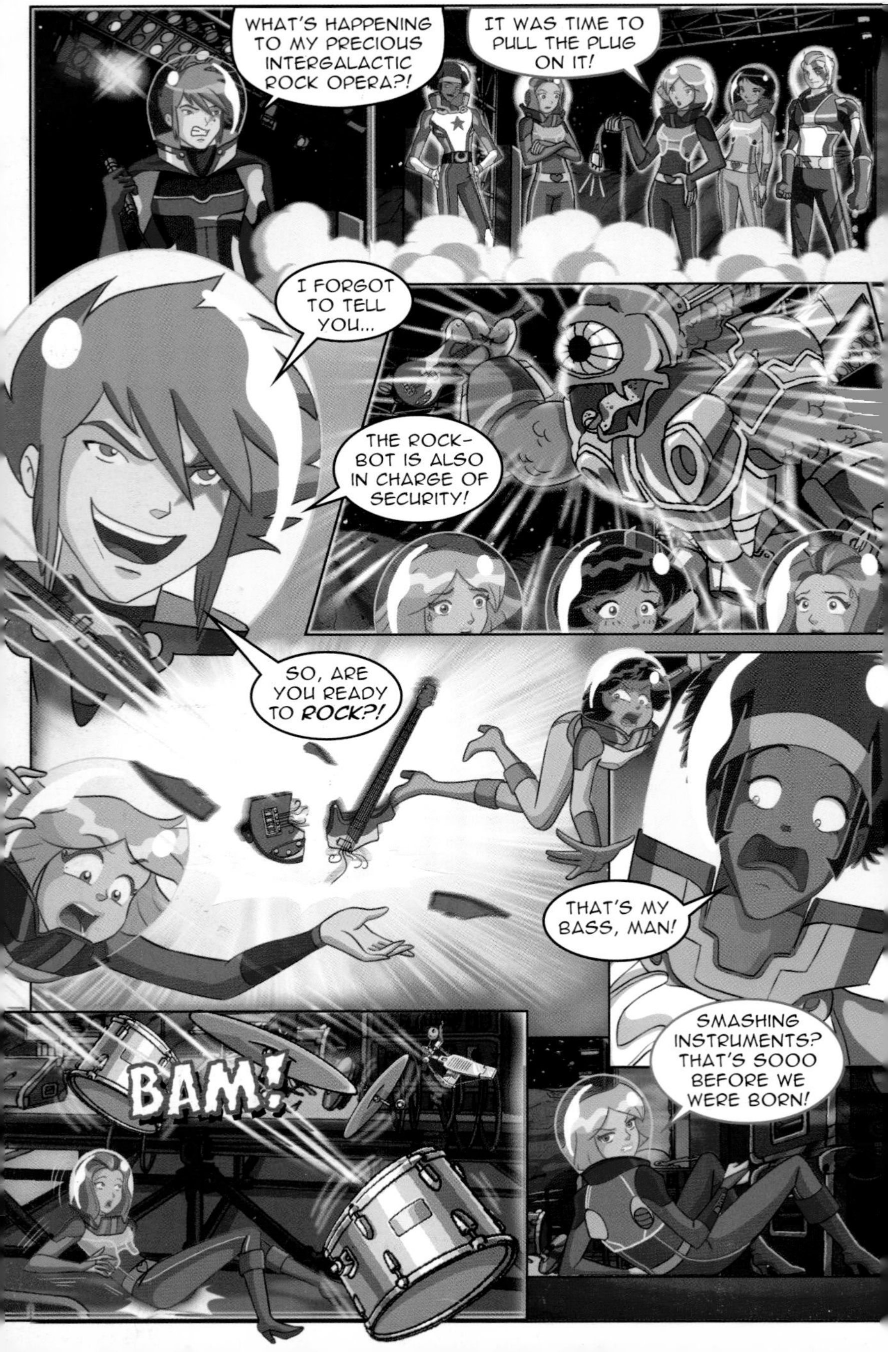
WHAT'S HAPPENING TO MY PRECIOUS INTERGALACTIC ROCK OPERA?!
IT WAS TIME TO PULL THE PLUG ON IT!
I FORGOT TO TELL YOU...
THE ROCK-BOT IS ALSO IN CHARGE OF SECURITY!
SO, ARE YOU READY TO ROCK?!
THAT'S MY BASS, MAN!
BAM!
SMASHING INSTRUMENTS? THAT'S SOOO BEFORE WE WERE BORN!

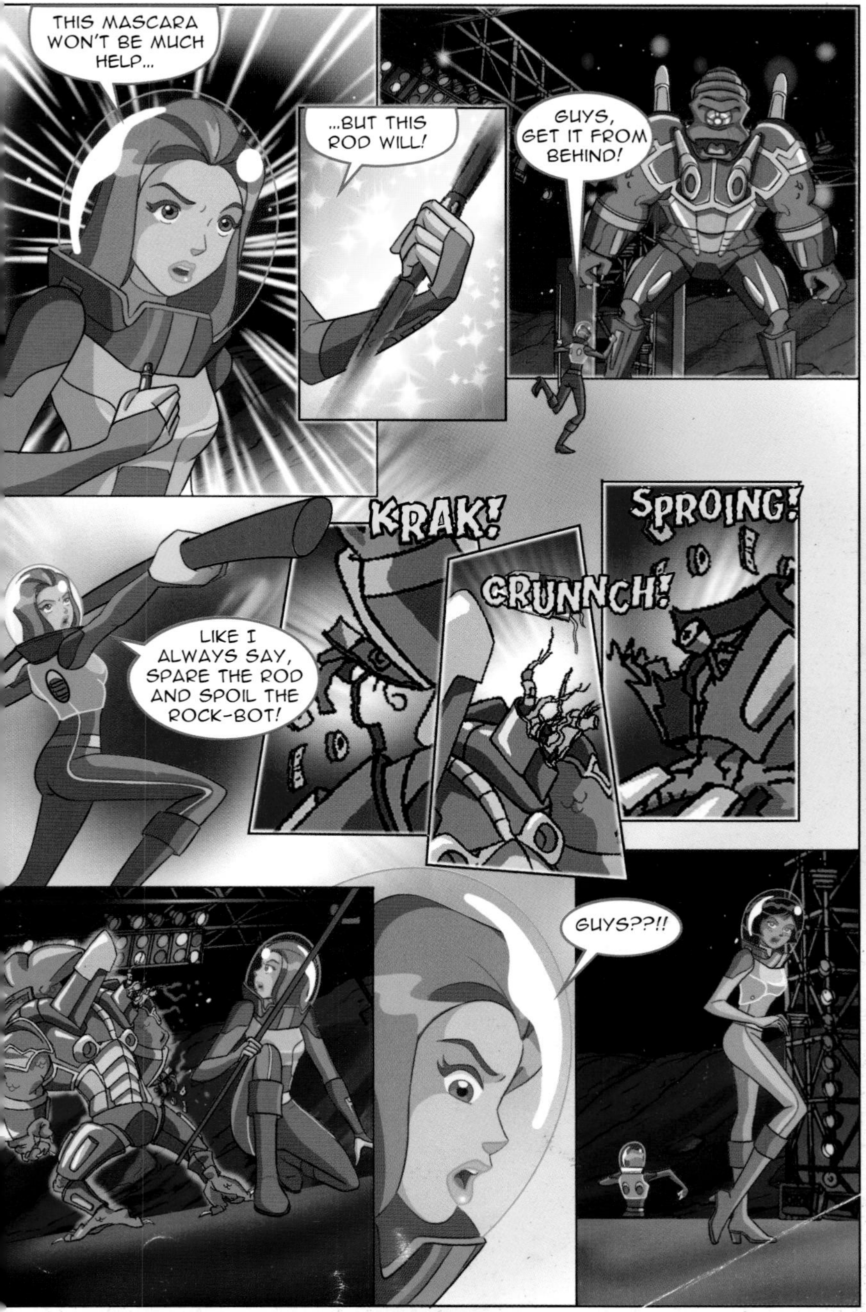
THIS MASCARA WON'T BE MUCH HELP...
...BUT THIS ROD WILL!
GUYS, GET IT FROM BEHIND!
LIKE I ALWAYS SAY, SPARE THE ROD AND SPOIL THE ROCK-BOT!
KRAK!
CRUNNCH!
SPROING!
GUYS??!!

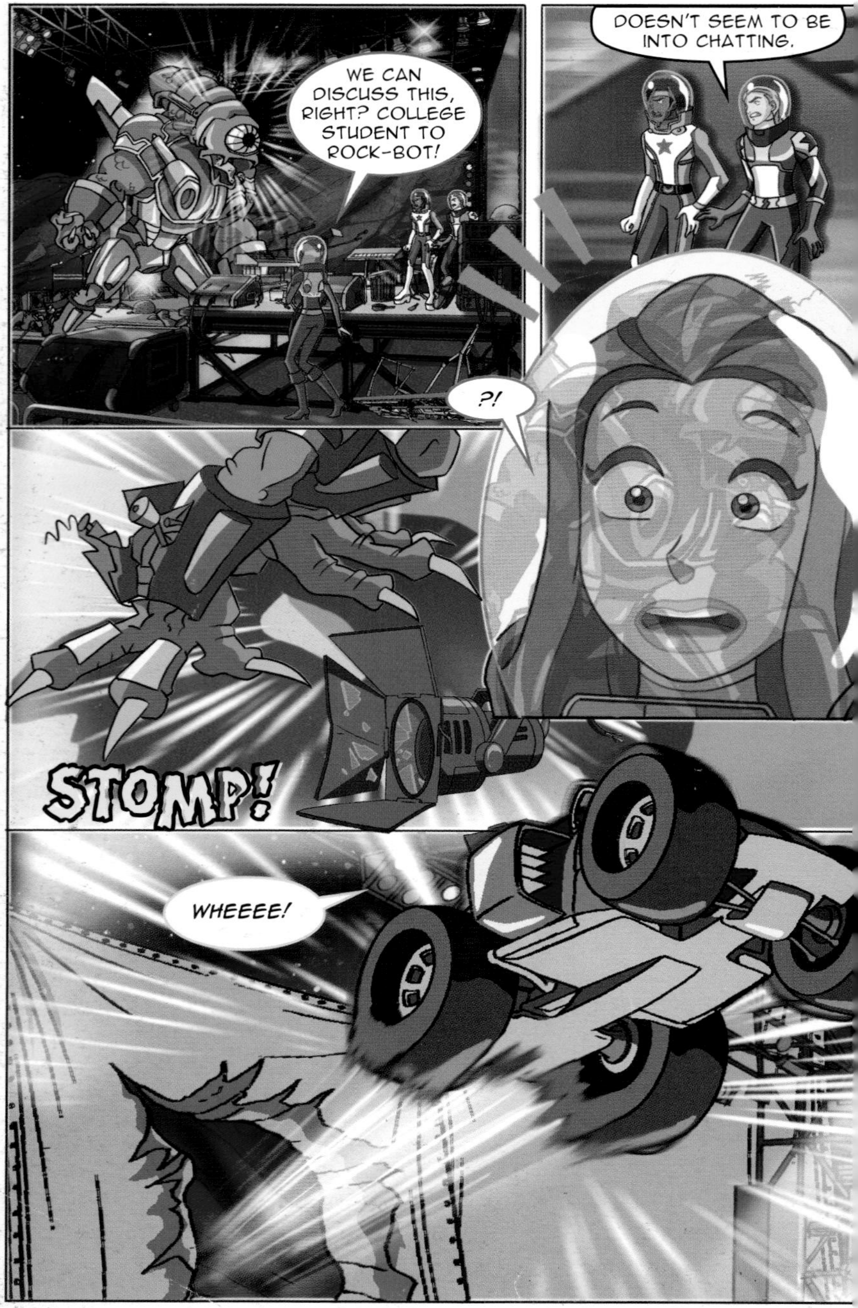
WE CAN DISCUSS THIS, RIGHT? COLLEGE STUDENT TO ROCK-BOT!
DOESN'T SEEM TO BE INTO CHATTING.
?!
STOMP!
WHEEEE!

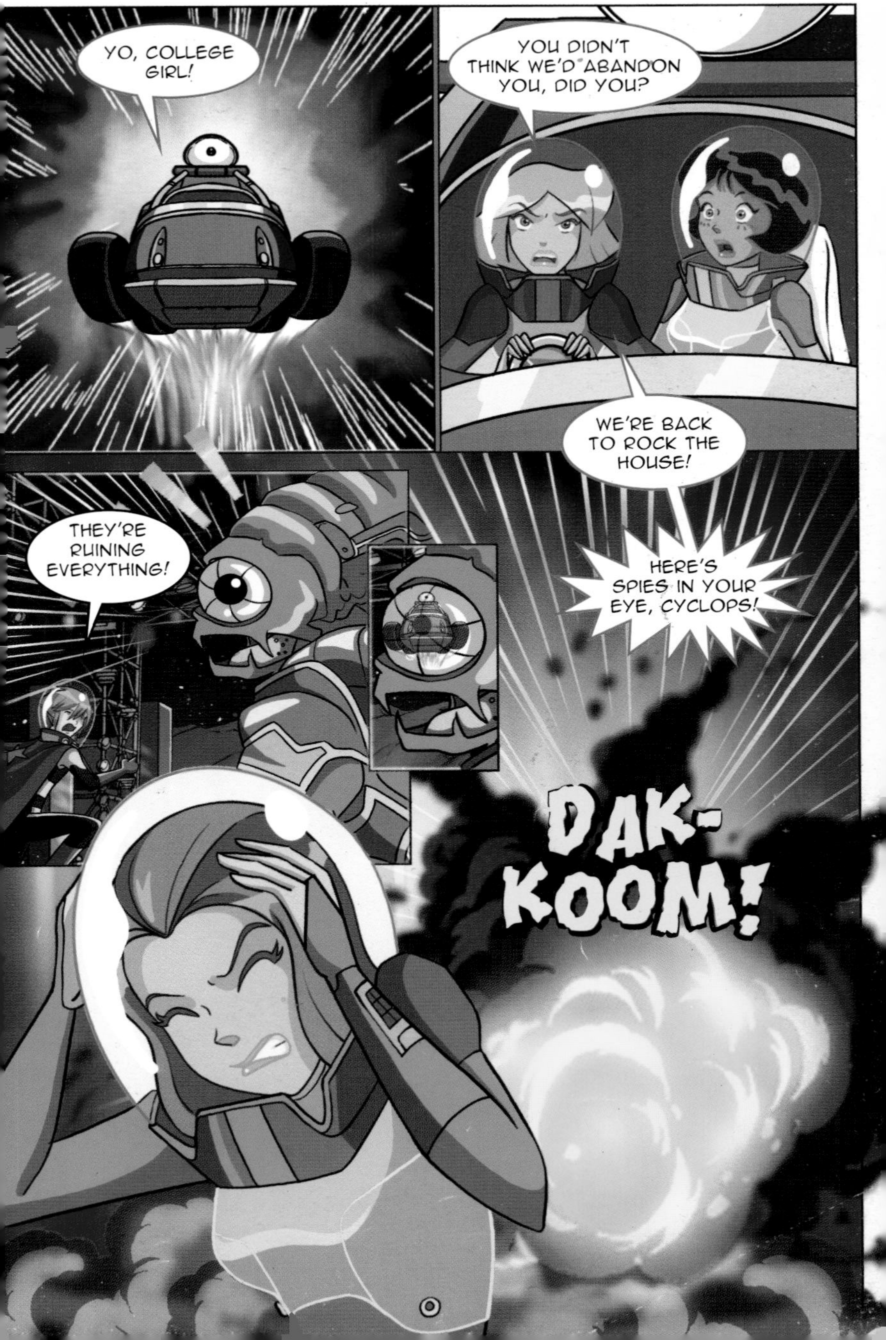
YO, COLLEGE GIRL!
YOU DIDN'T THINK WE'D ABANDON YOU, DID YOU?
WE'RE BACK TO ROCK THE HOUSE!
THEY'RE RUINING EVERYTHING!
HERE'S SPIES IN YOUR EYE, CYCLOPS!
DAK-KOOM!

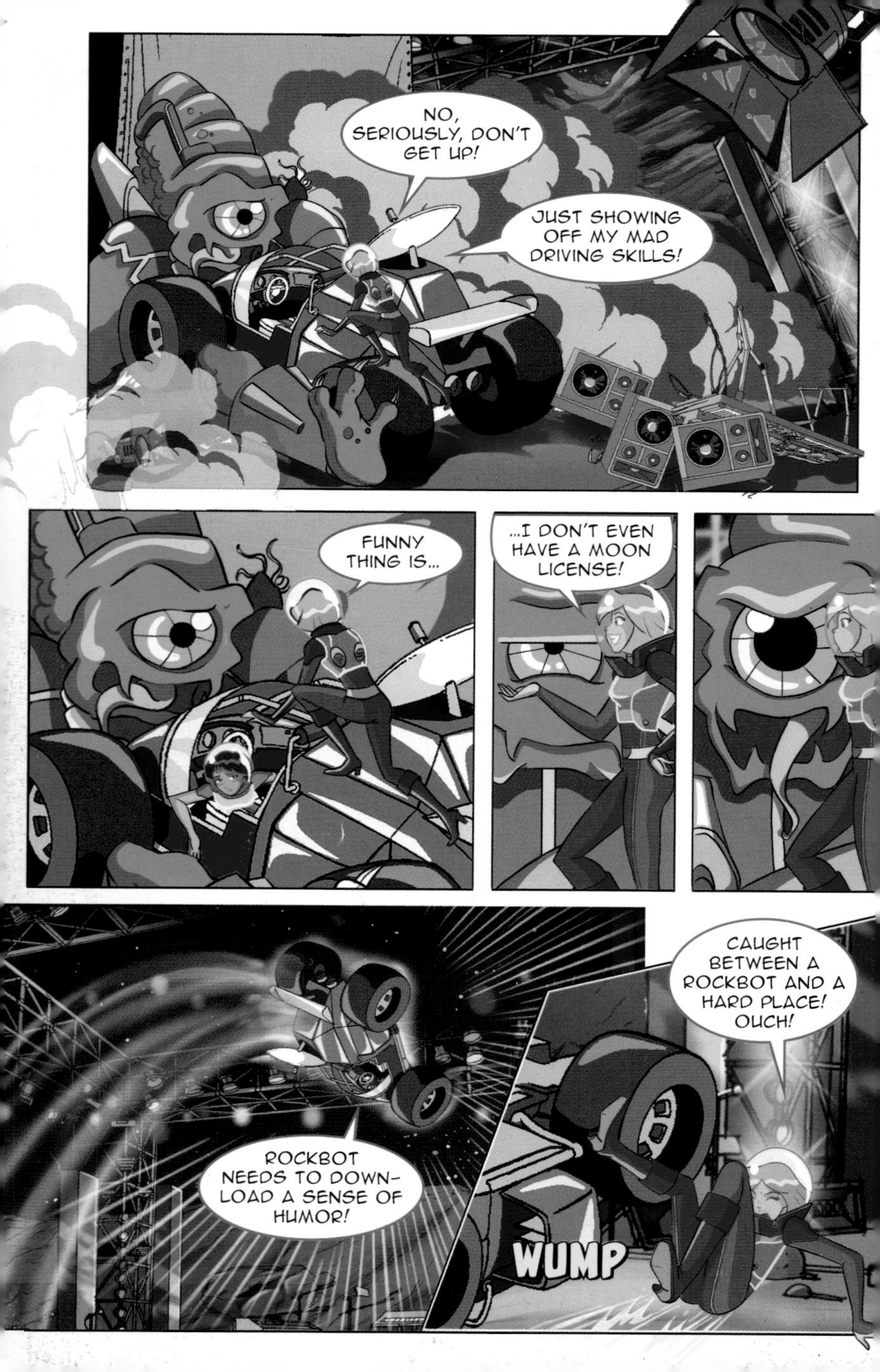
NO, SERIOUSLY, DON'T GET UP!
JUST SHOWING OFF MY MAD DRIVING SKILLS!
FUNNY THING IS...
...I DON'T EVEN HAVE A MOON LICENSE!
ROCKBOT NEEDS TO DOWN-LOAD A SENSE OF HUMOR!
CAUGHT BETWEEN A ROCKBOT AND A HARD PLACE! OUCH!
WUMP

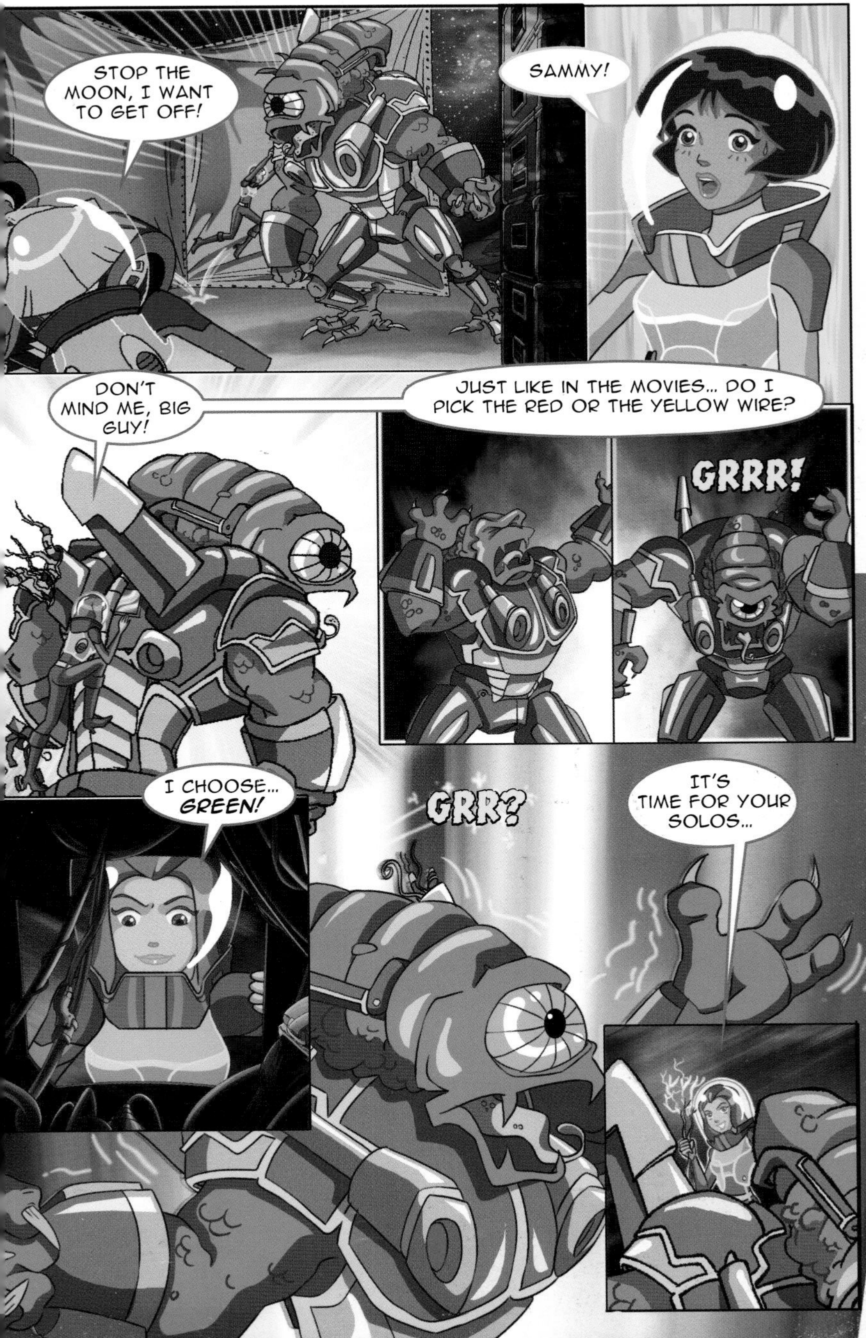
STOP THE MOON, I WANT TO GET OFF!
SAMMY!
DON'T MIND ME, BIG GUY!
JUST LIKE IN THE MOVIES... DO I PICK THE RED OR THE YELLOW WIRE?
GRRR!
I CHOOSE... GREEN!
GRR?
IT'S TIME FOR YOUR SOLOS...

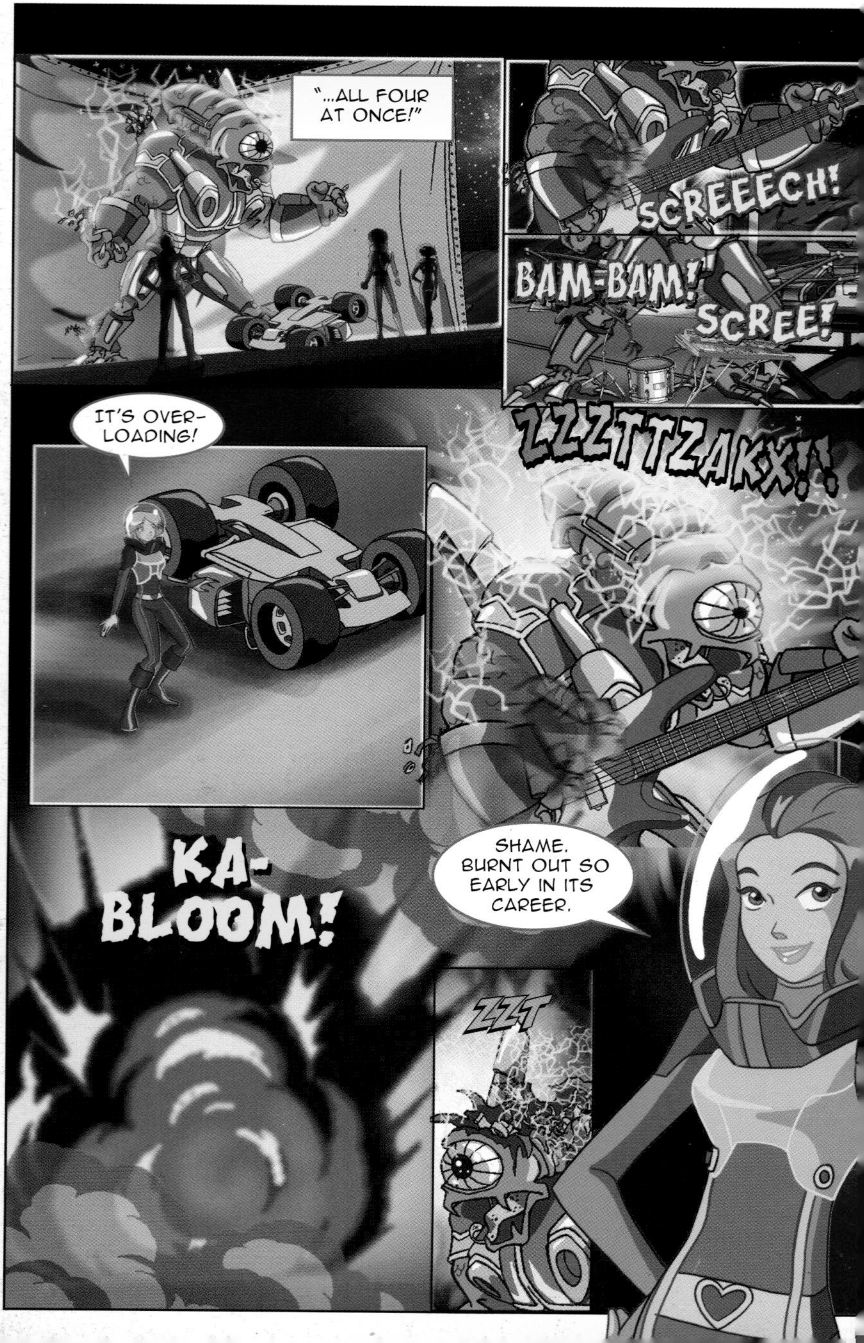
"...ALL FOUR AT ONCE!"
SCREEECH!
BAM-BAM!
SCREE!
IT'S OVER-LOADING!
ZZZTTZAKX!!
KA-BLOOM!
SHAME. BURNT OUT SO EARLY IN ITS CAREER.
ZZZT

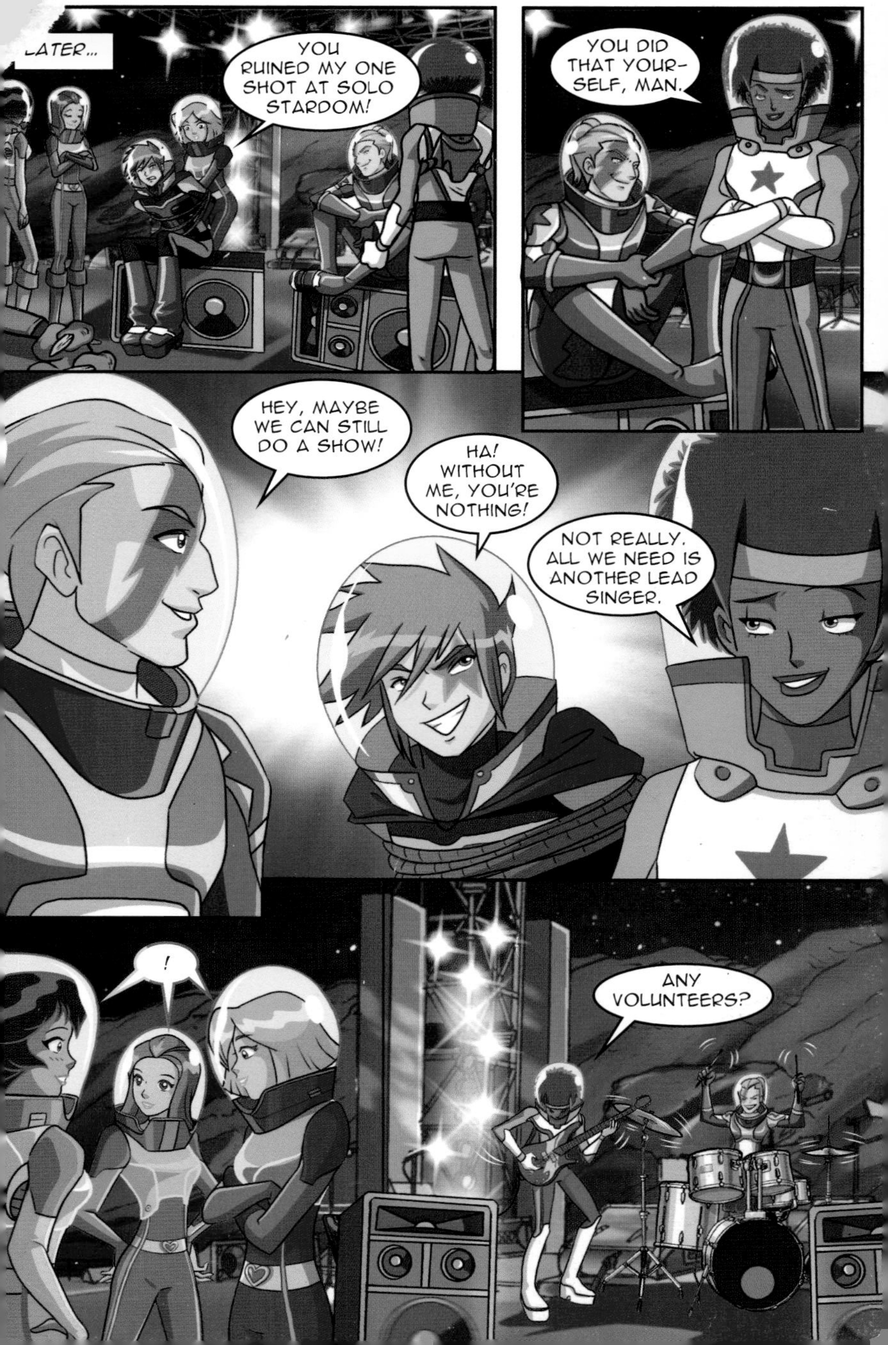
LATER...
YOU RUINED MY ONE SHOT AT SOLO STARDOM!
YOU DID THAT YOURSELF, MAN.
HEY, MAYBE WE CAN STILL DO A SHOW!
HA! WITHOUT ME, YOU'RE NOTHING!
NOT REALLY. ALL WE NEED IS ANOTHER LEAD SINGER.
!
ANY VOLUNTEERS?

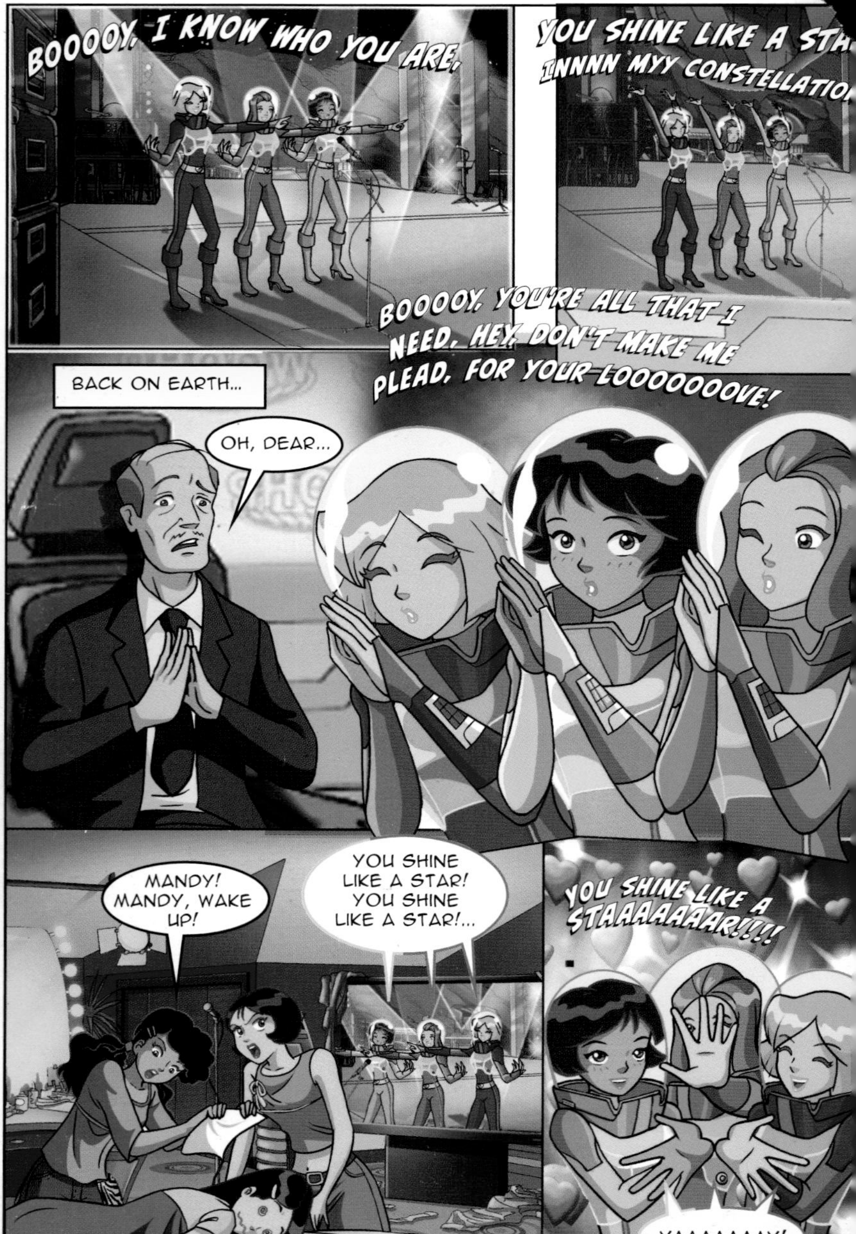
BOOOOY, I KNOW WHO YOU ARE,
YOU SHINE LIKE A STA
INNNN MYY CONSTELLATIO
BOOOOY, YOU'RE ALL THAT I NEED, HEY, DON'T MAKE ME PLEAD, FOR YOUR LOOOOOOOVE!
BACK ON EARTH...
OH, DEAR...
MANDY! MANDY, WAKE UP!
YOU SHINE LIKE A STAR! YOU SHINE LIKE A STAR!...
YOU SHINE LIKE A STAAAAAAAR!!!!
YAAAAAAAY!

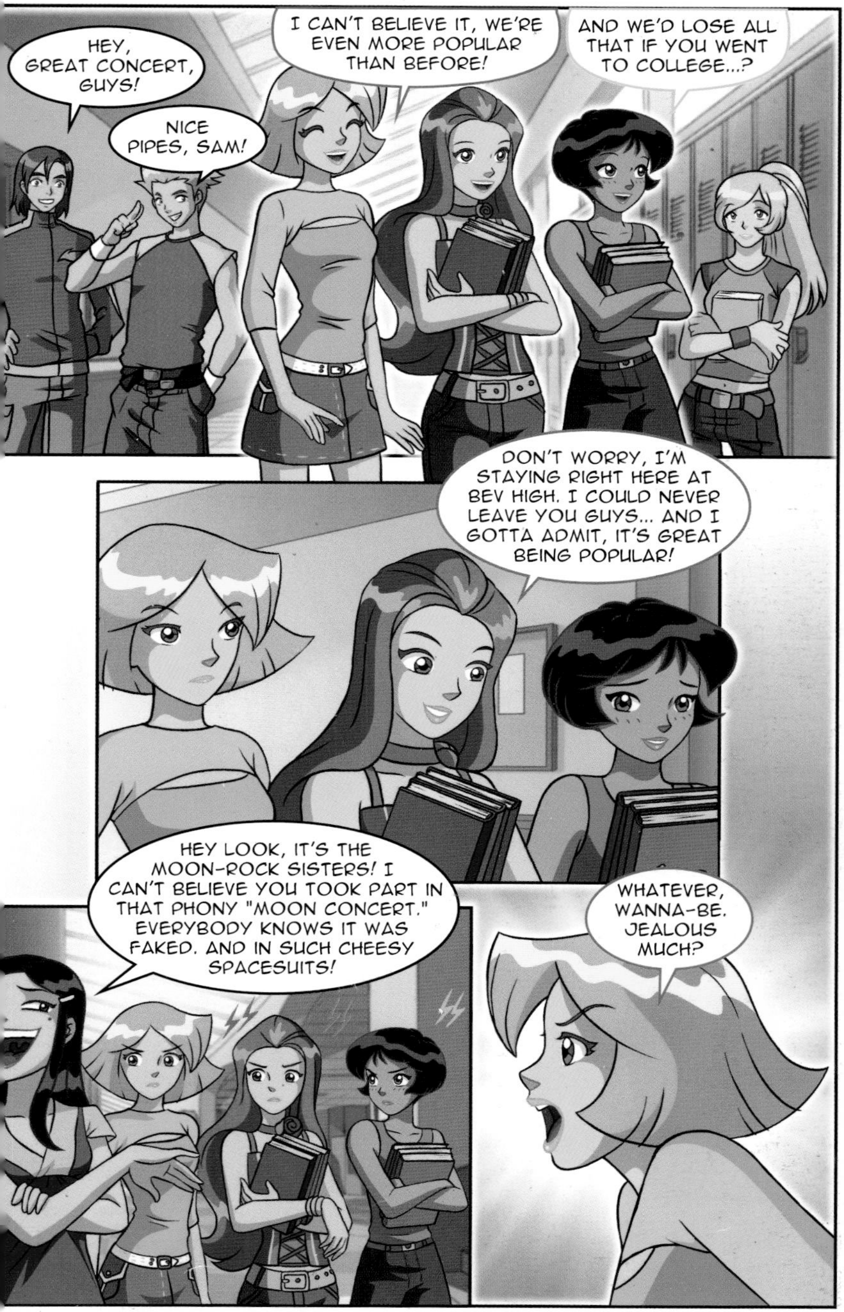
HEY, GREAT CONCERT, GUYS!
NICE PIPES, SAM!
I CAN'T BELIEVE IT, WE'RE EVEN MORE POPULAR THAN BEFORE!
AND WE'D LOSE ALL THAT IF YOU WENT TO COLLEGE...?
DON'T WORRY, I'M STAYING RIGHT HERE AT BEV HIGH. I COULD NEVER LEAVE YOU GUYS... AND I GOTTA ADMIT, IT'S GREAT BEING POPULAR!
HEY LOOK, IT'S THE MOON-ROCK SISTERS! I CAN'T BELIEVE YOU TOOK PART IN THAT PHONY "MOON CONCERT." EVERYBODY KNOWS IT WAS FAKED. AND IN SUCH CHEESY SPACESUITS!
WHATEVER, WANNA-BE. JEALOUS MUCH?

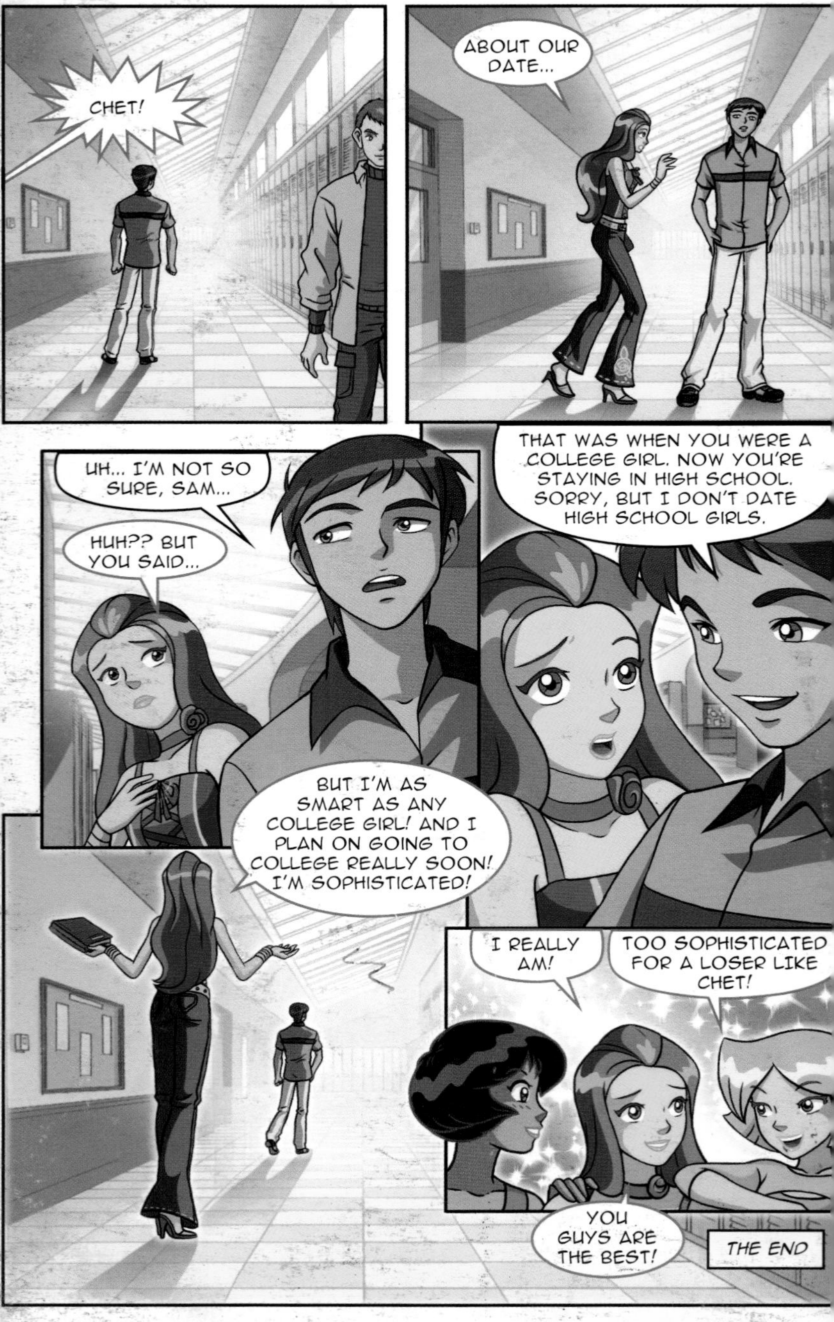
CHET!
ABOUT OUR DATE...
UH... I'M NOT SO SURE, SAM...
HUH?? BUT YOU SAID...
THAT WAS WHEN YOU WERE A COLLEGE GIRL. NOW YOU'RE STAYING IN HIGH SCHOOL. SORRY, BUT I DON'T DATE HIGH SCHOOL GIRLS.
BUT I'M AS SMART AS ANY COLLEGE GIRL! AND I PLAN ON GOING TO COLLEGE REALLY SOON! I'M SOPHISTICATED!
I REALLY AM!
TOO SOPHISTICATED FOR A LOSER LIKE CHET!
YOU GUYS ARE THE BEST!
THE END

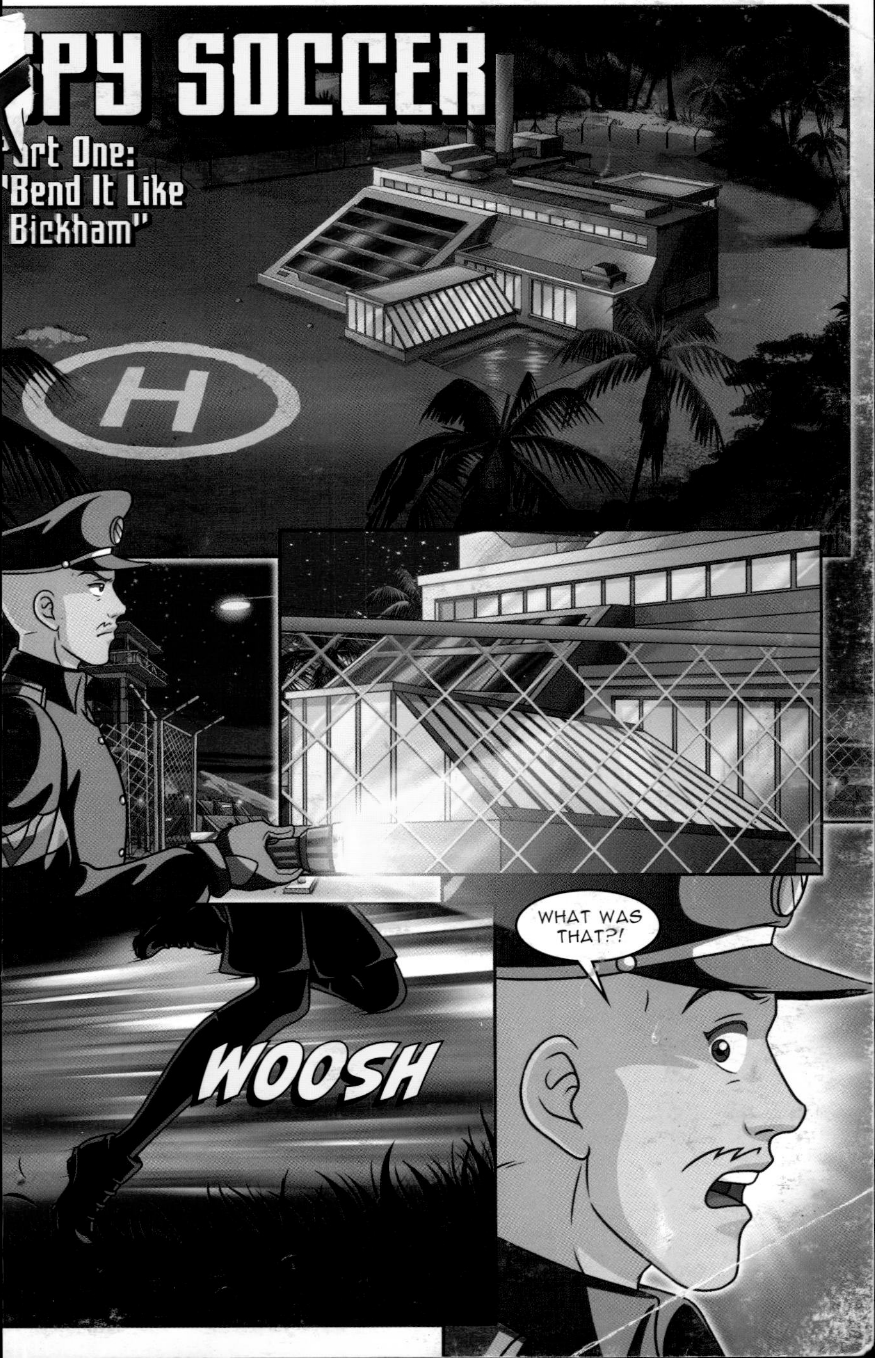
SPY SOCCER
Part One:
"Bend It Like
Bickham"
WOOSH
WHAT WAS THAT?!

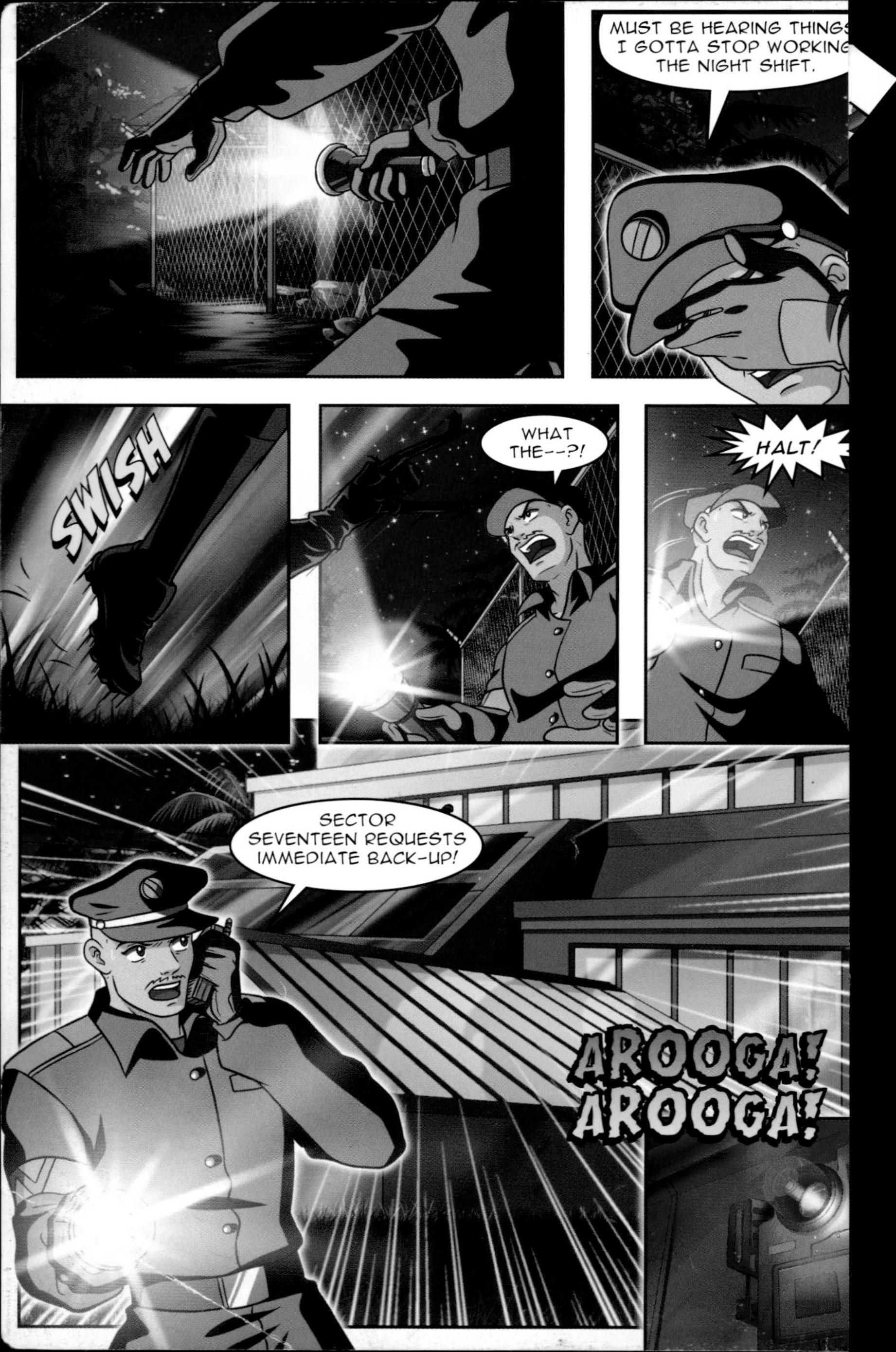
MUST BE HEARING THINGS I GOTTA STOP WORKING THE NIGHT SHIFT.
SWISH
WHAT THE--?!
HALT!
SECTOR SEVENTEEN REQUESTS IMMEDIATE BACK-UP!
AROOGA! AROOGA!

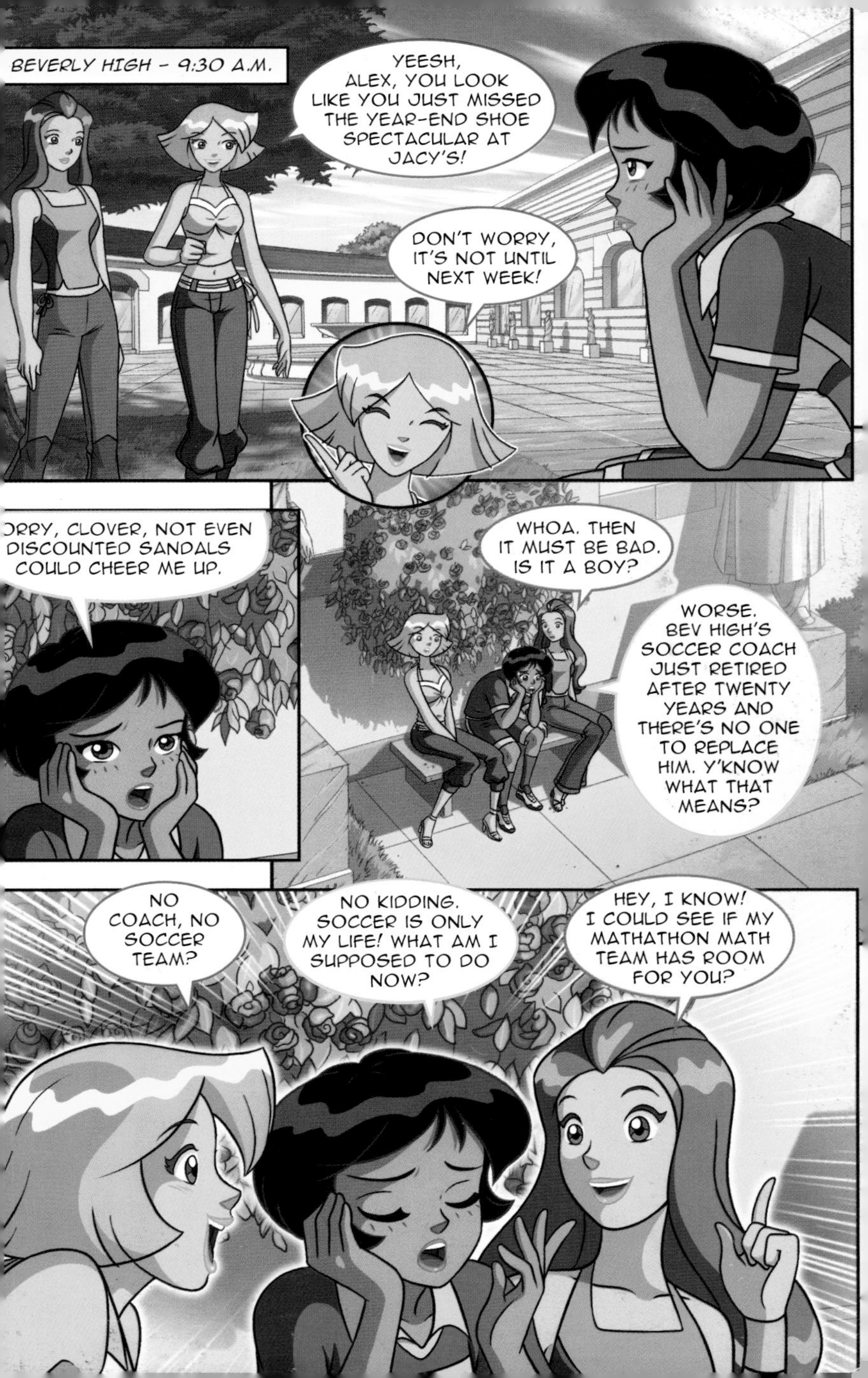
BEVERLY HIGH – 9:30 A.M.
YEESH, ALEX, YOU LOOK LIKE YOU JUST MISSED THE YEAR-END SHOE SPECTACULAR AT JACY'S!
DON'T WORRY, IT'S NOT UNTIL NEXT WEEK!
ORRY, CLOVER, NOT EVEN DISCOUNTED SANDALS COULD CHEER ME UP.
WHOA. THEN IT MUST BE BAD. IS IT A BOY?
WORSE. BEV HIGH'S SOCCER COACH JUST RETIRED AFTER TWENTY YEARS AND THERE'S NO ONE TO REPLACE HIM. Y'KNOW WHAT THAT MEANS?
NO COACH, NO SOCCER TEAM?
NO KIDDING. SOCCER IS ONLY MY LIFE! WHAT AM I SUPPOSED TO DO NOW?
HEY, I KNOW! I COULD SEE IF MY MATHATHON MATH TEAM HAS ROOM FOR YOU?

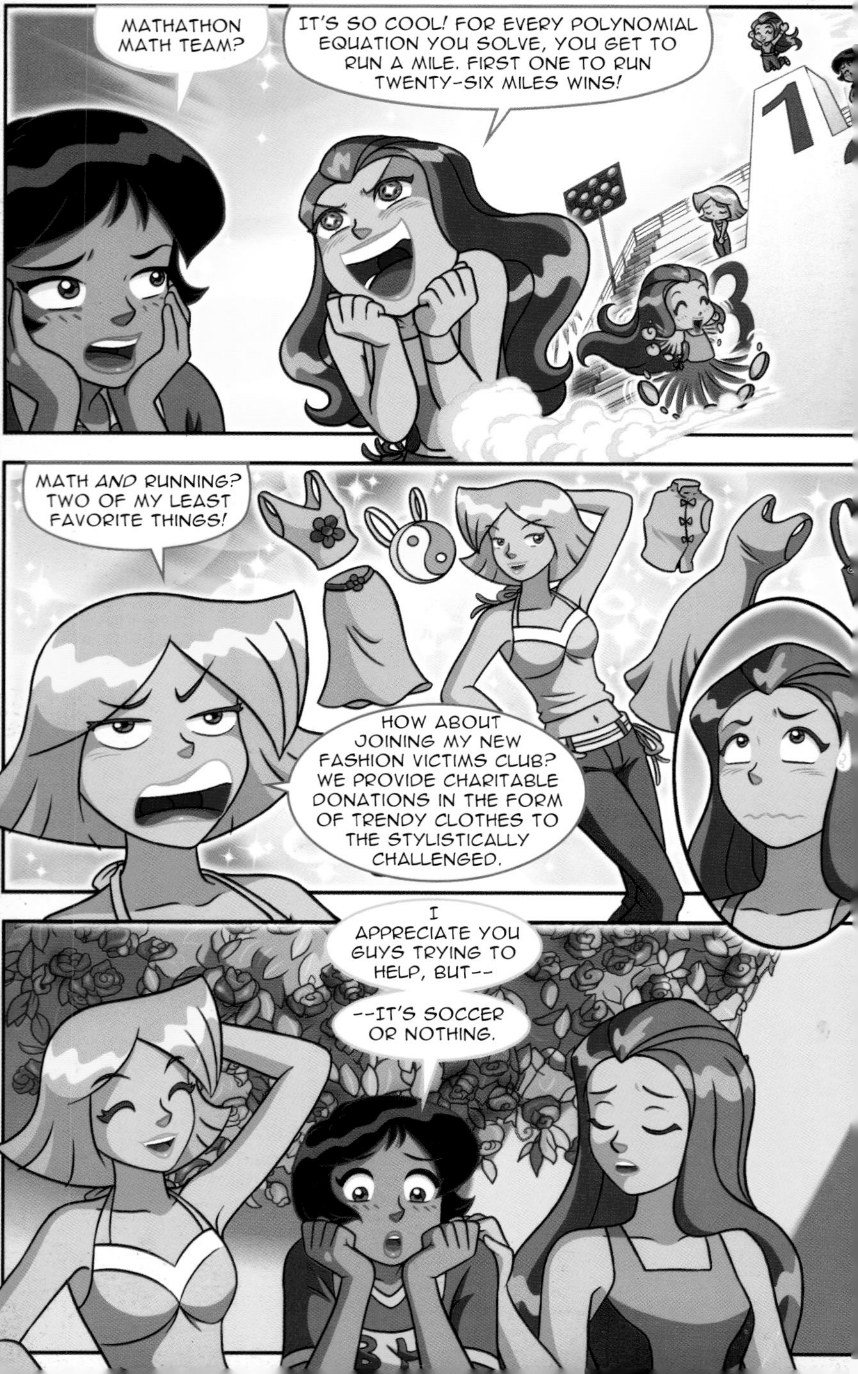
MATHATHON MATH TEAM?
IT'S SO COOL! FOR EVERY POLYNOMIAL EQUATION YOU SOLVE, YOU GET TO RUN A MILE. FIRST ONE TO RUN TWENTY-SIX MILES WINS!
MATH *AND* RUNNING? TWO OF MY LEAST FAVORITE THINGS!
HOW ABOUT JOINING MY NEW FASHION VICTIMS CLUB? WE PROVIDE CHARITABLE DONATIONS IN THE FORM OF TRENDY CLOTHES TO THE STYLISTICALLY CHALLENGED.
I APPRECIATE YOU GUYS TRYING TO HELP, BUT--
--IT'S SOCCER OR NOTHING.

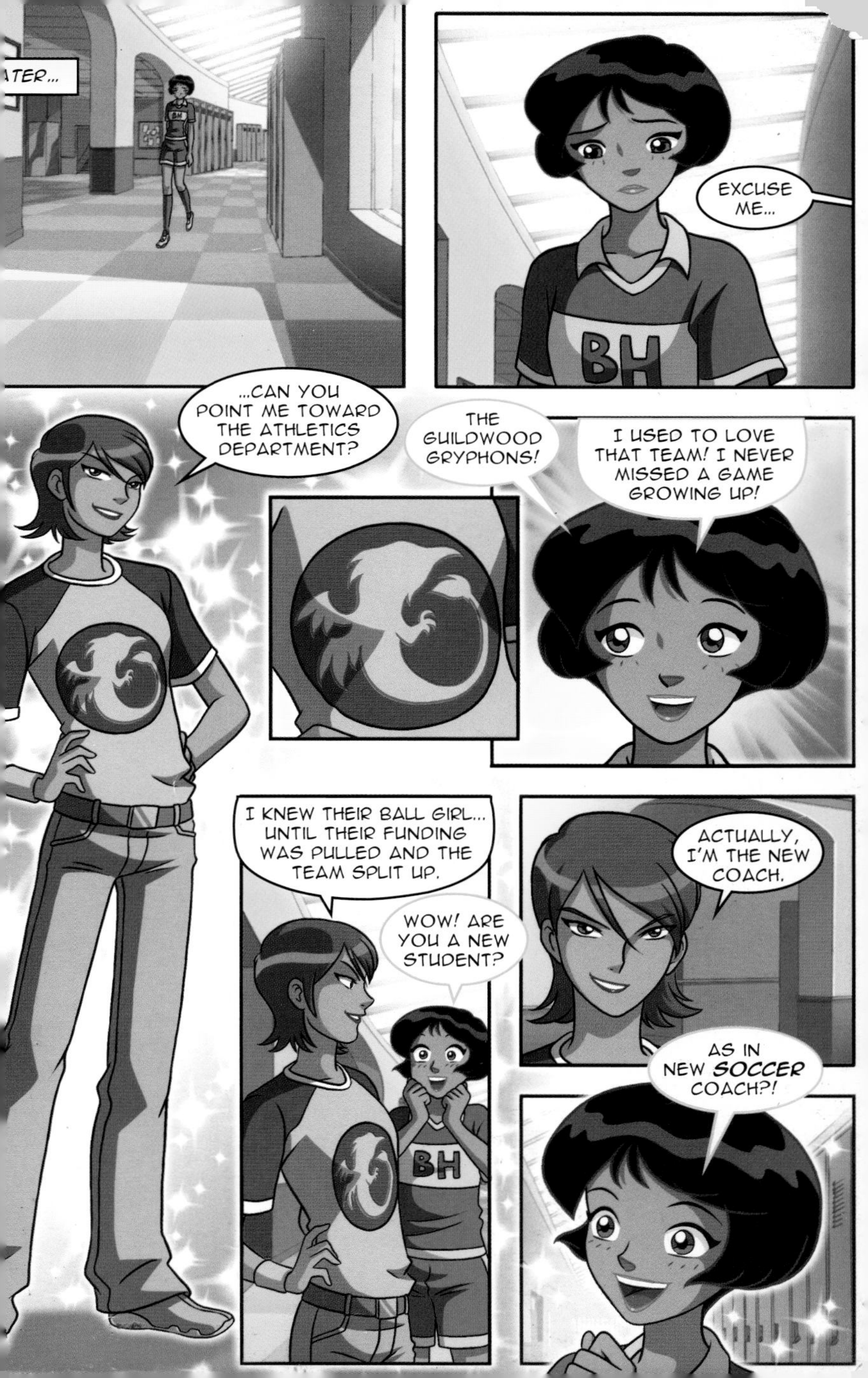
ATER...
EXCUSE ME...
...CAN YOU POINT ME TOWARD THE ATHLETICS DEPARTMENT?
THE GUILDWOOD GRYPHONS!
I USED TO LOVE THAT TEAM! I NEVER MISSED A GAME GROWING UP!
I KNEW THEIR BALL GIRL... UNTIL THEIR FUNDING WAS PULLED AND THE TEAM SPLIT UP.
WOW! ARE YOU A NEW STUDENT?
ACTUALLY, I'M THE NEW COACH.
AS IN NEW SOCCER COACH?!

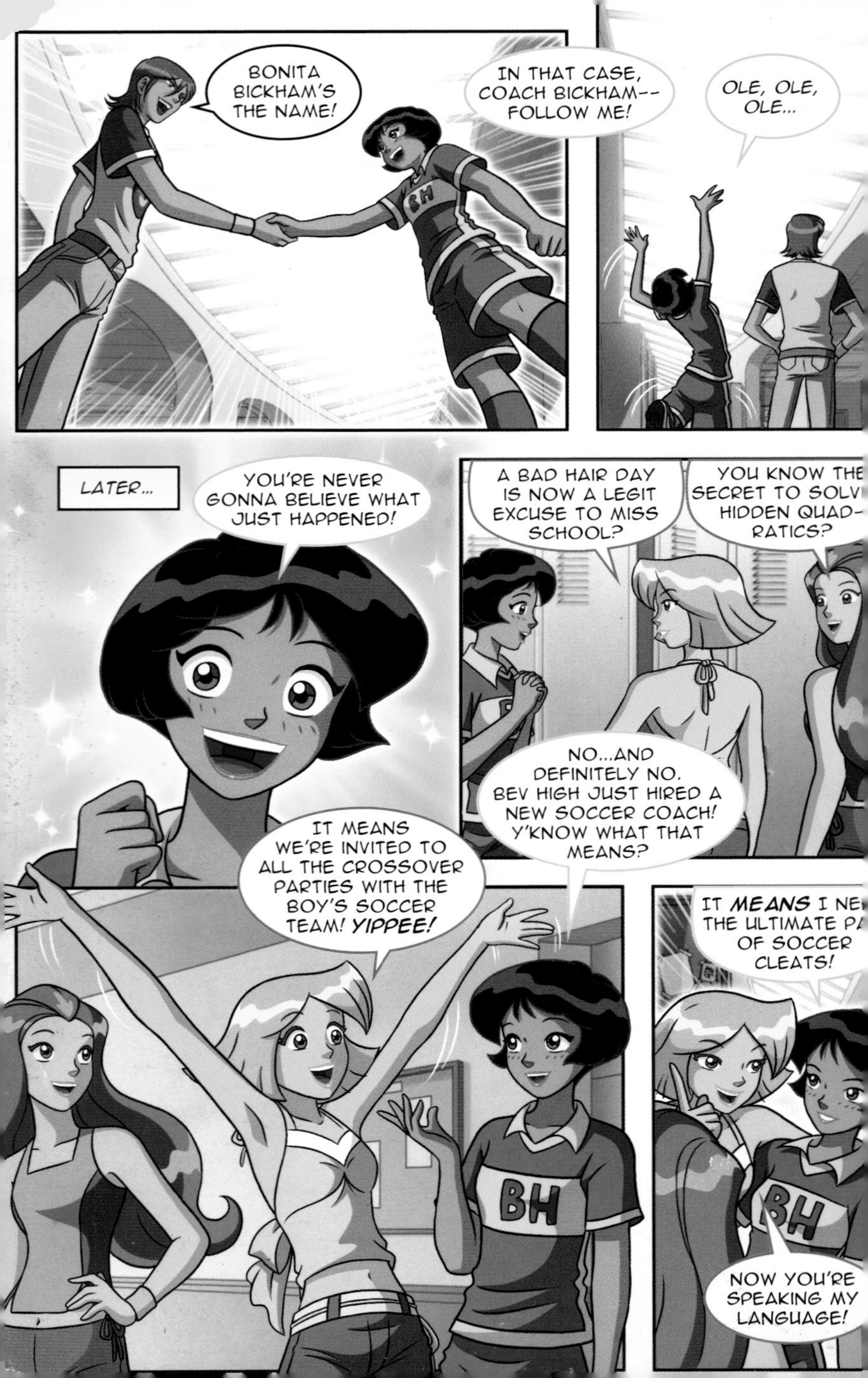
BONITA BICKHAM'S THE NAME!
IN THAT CASE, COACH BICKHAM-- FOLLOW ME!
OLE, OLE, OLE...
LATER...
YOU'RE NEVER GONNA BELIEVE WHAT JUST HAPPENED!
A BAD HAIR DAY IS NOW A LEGIT EXCUSE TO MISS SCHOOL?
YOU KNOW THE SECRET TO SOLV HIDDEN QUAD-RATICS?
NO...AND DEFINITELY NO. BEV HIGH JUST HIRED A NEW SOCCER COACH! Y'KNOW WHAT THAT MEANS?
IT MEANS WE'RE INVITED TO ALL THE CROSSOVER PARTIES WITH THE BOY'S SOCCER TEAM! *YIPPEE!*
IT *MEANS* I NE THE ULTIMATE PA OF SOCCER CLEATS!
NOW YOU'RE SPEAKING MY LANGUAGE!

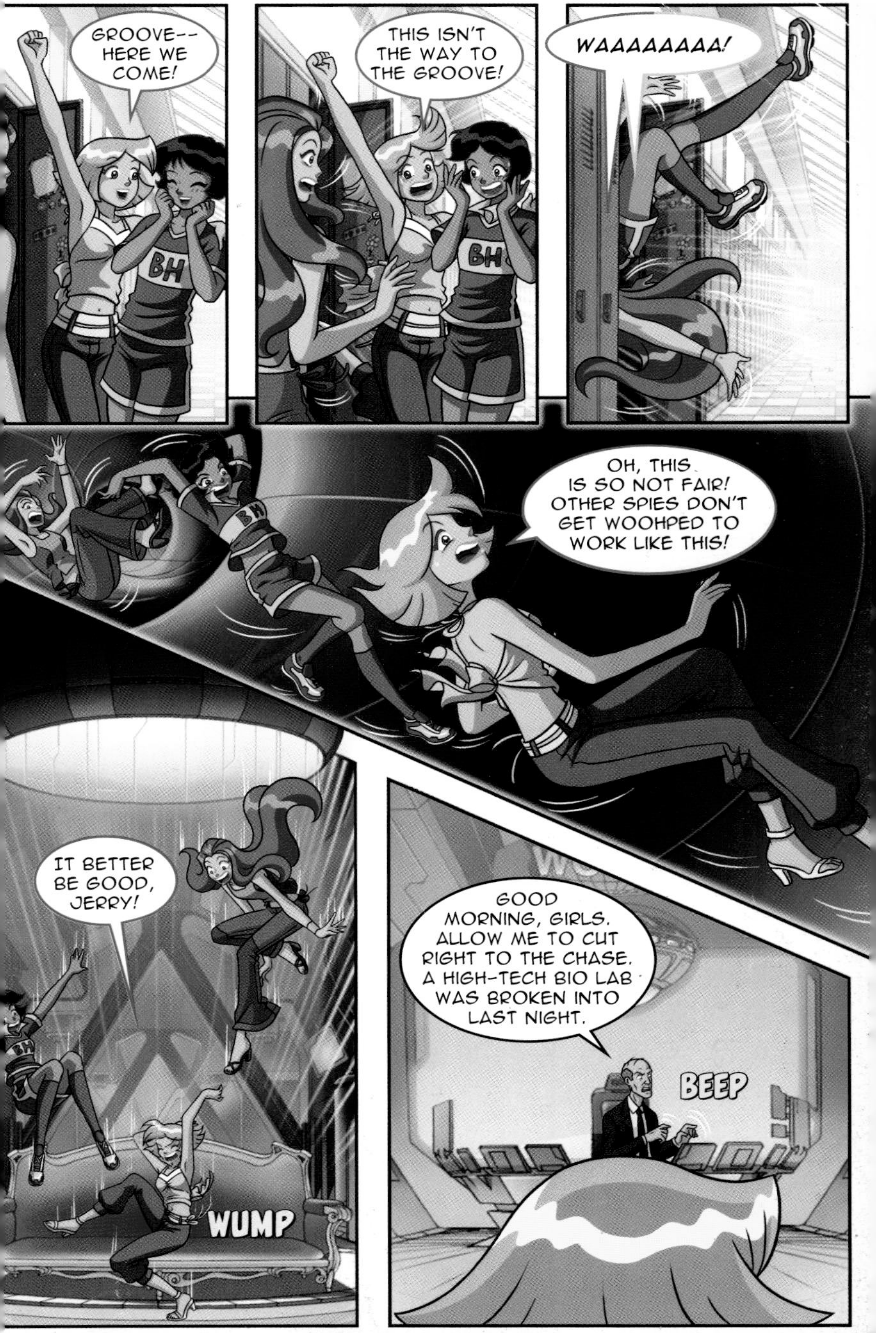
GROOVE-- HERE WE COME!
THIS ISN'T THE WAY TO THE GROOVE!
WAAAAAAAA!
OH, THIS IS SO NOT FAIR! OTHER SPIES DON'T GET WOOHPED TO WORK LIKE THIS!
IT BETTER BE GOOD, JERRY!
WUMP
GOOD MORNING, GIRLS. ALLOW ME TO CUT RIGHT TO THE CHASE. A HIGH-TECH BIO LAB WAS BROKEN INTO LAST NIGHT.
BEEP

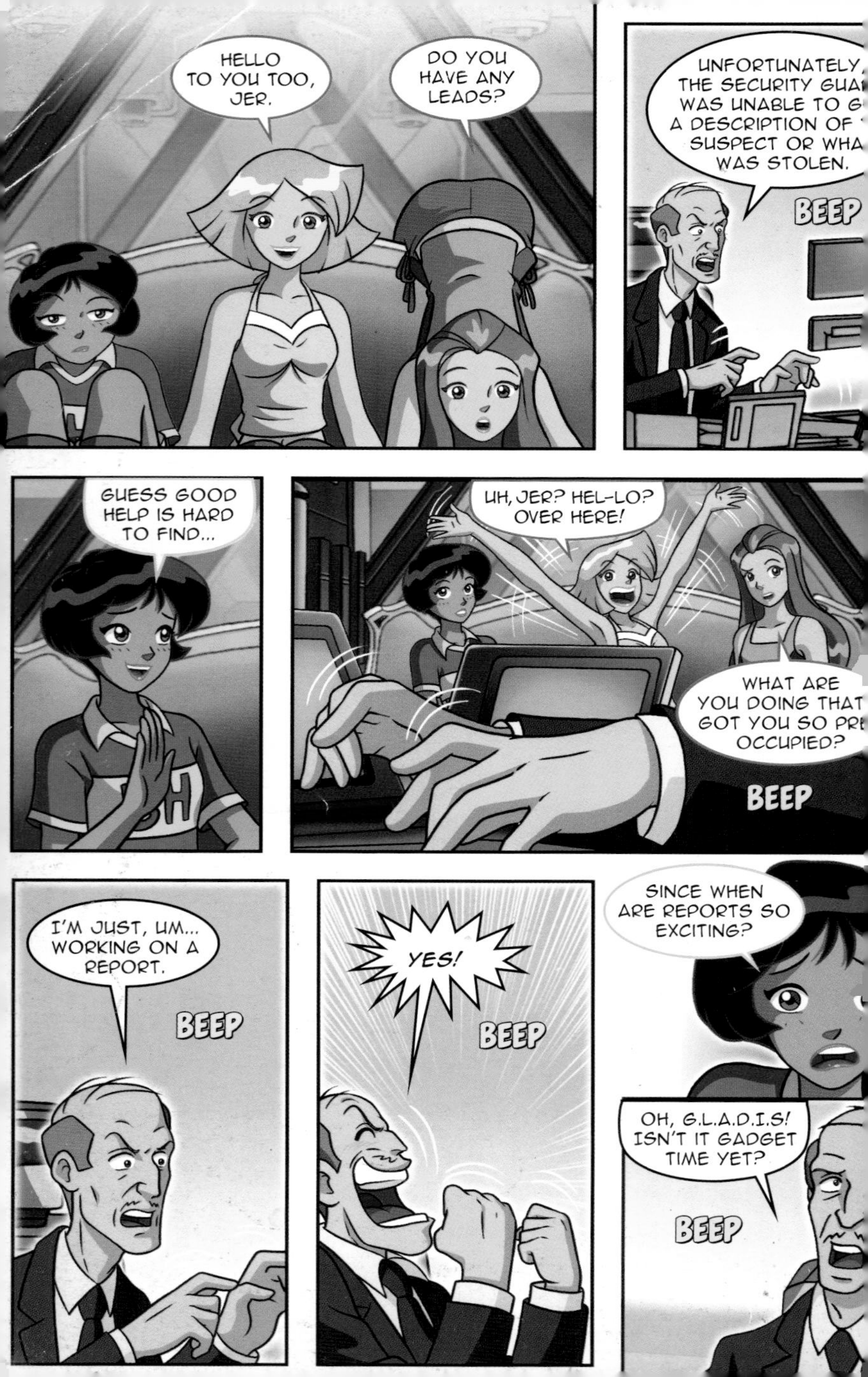
HELLO TO YOU TOO, JER.
DO YOU HAVE ANY LEADS?
UNFORTUNATELY, THE SECURITY GUA WAS UNABLE TO G A DESCRIPTION OF SUSPECT OR WHA WAS STOLEN.
BEEP
GUESS GOOD HELP IS HARD TO FIND...
UH, JER? HEL-LO? OVER HERE!
WHAT ARE YOU DOING THAT GOT YOU SO PR OCCUPIED?
BEEP
I'M JUST, UM... WORKING ON A REPORT.
BEEP
YES!
BEEP
SINCE WHEN ARE REPORTS SO EXCITING?
OH, G.L.A.D.I.S! ISN'T IT GADGET TIME YET?
BEEP

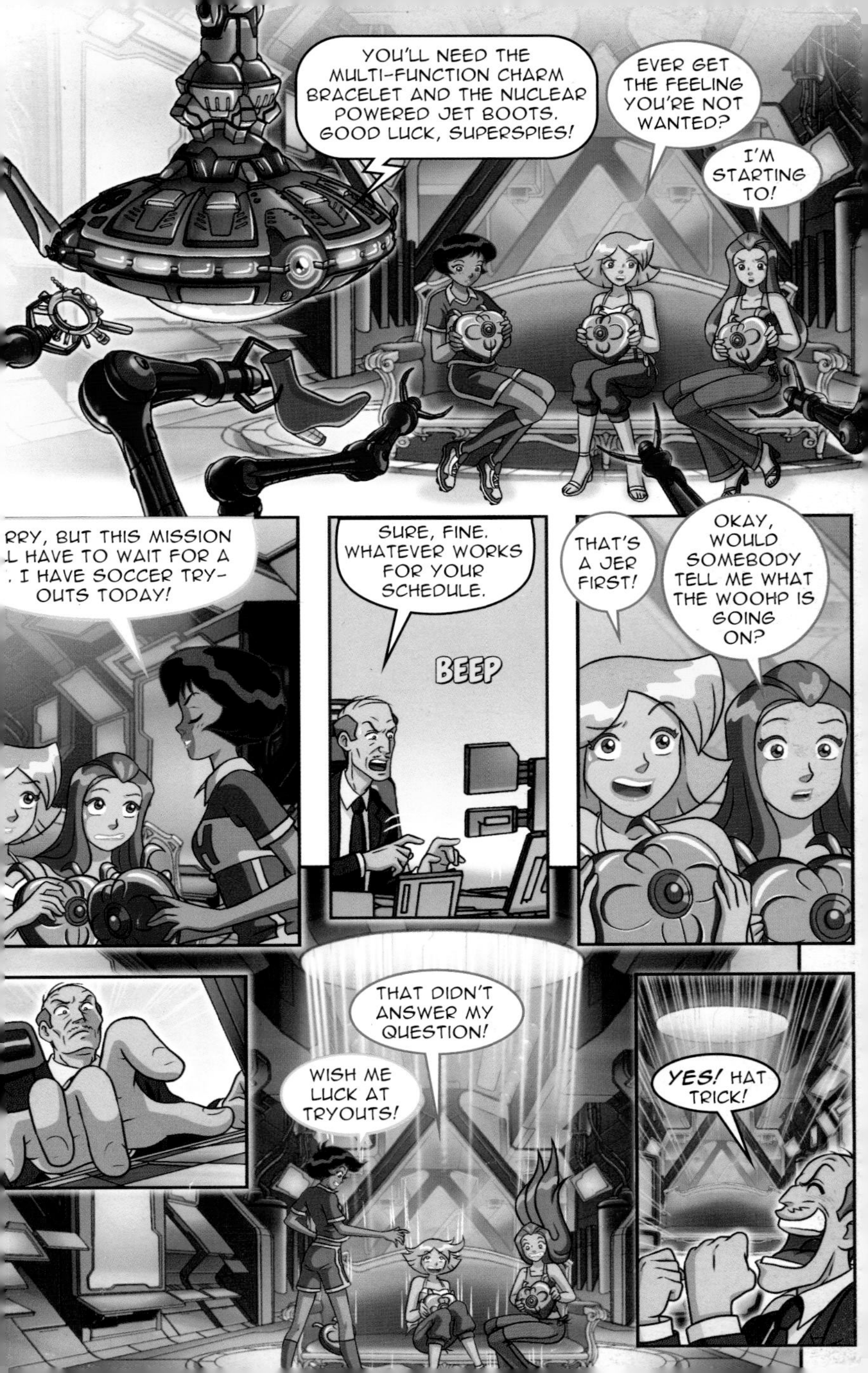
YOU'LL NEED THE MULTI-FUNCTION CHARM BRACELET AND THE NUCLEAR POWERED JET BOOTS. GOOD LUCK, SUPERSPIES!
EVER GET THE FEELING YOU'RE NOT WANTED?
I'M STARTING TO!
RRY, BUT THIS MISSION L HAVE TO WAIT FOR A . I HAVE SOCCER TRY-OUTS TODAY!
SURE, FINE. WHATEVER WORKS FOR YOUR SCHEDULE.
BEEP
THAT'S A JER FIRST!
OKAY, WOULD SOMEBODY TELL ME WHAT THE WOOHP IS GOING ON?
THAT DIDN'T ANSWER MY QUESTION!
WISH ME LUCK AT TRYOUTS!
YES! HAT TRICK!

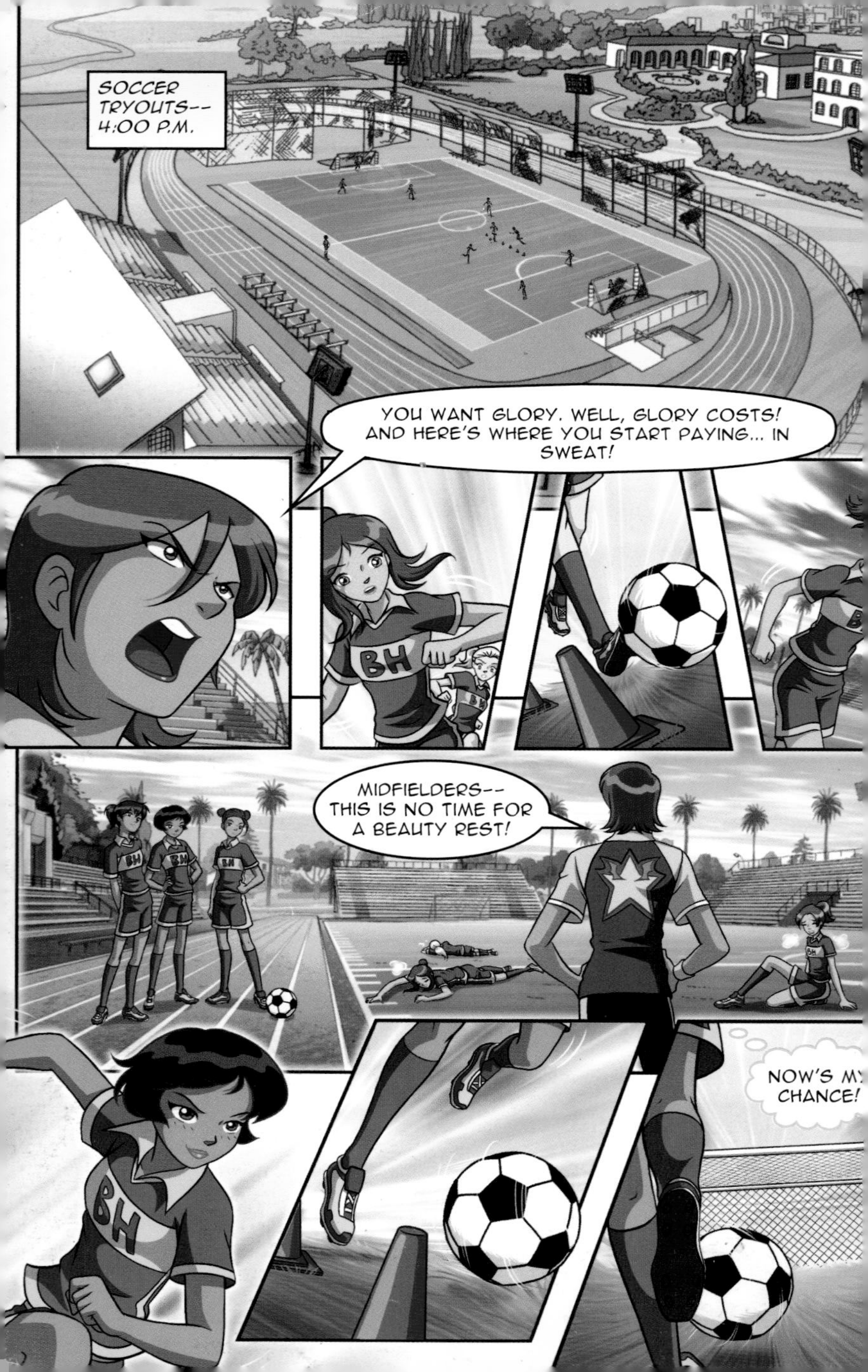
SOCCER TRYOUTS-- 4:00 P.M.
YOU WANT GLORY. WELL, GLORY COSTS! AND HERE'S WHERE YOU START PAYING... IN SWEAT!
MIDFIELDERS-- THIS IS NO TIME FOR A BEAUTY REST!
NOW'S MY CHANCE!

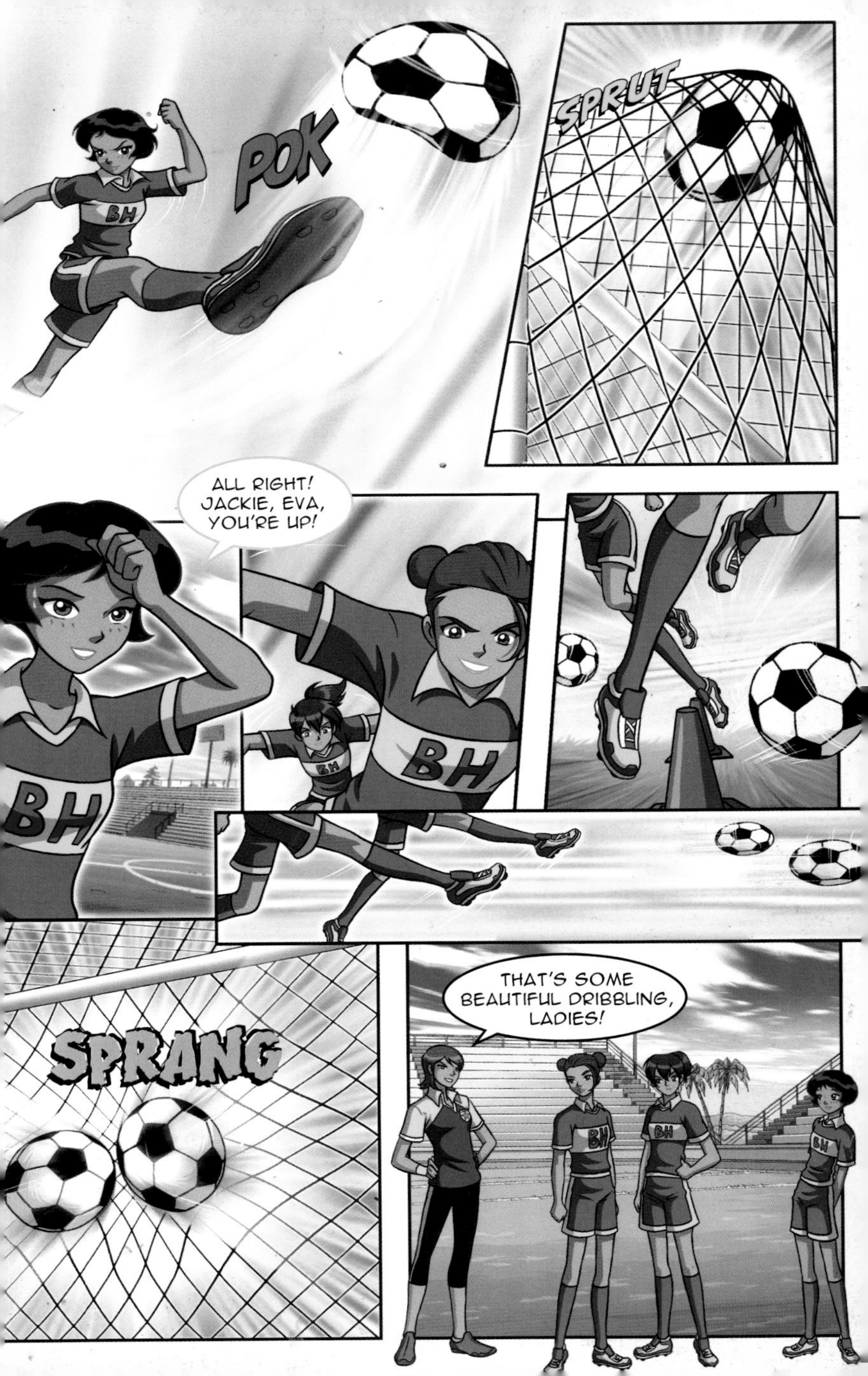
POK
SPRUT
ALL RIGHT! JACKIE, EVA, YOU'RE UP!
SPRANG
THAT'S SOME BEAUTIFUL DRIBBLING, LADIES!

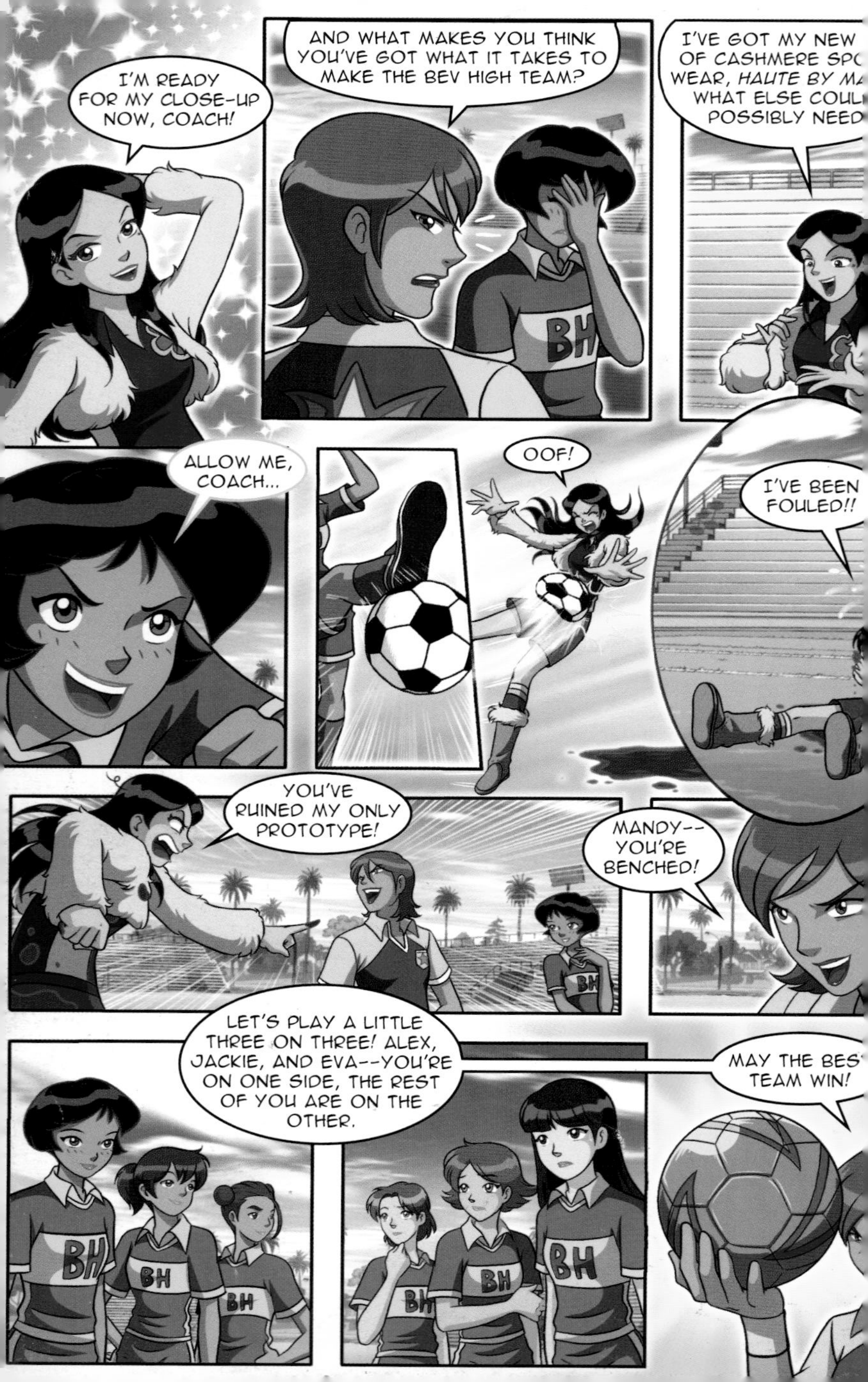
I'M READY FOR MY CLOSE-UP NOW, COACH!
AND WHAT MAKES YOU THINK YOU'VE GOT WHAT IT TAKES TO MAKE THE BEV HIGH TEAM?
I'VE GOT MY NEW OF CASHMERE SPO WEAR, *HAUTE BY MA* WHAT ELSE COUL POSSIBLY NEED
ALLOW ME, COACH...
OOF!
I'VE BEEN FOULED!!
YOU'VE RUINED MY ONLY PROTOTYPE!
MANDY-- YOU'RE BENCHED!
LET'S PLAY A LITTLE THREE ON THREE! ALEX, JACKIE, AND EVA--YOU'RE ON ONE SIDE, THE REST OF YOU ARE ON THE OTHER.
MAY THE BES TEAM WIN!

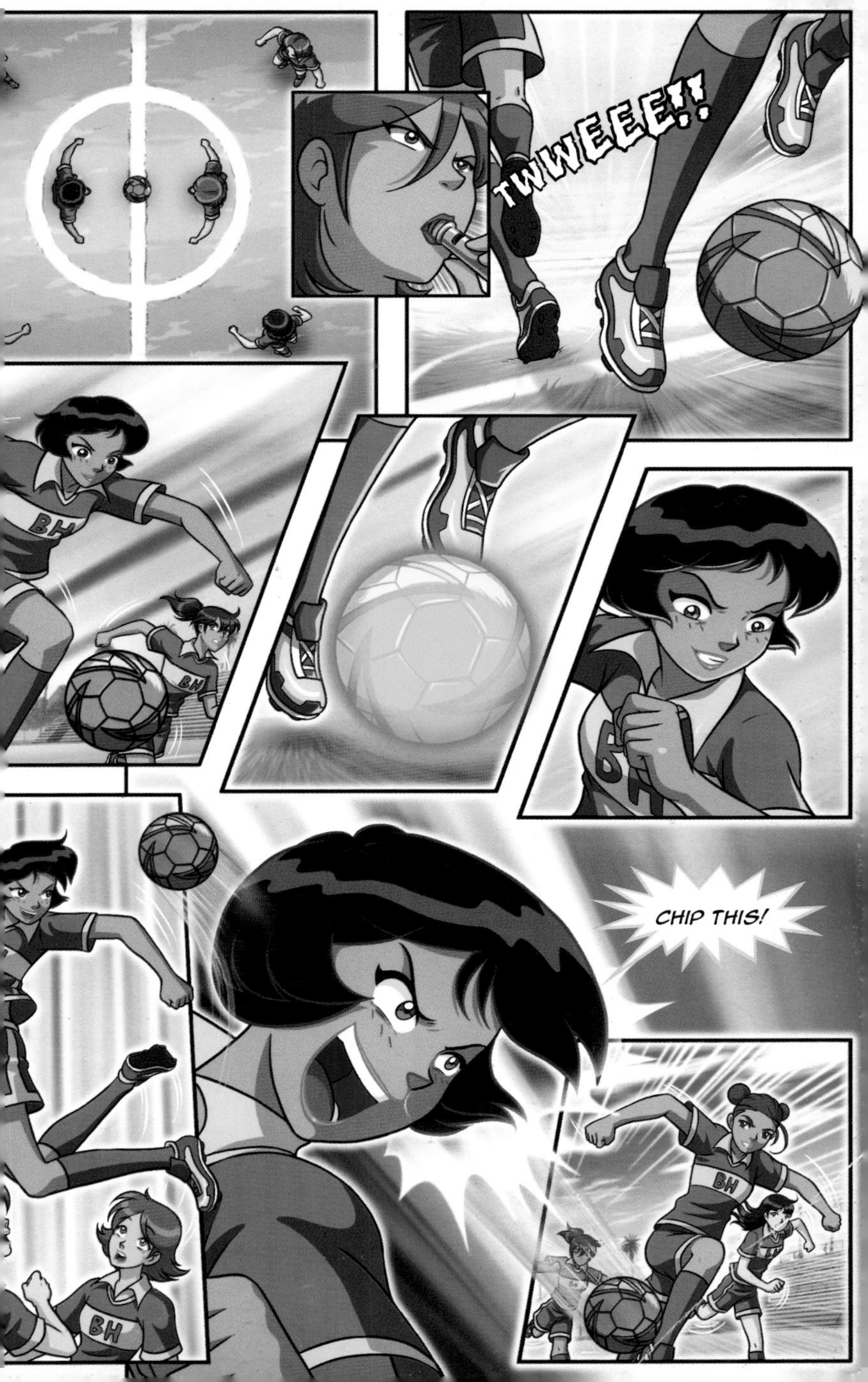
TWWEEE!!
BH
BH
BH
CHIP THIS!
BH
BH

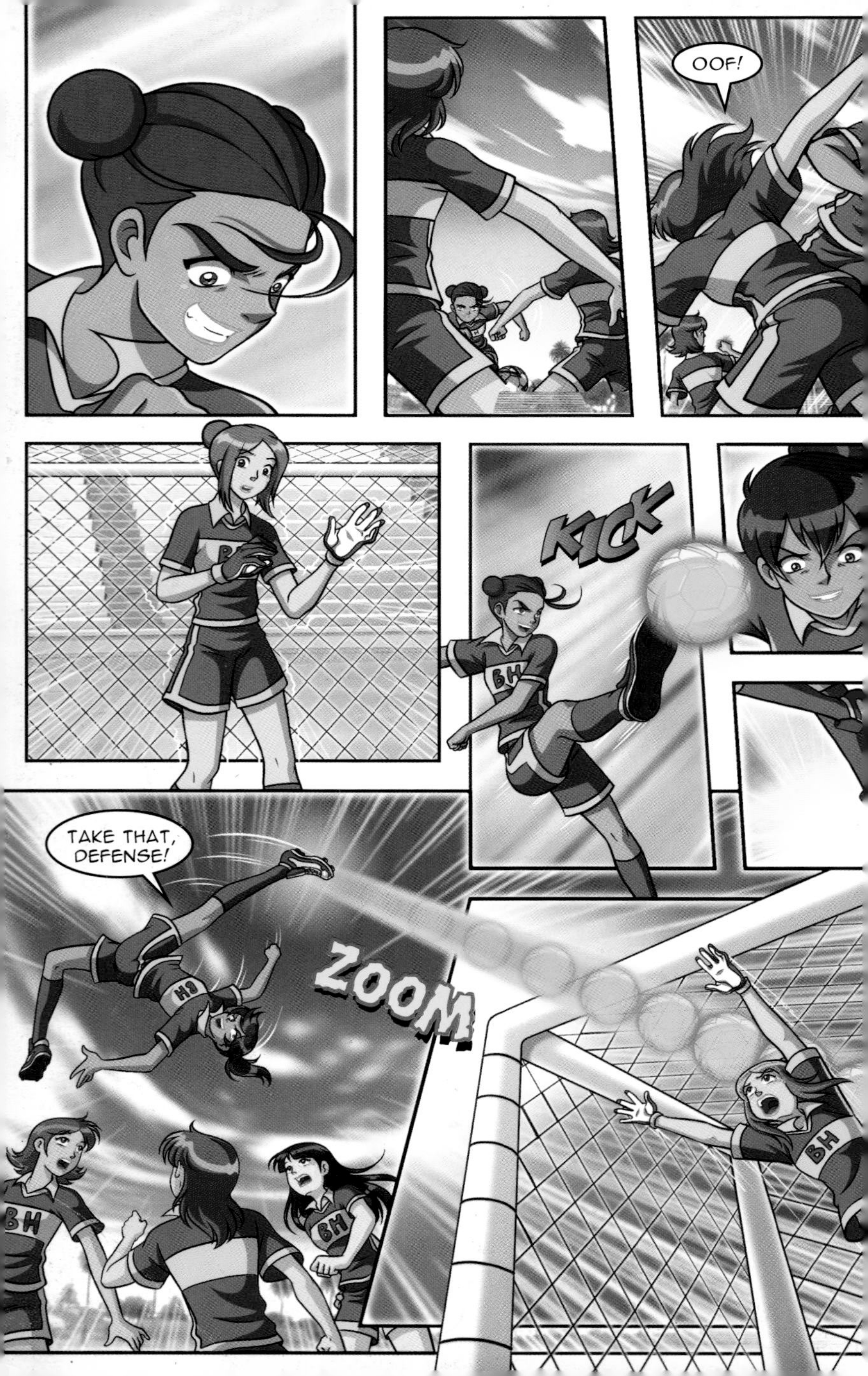
OOF!
KICK
TAKE THAT, DEFENSE!
ZOOM

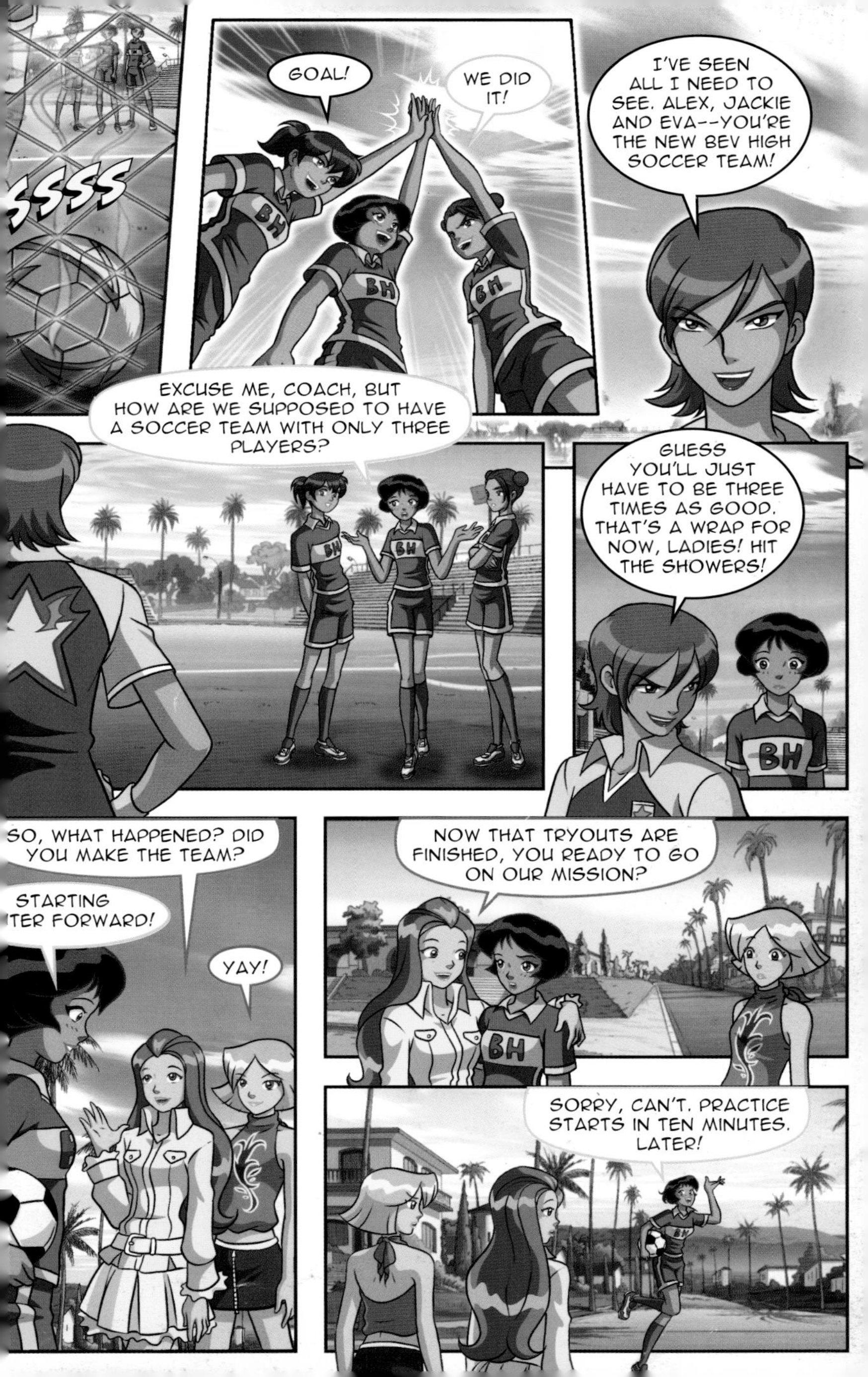
SSSS
GOAL!
WE DID IT!
I'VE SEEN ALL I NEED TO SEE. ALEX, JACKIE AND EVA--YOU'RE THE NEW BEV HIGH SOCCER TEAM!
EXCUSE ME, COACH, BUT HOW ARE WE SUPPOSED TO HAVE A SOCCER TEAM WITH ONLY THREE PLAYERS?
GUESS YOU'LL JUST HAVE TO BE THREE TIMES AS GOOD. THAT'S A WRAP FOR NOW, LADIES! HIT THE SHOWERS!
SO, WHAT HAPPENED? DID YOU MAKE THE TEAM?
STARTING
TER FORWARD!
YAY!
NOW THAT TRYOUTS ARE FINISHED, YOU READY TO GO ON OUR MISSION?
SORRY, CAN'T. PRACTICE STARTS IN TEN MINUTES. LATER!

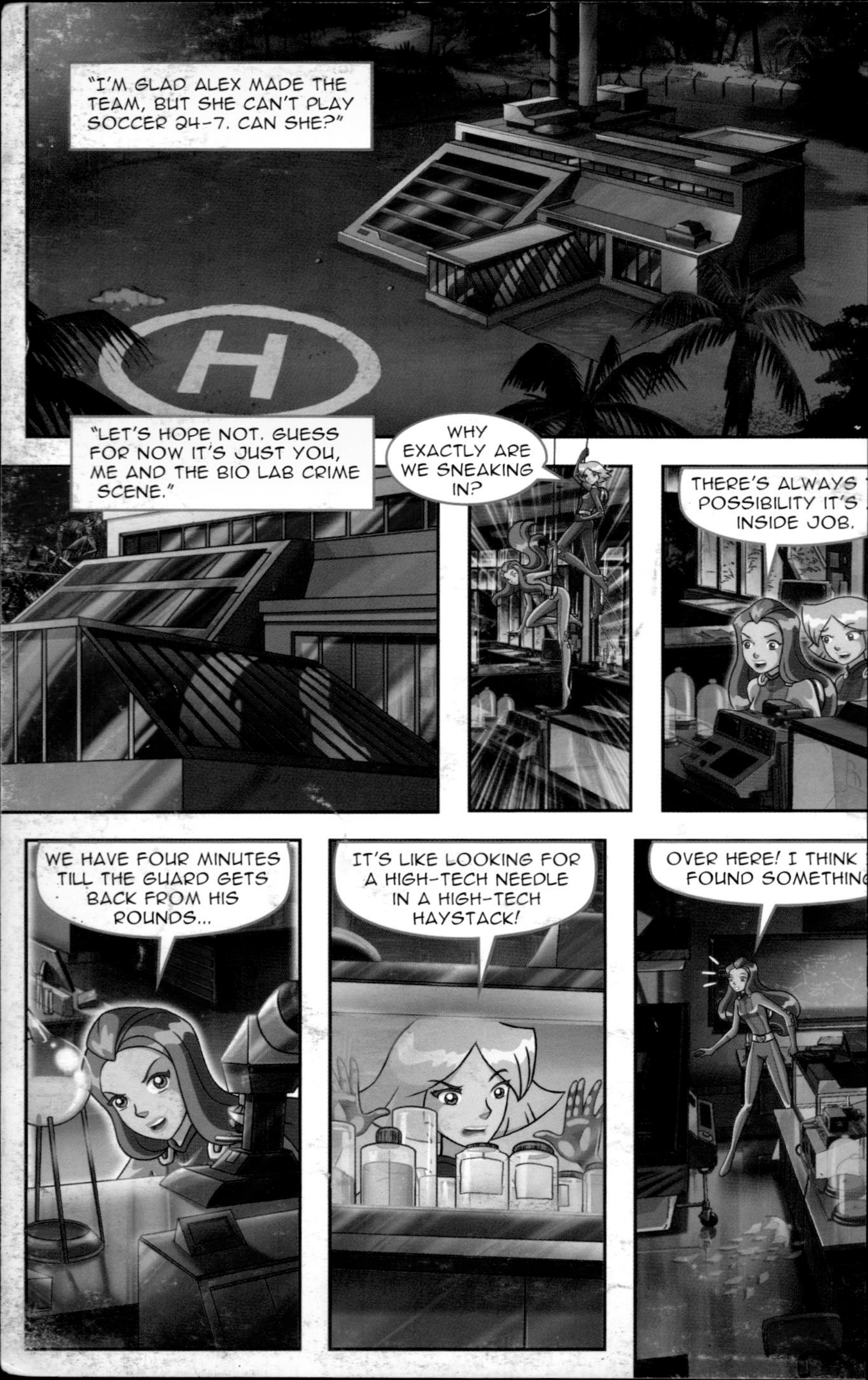
"I'M GLAD ALEX MADE THE TEAM, BUT SHE CAN'T PLAY SOCCER 24-7. CAN SHE?"
"LET'S HOPE NOT. GUESS FOR NOW IT'S JUST YOU, ME AND THE BIO LAB CRIME SCENE."
WHY EXACTLY ARE WE SNEAKING IN?
THERE'S ALWAYS POSSIBILITY IT'S INSIDE JOB.
WE HAVE FOUR MINUTES TILL THE GUARD GETS BACK FROM HIS ROUNDS...
IT'S LIKE LOOKING FOR A HIGH-TECH NEEDLE IN A HIGH-TECH HAYSTACK!
OVER HERE! I THINK FOUND SOMETHIN

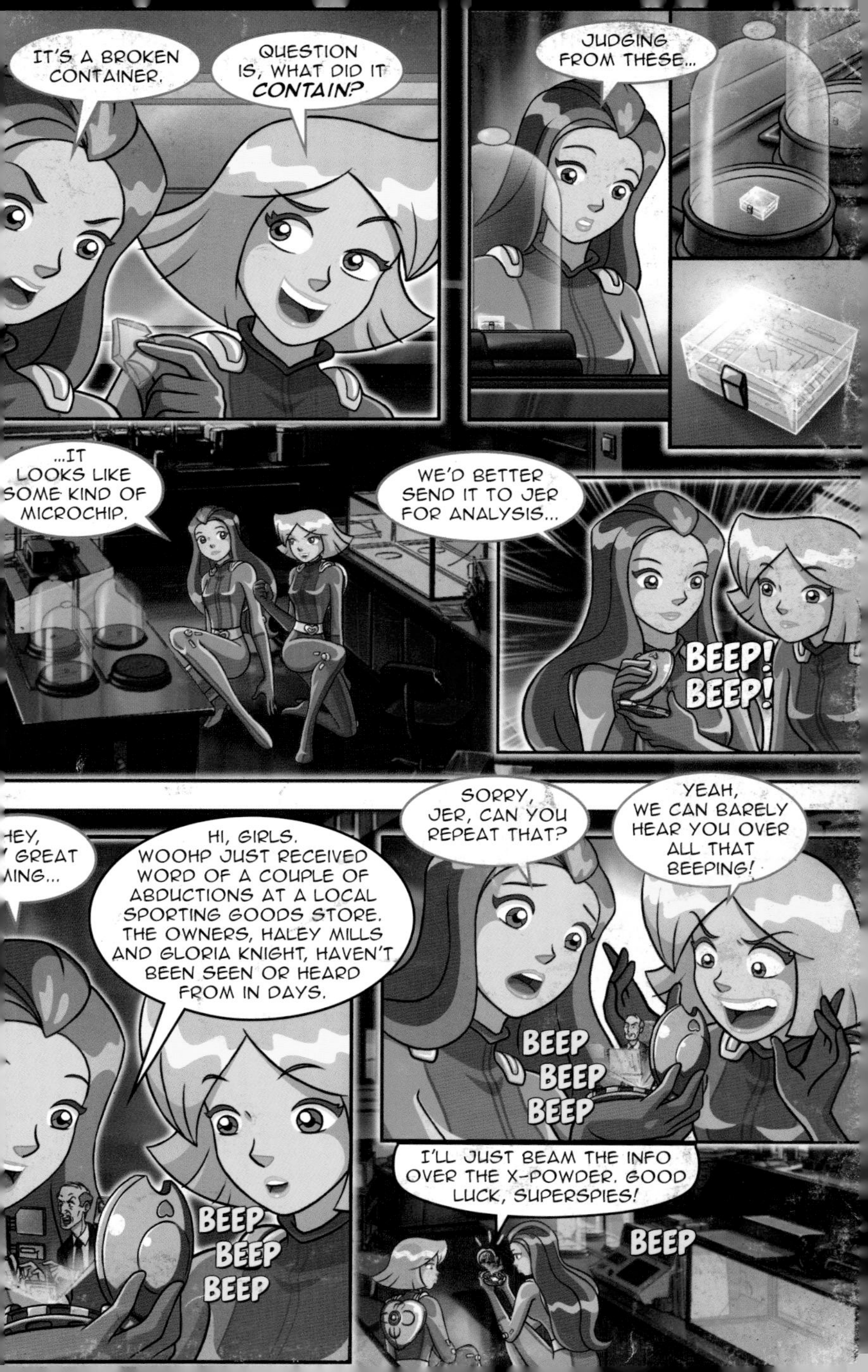
IT'S A BROKEN CONTAINER.
QUESTION IS, WHAT DID IT CONTAIN?
JUDGING FROM THESE...
...IT LOOKS LIKE SOME KIND OF MICROCHIP.
WE'D BETTER SEND IT TO JER FOR ANALYSIS...
BEEP! BEEP!
HI, GIRLS. WOOHP JUST RECEIVED WORD OF A COUPLE OF ABDUCTIONS AT A LOCAL SPORTING GOODS STORE. THE OWNERS, HALEY MILLS AND GLORIA KNIGHT, HAVEN'T BEEN SEEN OR HEARD FROM IN DAYS.
BEEP BEEP BEEP
SORRY, JER, CAN YOU REPEAT THAT?
YEAH, WE CAN BARELY HEAR YOU OVER ALL THAT BEEPING!
BEEP BEEP BEEP
I'LL JUST BEAM THE INFO OVER THE X-POWDER. GOOD LUCK, SUPERSPIES!
BEEP

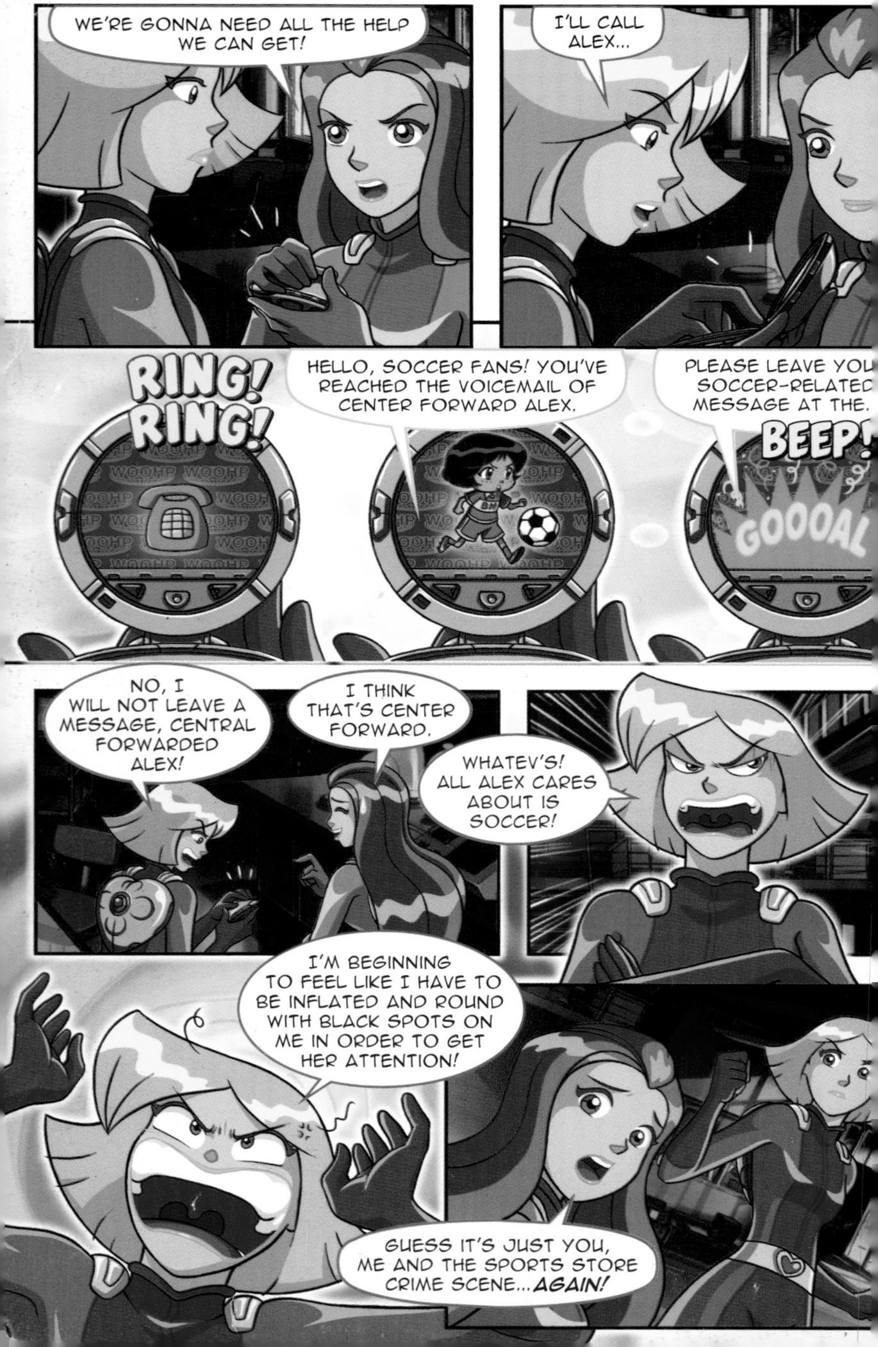

WE'RE GONNA NEED ALL THE HELP WE CAN GET!
I'LL CALL ALEX...
RING! RING!
WOOHP
HELLO, SOCCER FANS! YOU'VE REACHED THE VOICEMAIL OF CENTER FORWARD ALEX.
PLEASE LEAVE YOU SOCCER-RELATED MESSAGE AT THE.
BEEP!
GOOOAL
NO, I WILL NOT LEAVE A MESSAGE, CENTRAL FORWARDED ALEX!
I THINK THAT'S CENTER FORWARD.
WHATEV'S! ALL ALEX CARES ABOUT IS SOCCER!
I'M BEGINNING TO FEEL LIKE I HAVE TO BE INFLATED AND ROUND WITH BLACK SPOTS ON ME IN ORDER TO GET HER ATTENTION!
GUESS IT'S JUST YOU, ME AND THE SPORTS STORE CRIME SCENE... *AGAIN!*

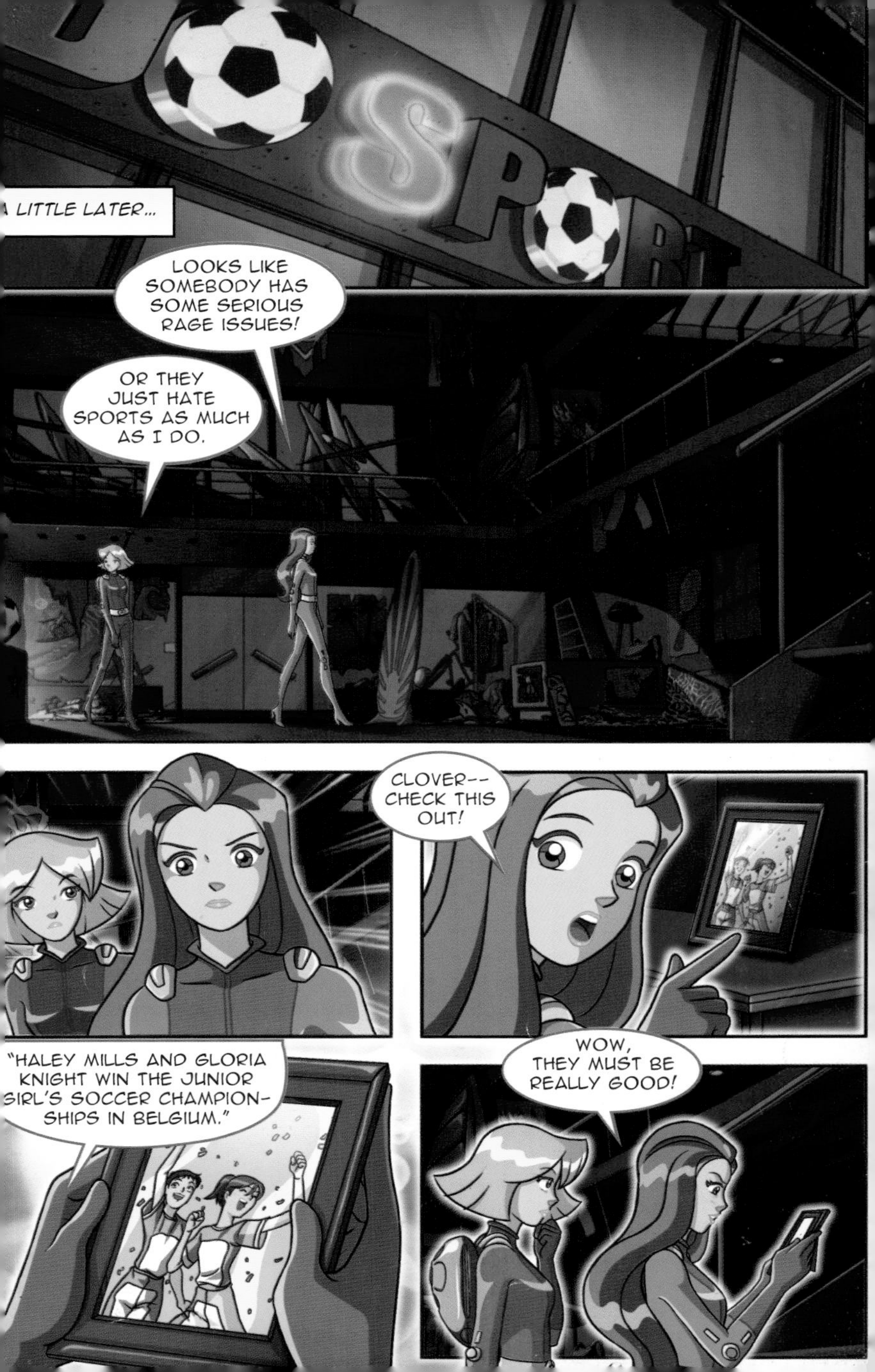

A LITTLE LATER...
LOOKS LIKE SOMEBODY HAS SOME SERIOUS RAGE ISSUES!
OR THEY JUST HATE SPORTS AS MUCH AS I DO.
CLOVER-- CHECK THIS OUT!
"HALEY MILLS AND GLORIA KNIGHT WIN THE JUNIOR GIRL'S SOCCER CHAMPIONSHIPS IN BELGIUM."
WOW, THEY MUST BE REALLY GOOD!

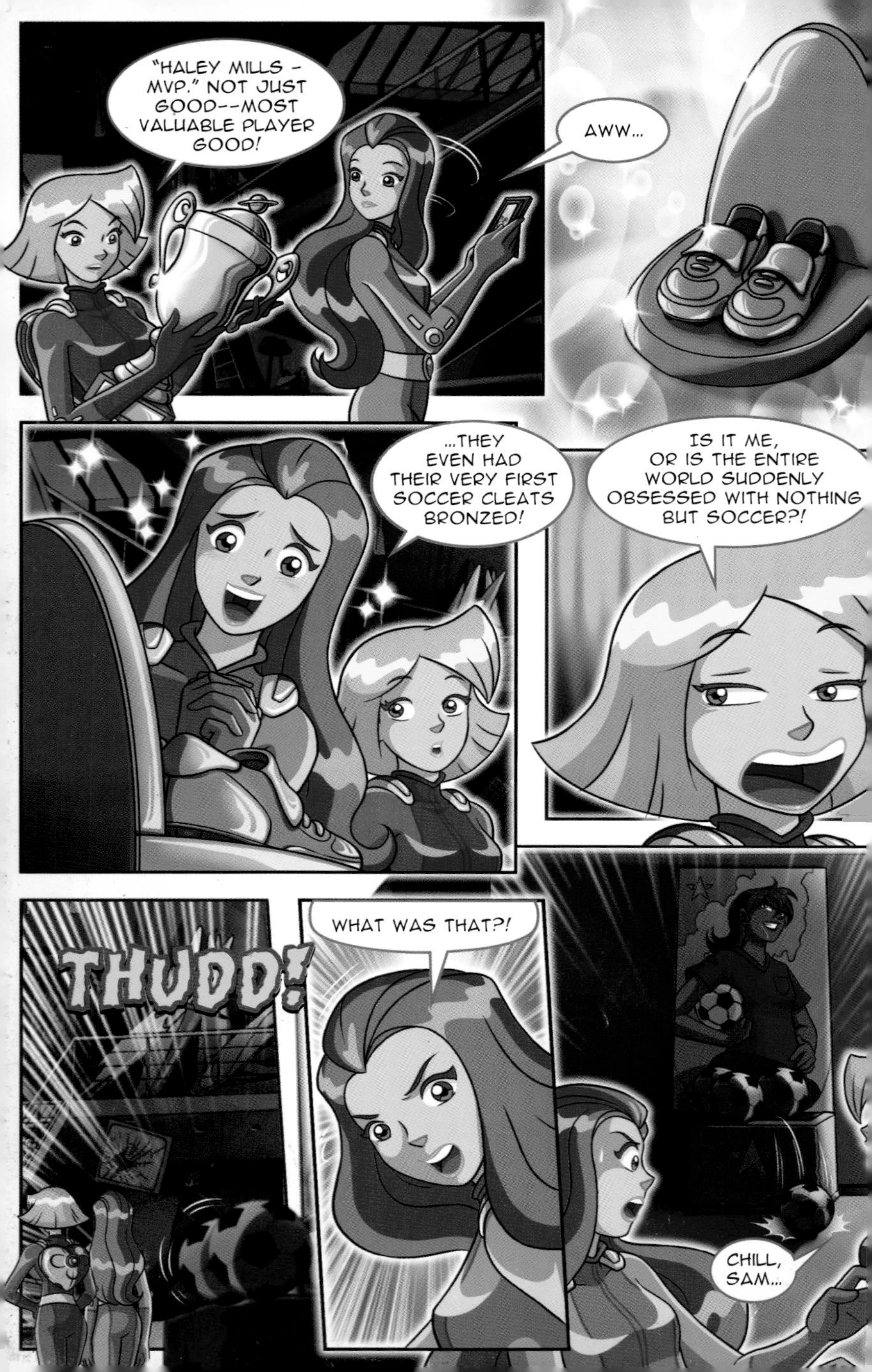
"HALEY MILLS - MVP." NOT JUST GOOD--MOST VALUABLE PLAYER GOOD!
AWW...
...THEY EVEN HAD THEIR VERY FIRST SOCCER CLEATS BRONZED!
IS IT ME, OR IS THE ENTIRE WORLD SUDDENLY OBSESSED WITH NOTHING BUT SOCCER?!
THUDD!
WHAT WAS THAT?!
CHILL, SAM...

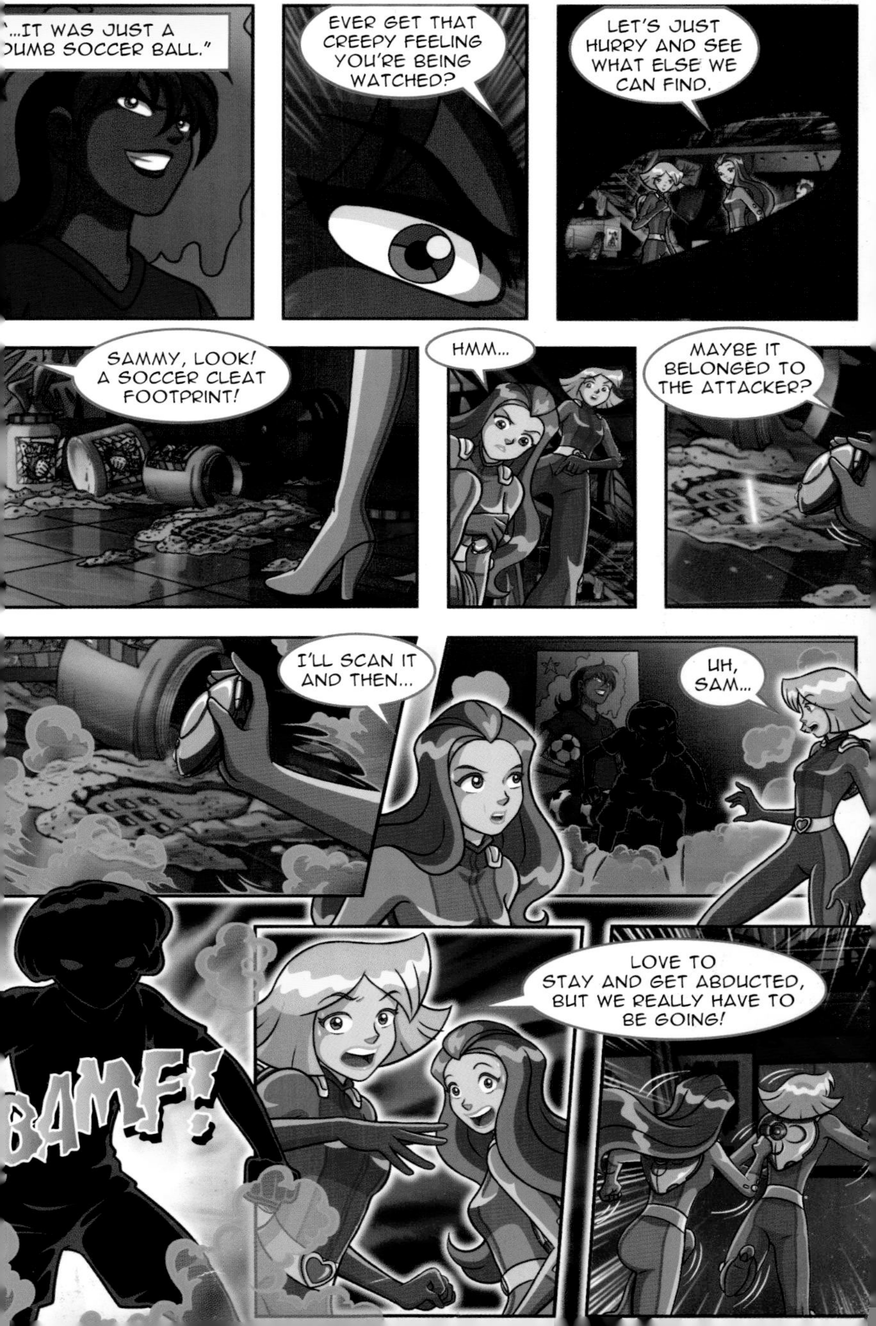
"...IT WAS JUST A
DUMB SOCCER BALL."
EVER GET THAT CREEPY FEELING YOU'RE BEING WATCHED?
LET'S JUST HURRY AND SEE WHAT ELSE WE CAN FIND.
SAMMY, LOOK! A SOCCER CLEAT FOOTPRINT!
HMM...
MAYBE IT BELONGED TO THE ATTACKER?
I'LL SCAN IT AND THEN...
UH, SAM...
BAMF!
LOVE TO STAY AND GET ABDUCTED, BUT WE REALLY HAVE TO BE GOING!

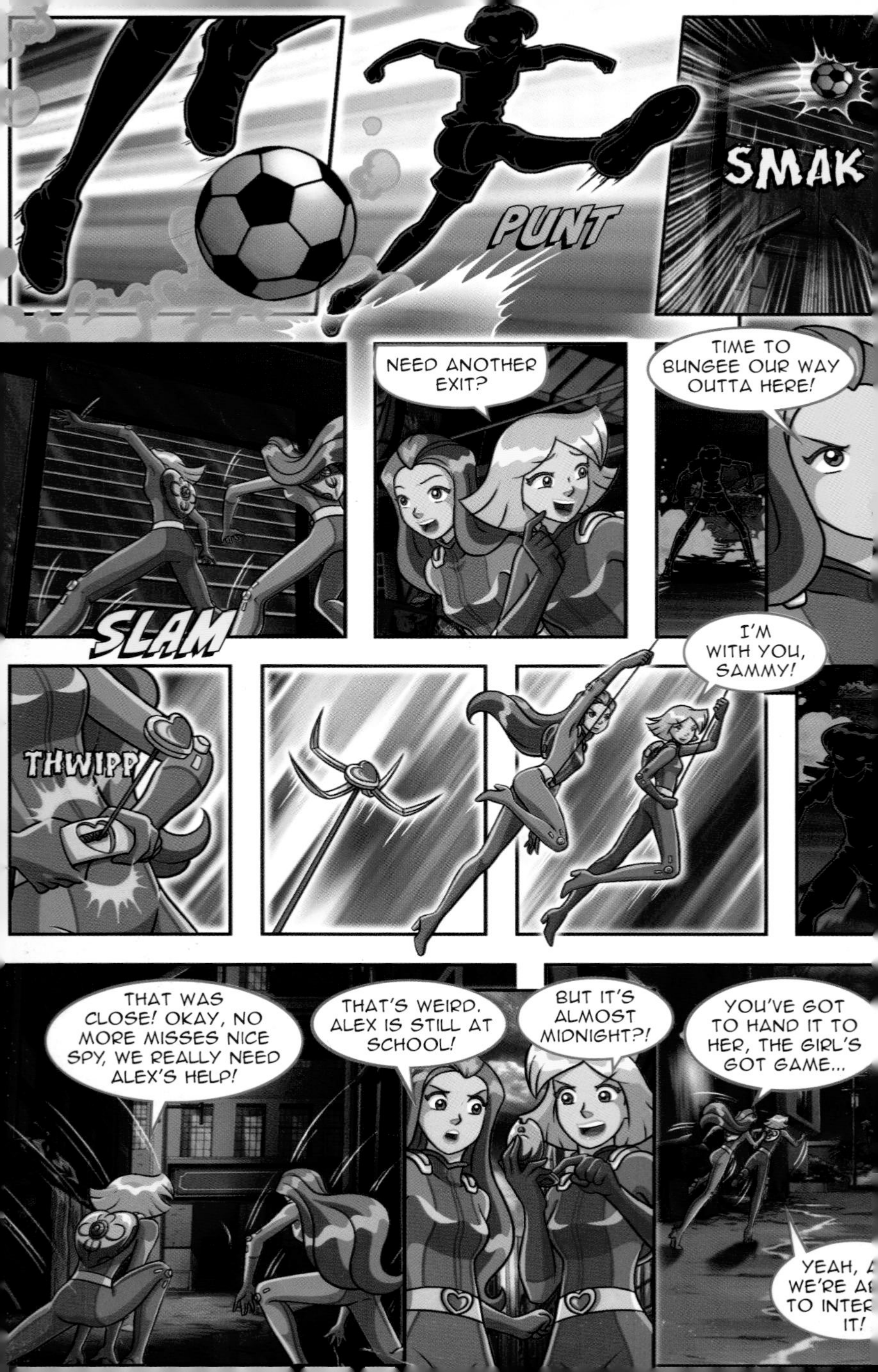
PUNT
SMAK
SLAM
NEED ANOTHER EXIT?
TIME TO BUNGEE OUR WAY OUTTA HERE!
THWIPP
I'M WITH YOU, SAMMY!
THAT WAS CLOSE! OKAY, NO MORE MISSES NICE SPY, WE REALLY NEED ALEX'S HELP!
THAT'S WEIRD. ALEX IS STILL AT SCHOOL!
BUT IT'S ALMOST MIDNIGHT?!
YOU'VE GOT TO HAND IT TO HER, THE GIRL'S GOT GAME...

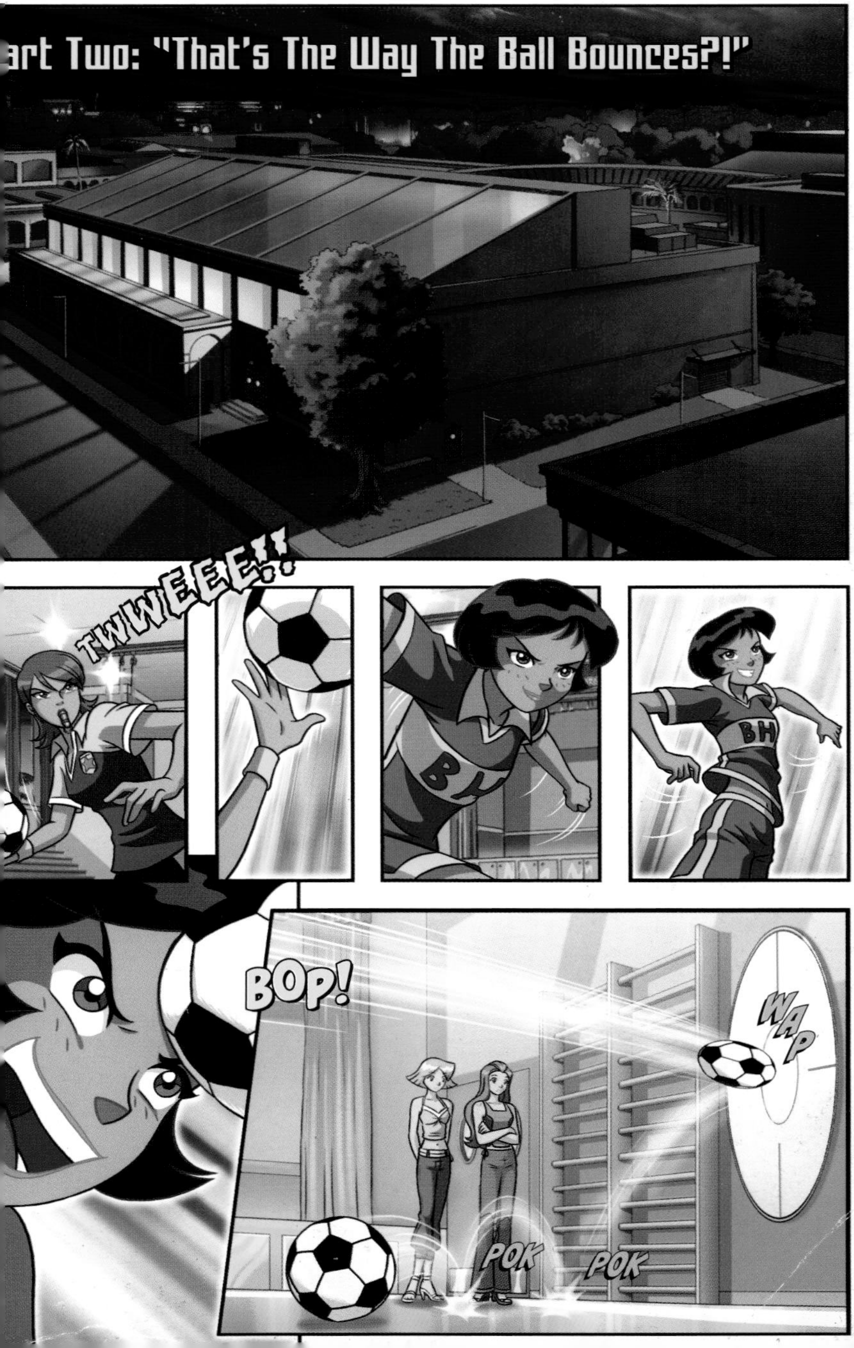
art Two: "That's The Way The Ball Bounces?!"
TWWEEE!!
BOP!
WAP
POK
POK

CLOVER? SAMMY?

SORRY TO DISTURB YOU, ALEX.

BUT CAN WE TALK IN THE HALLWAY FOR A SEC?

DON'T YOU THINK YO[U] TAKING THIS SOCCE[R] THING A LITTLE TOO FAR?

FIRST IT [WAS] TRYOUTS, [THEN] PRACTICE [TILL] MIDNIGH[T]

I KNOW I HAVEN'T EXACTLY BEEN PULLING MY WEIGHT ON MISSIONS LATELY. BUT DON'T WORRY, THAT'S ALL GONNA CHANGE!

WE'RE TOTALLY GLAD TO HEAR YOU SAY...

JUST AS SOON AS BEVE[RLY] WINS REGIONALS IN A COUPLE OF MONTHS!

BEEP!

SORRY TO INTERRUPT, GIRLS, BUT I JUST GOT THE RESULTS. FIRST UP, THE D[OG] CONTAINED AN EXPERIMENTAL MICROCHI[P] DESIGNED TO TAP INTO PEOPLE'S NATURA[L] AGGRESSION.

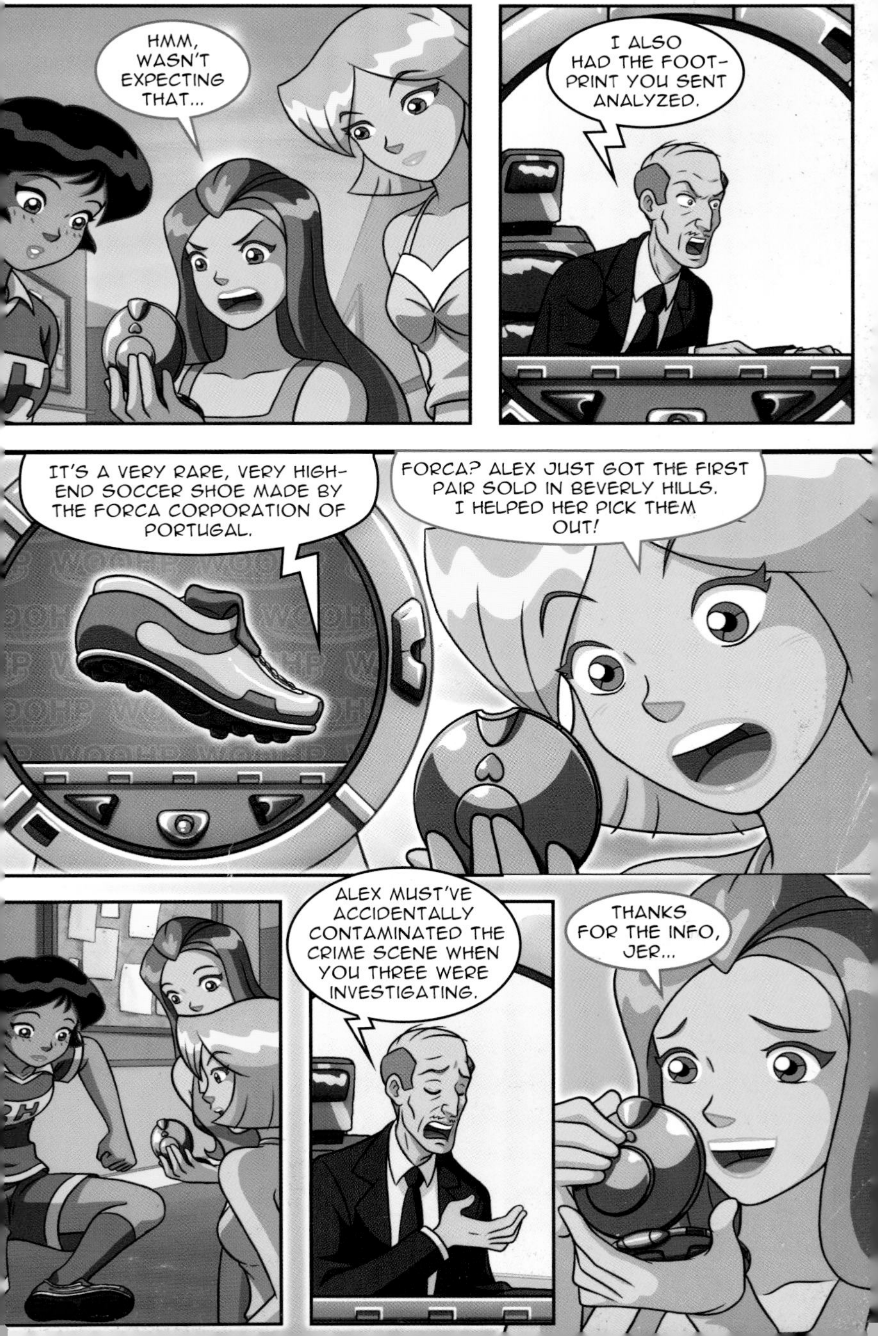
HMM, WASN'T EXPECTING THAT...
I ALSO HAD THE FOOT-PRINT YOU SENT ANALYZED.
IT'S A VERY RARE, VERY HIGH-END SOCCER SHOE MADE BY THE FORCA CORPORATION OF PORTUGAL.
FORCA? ALEX JUST GOT THE FIRST PAIR SOLD IN BEVERLY HILLS. I HELPED HER PICK THEM OUT!
ALEX MUST'VE ACCIDENTALLY CONTAMINATED THE CRIME SCENE WHEN YOU THREE WERE INVESTIGATING.
THANKS FOR THE INFO, JER...

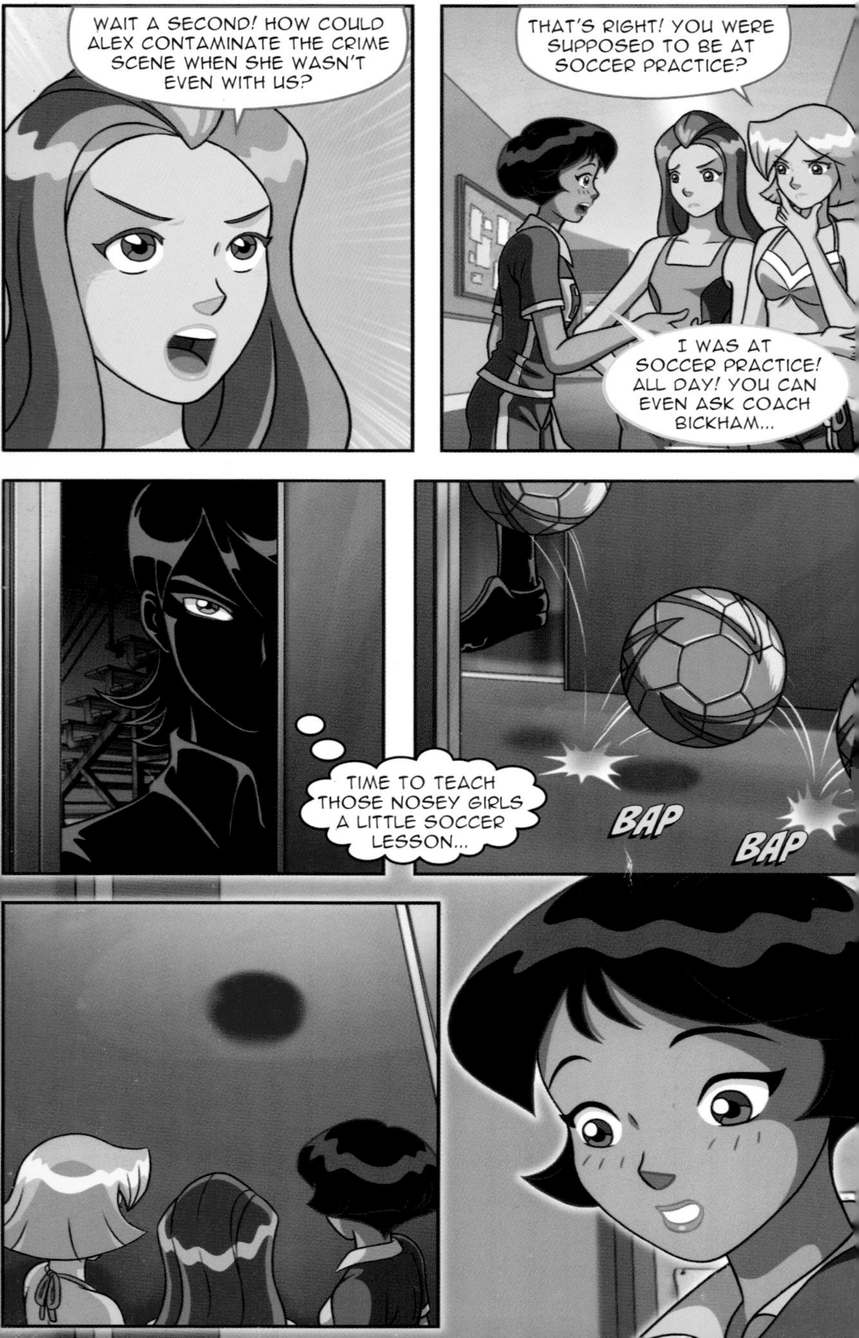
WAIT A SECOND! HOW COULD ALEX CONTAMINATE THE CRIME SCENE WHEN SHE WASN'T EVEN WITH US?
THAT'S RIGHT! YOU WERE SUPPOSED TO BE AT SOCCER PRACTICE?
I WAS AT SOCCER PRACTICE! ALL DAY! YOU CAN EVEN ASK COACH BICKHAM...
TIME TO TEACH THOSE NOSEY GIRLS A LITTLE SOCCER LESSON...
BAP
BAP

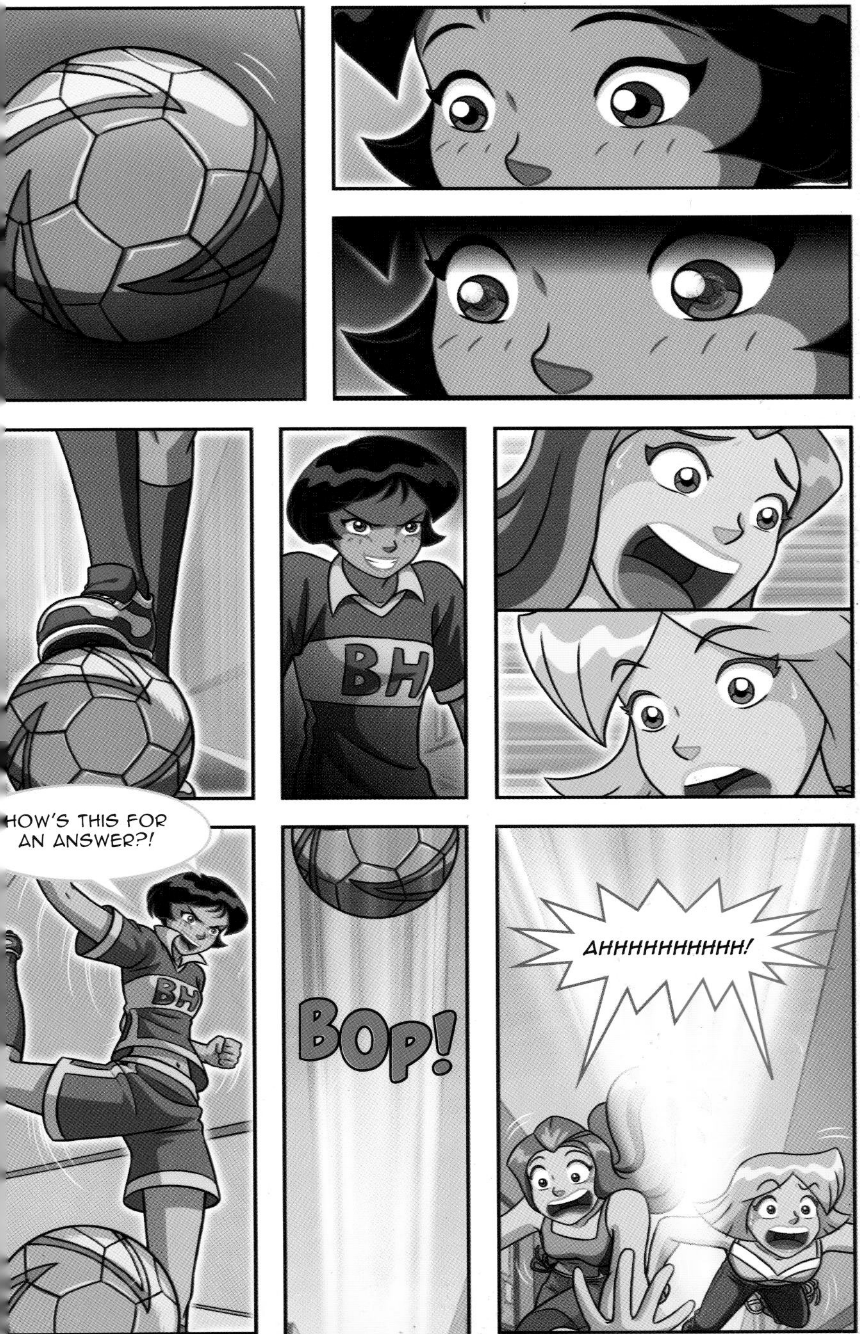
HOW'S THIS FOR AN ANSWER?!
BOP!
AHHHHHHHHHHH!

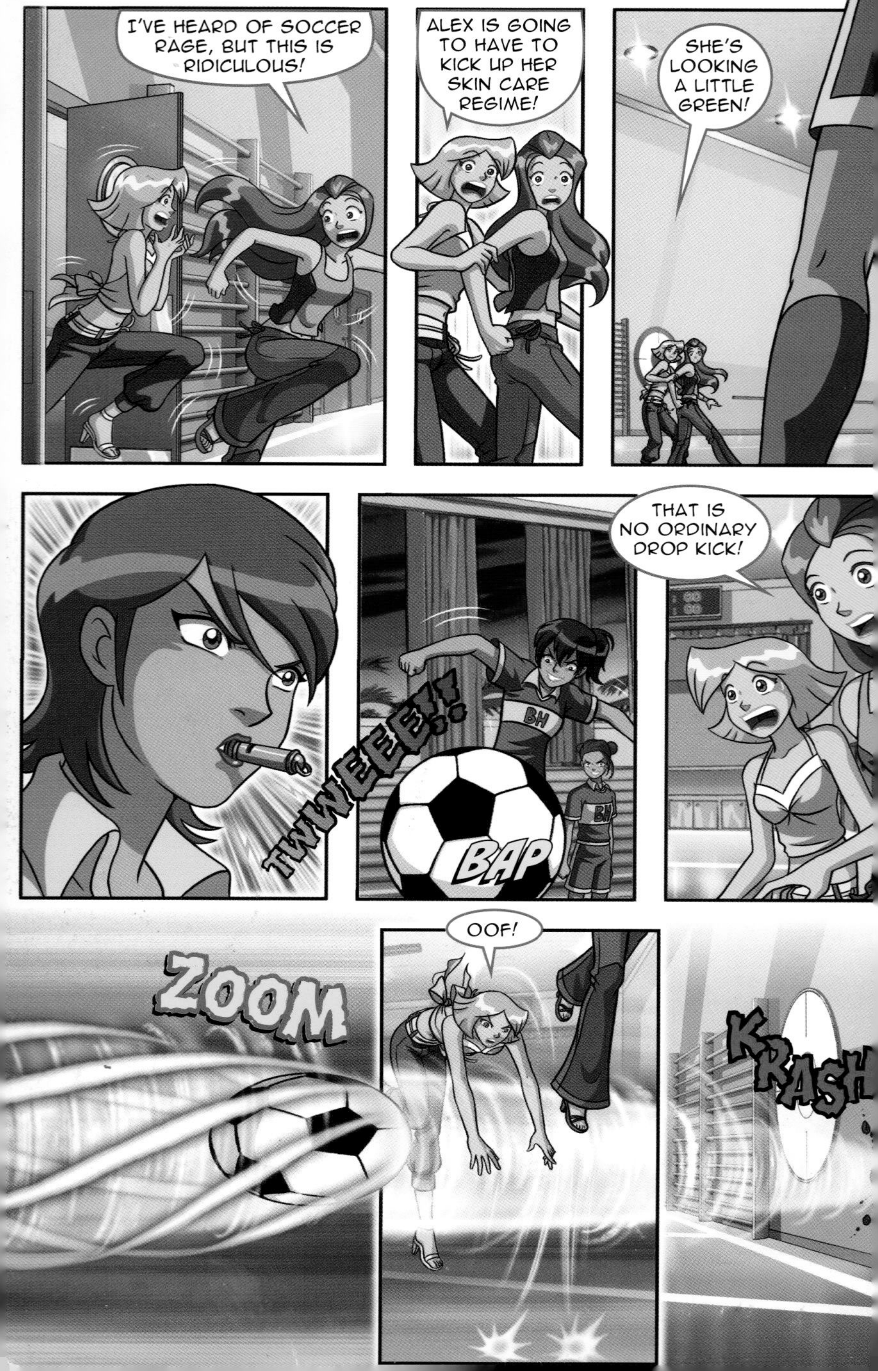
I'VE HEARD OF SOCCER RAGE, BUT THIS IS RIDICULOUS!
ALEX IS GOING TO HAVE TO KICK UP HER SKIN CARE REGIME!
SHE'S LOOKING A LITTLE GREEN!
TWWEEEE!!
BH
BAP
BH
THAT IS NO ORDINARY DROP KICK!
ZOOM
OOF!
KRASH

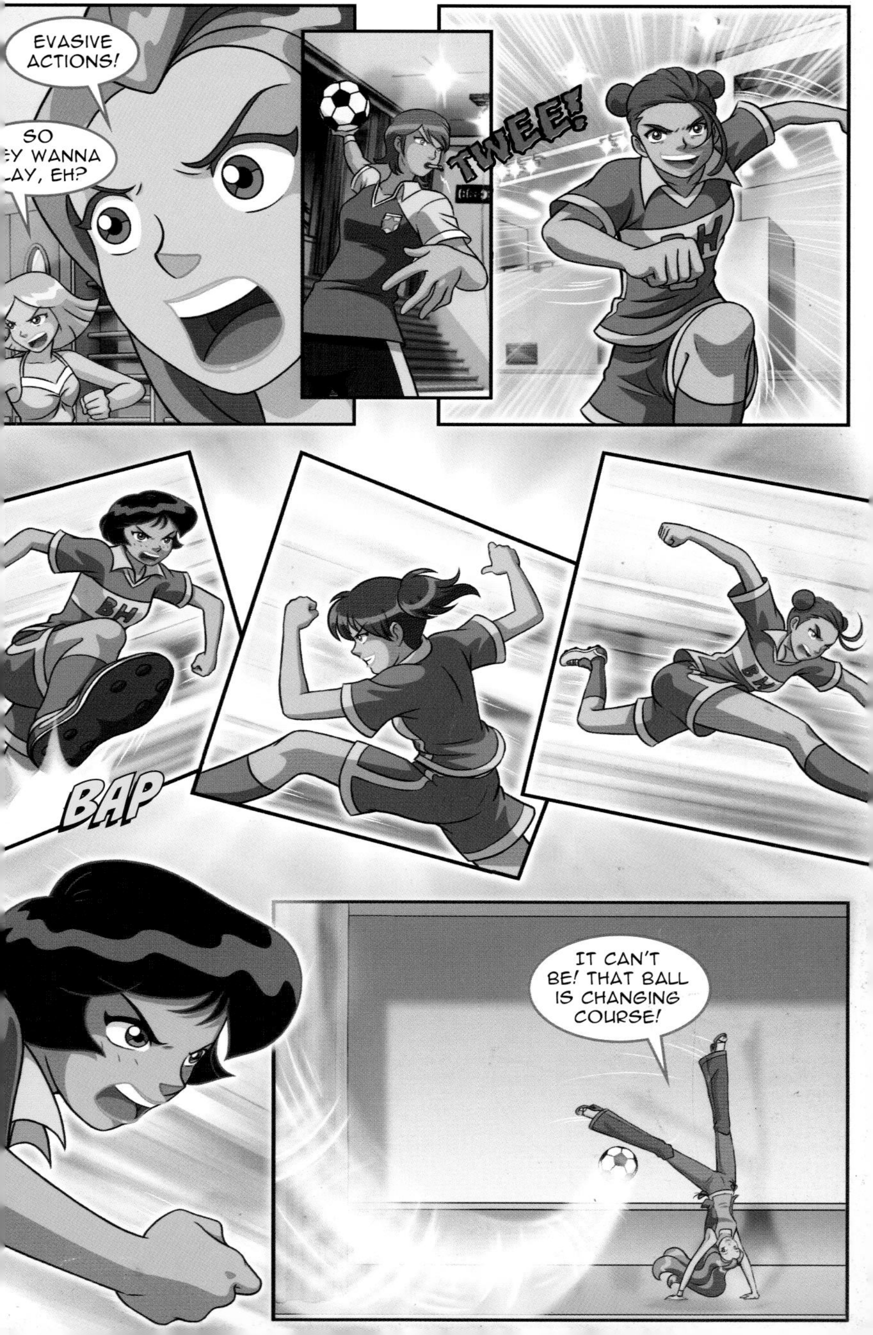
EVASIVE ACTIONS!
SO
EY WANNA
LAY, EH?
TWEEE!
BAP
IT CAN'T BE! THAT BALL IS CHANGING COURSE!

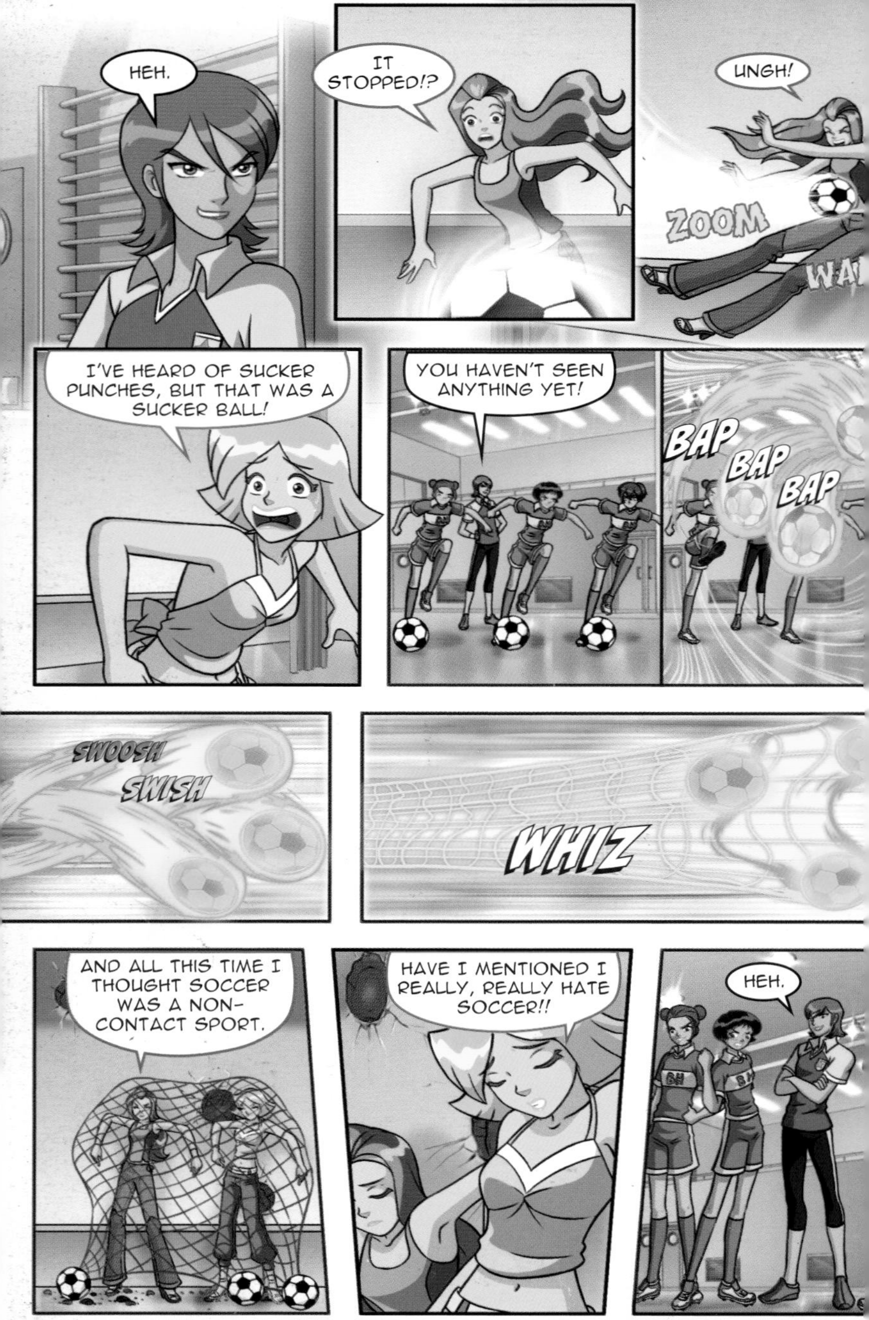
HEH.
IT STOPPED!?
UNGH!
ZOOM
I'VE HEARD OF SUCKER PUNCHES, BUT THAT WAS A SUCKER BALL!
YOU HAVEN'T SEEN ANYTHING YET!
BAP
BAP
BAP
SWOOSH
SWISH
WHIZ
AND ALL THIS TIME I THOUGHT SOCCER WAS A NON-CONTACT SPORT.
HAVE I MENTIONED I REALLY, REALLY HATE SOCCER!!
HEH.

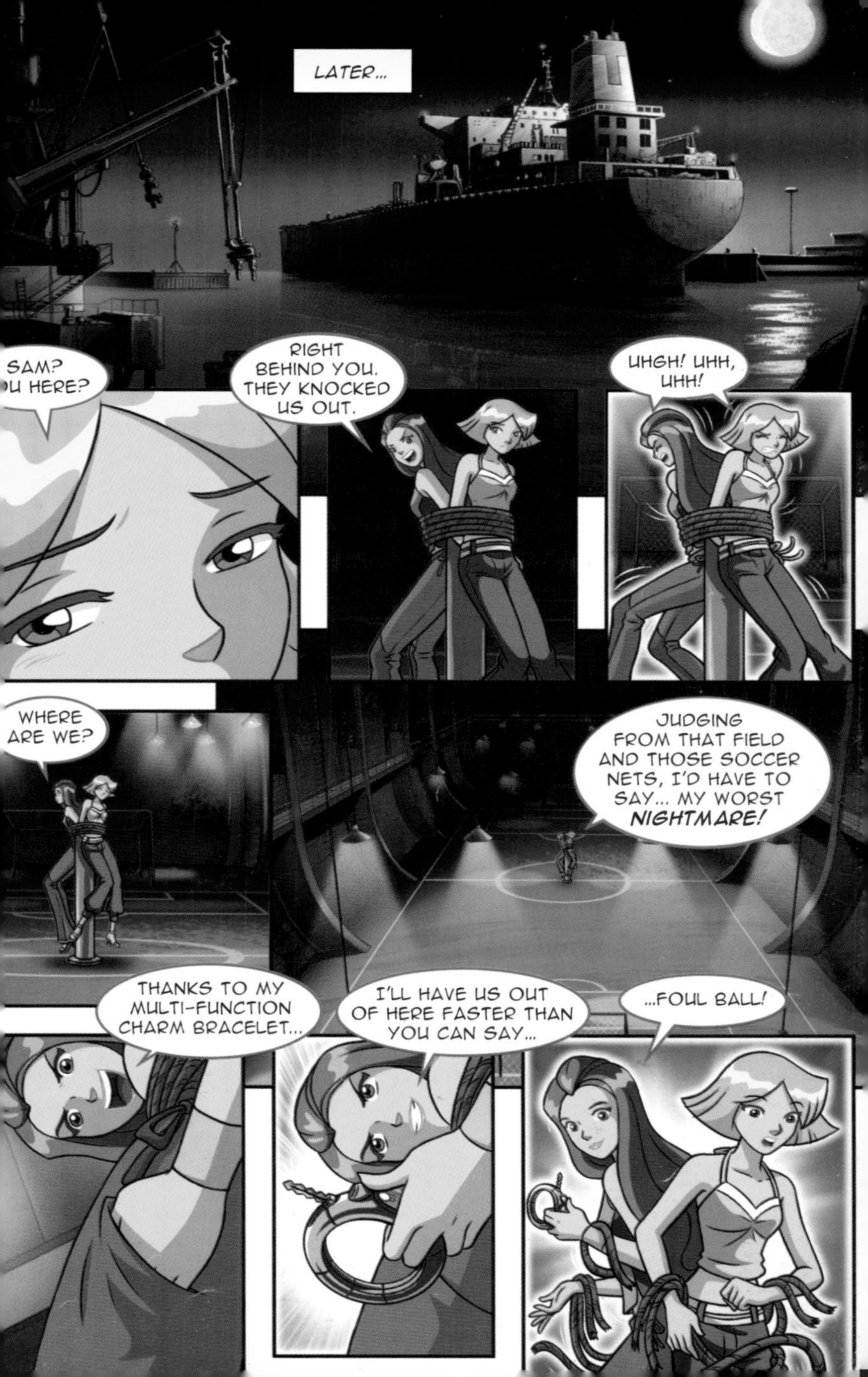
LATER...
SAM? ...U HERE?
RIGHT BEHIND YOU. THEY KNOCKED US OUT.
UHGH! UHH, UHH!
WHERE ARE WE?
JUDGING FROM THAT FIELD AND THOSE SOCCER NETS, I'D HAVE TO SAY... MY WORST NIGHTMARE!
THANKS TO MY MULTI-FUNCTION CHARM BRACELET...
I'LL HAVE US OUT OF HERE FASTER THAN YOU CAN SAY...
...FOUL BALL!

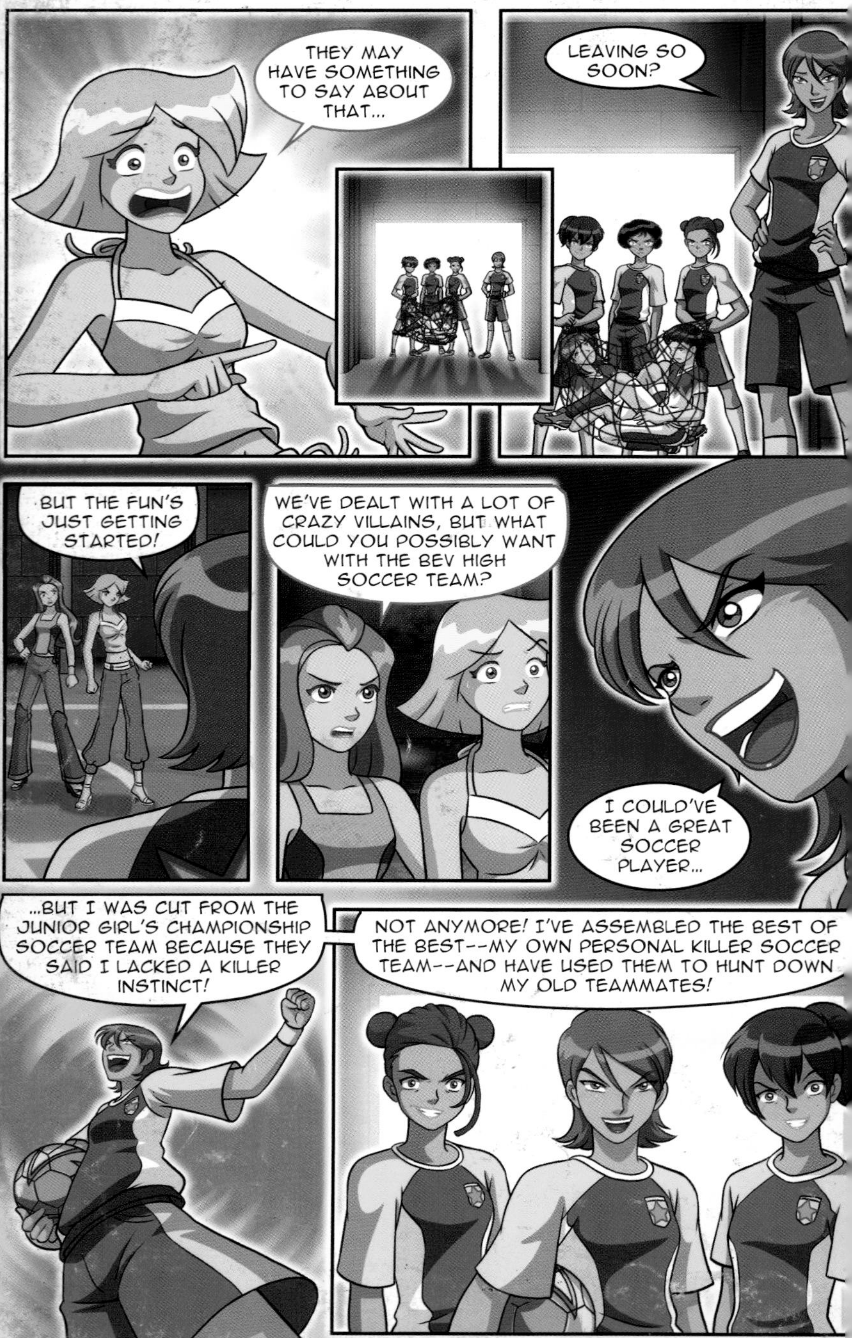

THEY MAY HAVE SOMETHING TO SAY ABOUT THAT...
LEAVING SO SOON?
...BUT THE FUN'S JUST GETTING STARTED!
WE'VE DEALT WITH A LOT OF CRAZY VILLAINS, BUT WHAT COULD YOU POSSIBLY WANT WITH THE BEV HIGH SOCCER TEAM?
I COULD'VE BEEN A GREAT SOCCER PLAYER...
...BUT I WAS CUT FROM THE JUNIOR GIRL'S CHAMPIONSHIP SOCCER TEAM BECAUSE THEY SAID I LACKED A KILLER INSTINCT!
NOT ANYMORE! I'VE ASSEMBLED THE BEST OF THE BEST--MY OWN PERSONAL KILLER SOCCER TEAM--AND HAVE USED THEM TO HUNT DOWN MY OLD TEAMMATES!

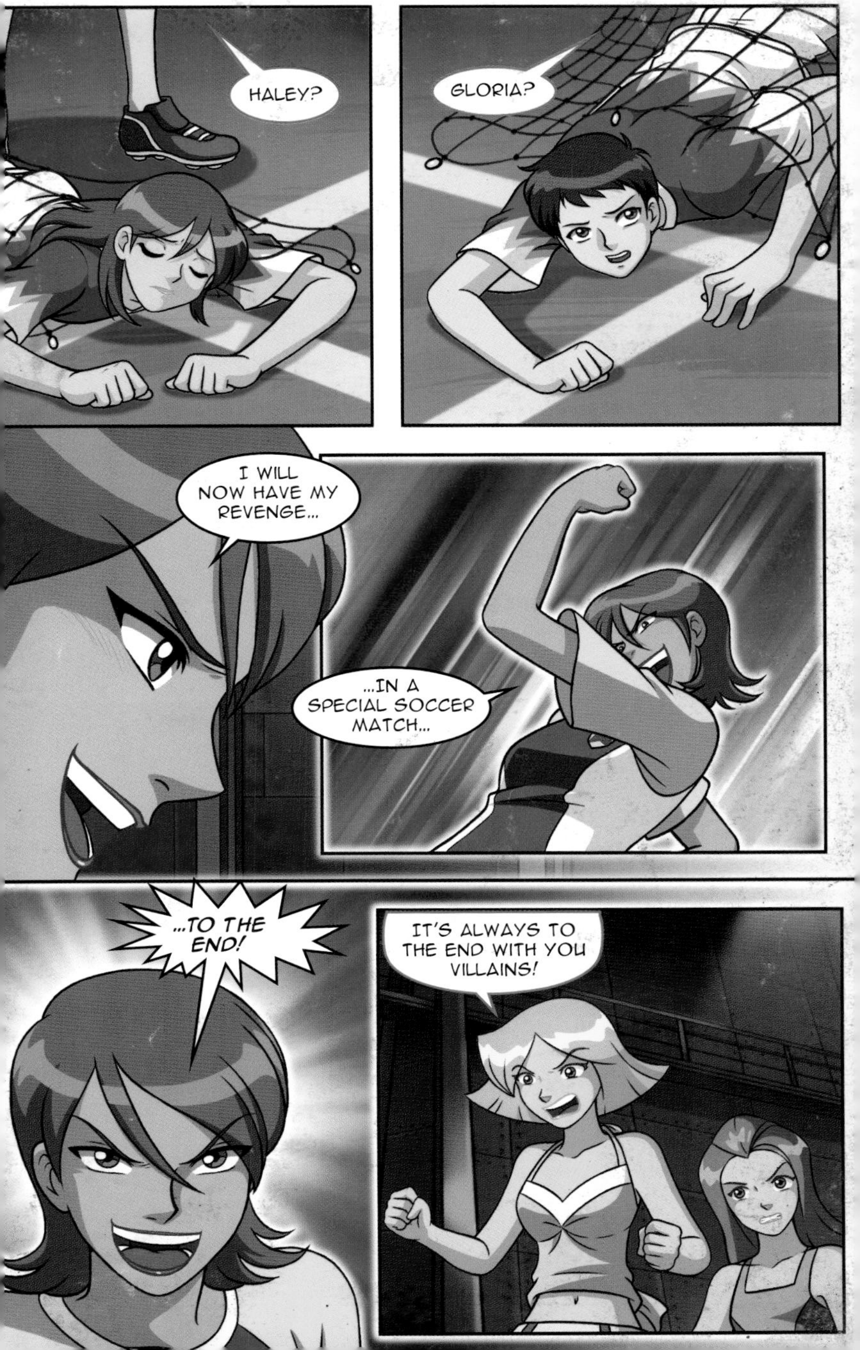
HALEY?
GLORIA?
I WILL NOW HAVE MY REVENGE...
...IN A SPECIAL SOCCER MATCH...
...TO THE END!
IT'S ALWAYS TO THE END WITH YOU VILLAINS!

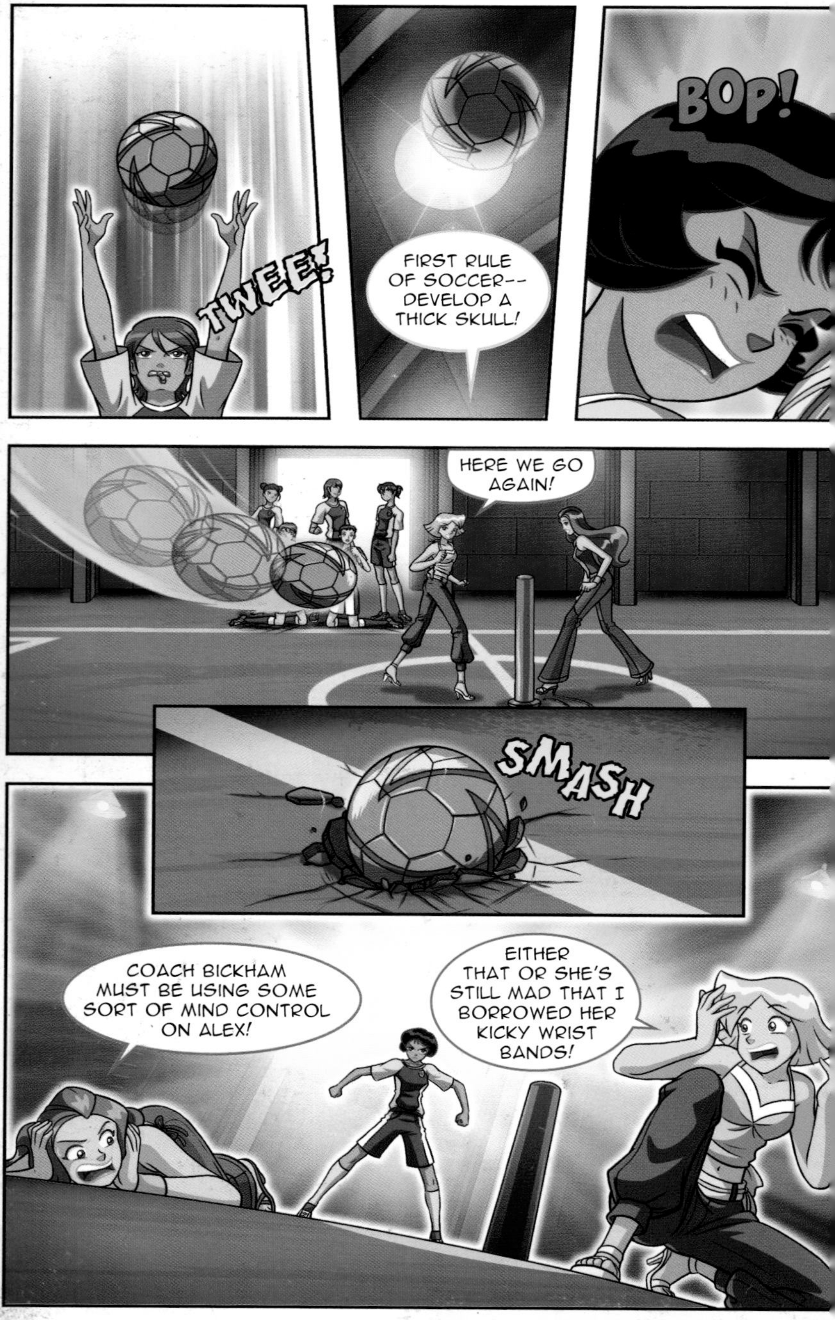
TWEE!
FIRST RULE OF SOCCER-- DEVELOP A THICK SKULL!
BOP!
HERE WE GO AGAIN!
SMASH
COACH BICKHAM MUST BE USING SOME SORT OF MIND CONTROL ON ALEX!
EITHER THAT OR SHE'S STILL MAD THAT I BORROWED HER KICKY WRIST BANDS!

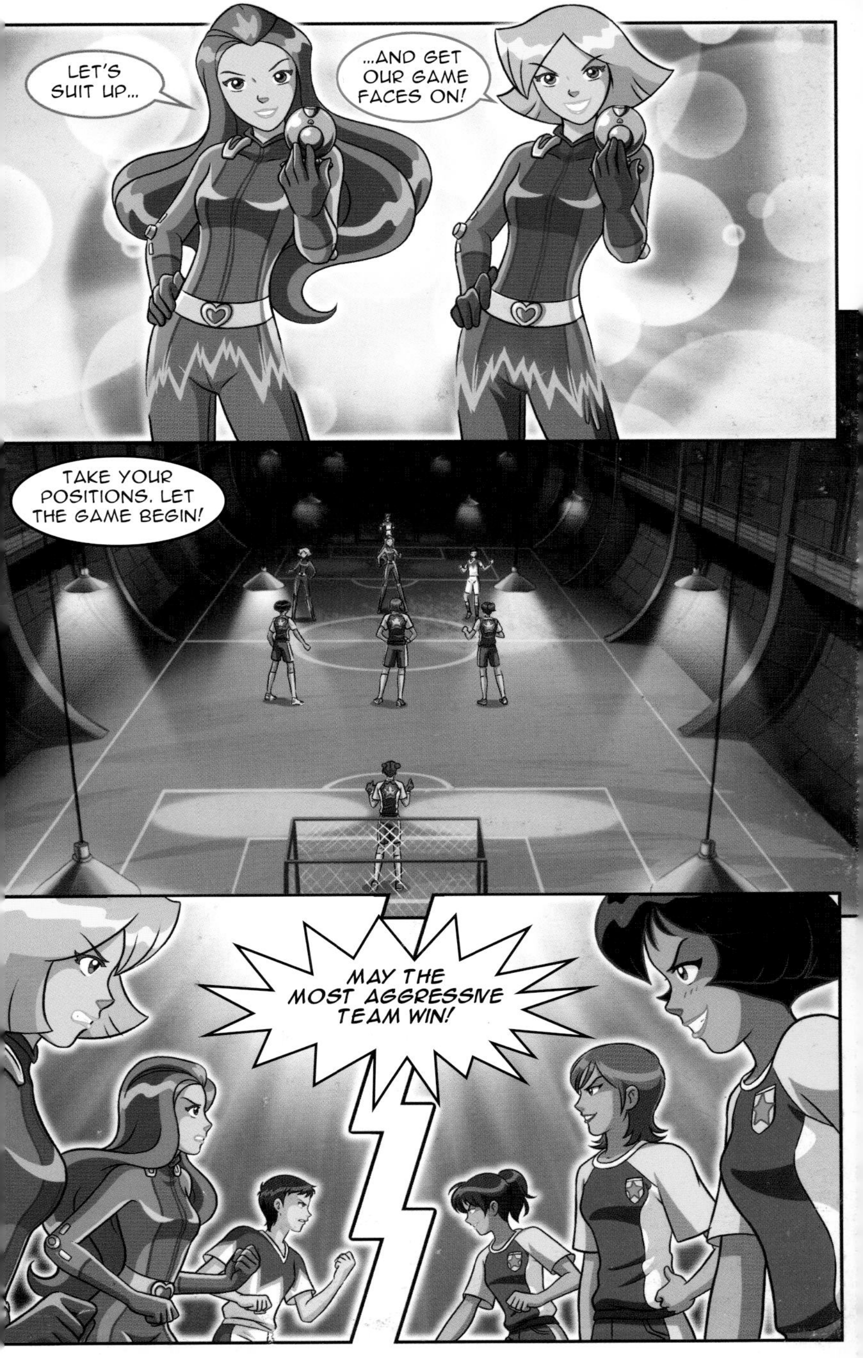
LET'S SUIT UP...
...AND GET OUR GAME FACES ON!
TAKE YOUR POSITIONS. LET THE GAME BEGIN!
MAY THE MOST AGGRESSIVE TEAM WIN!

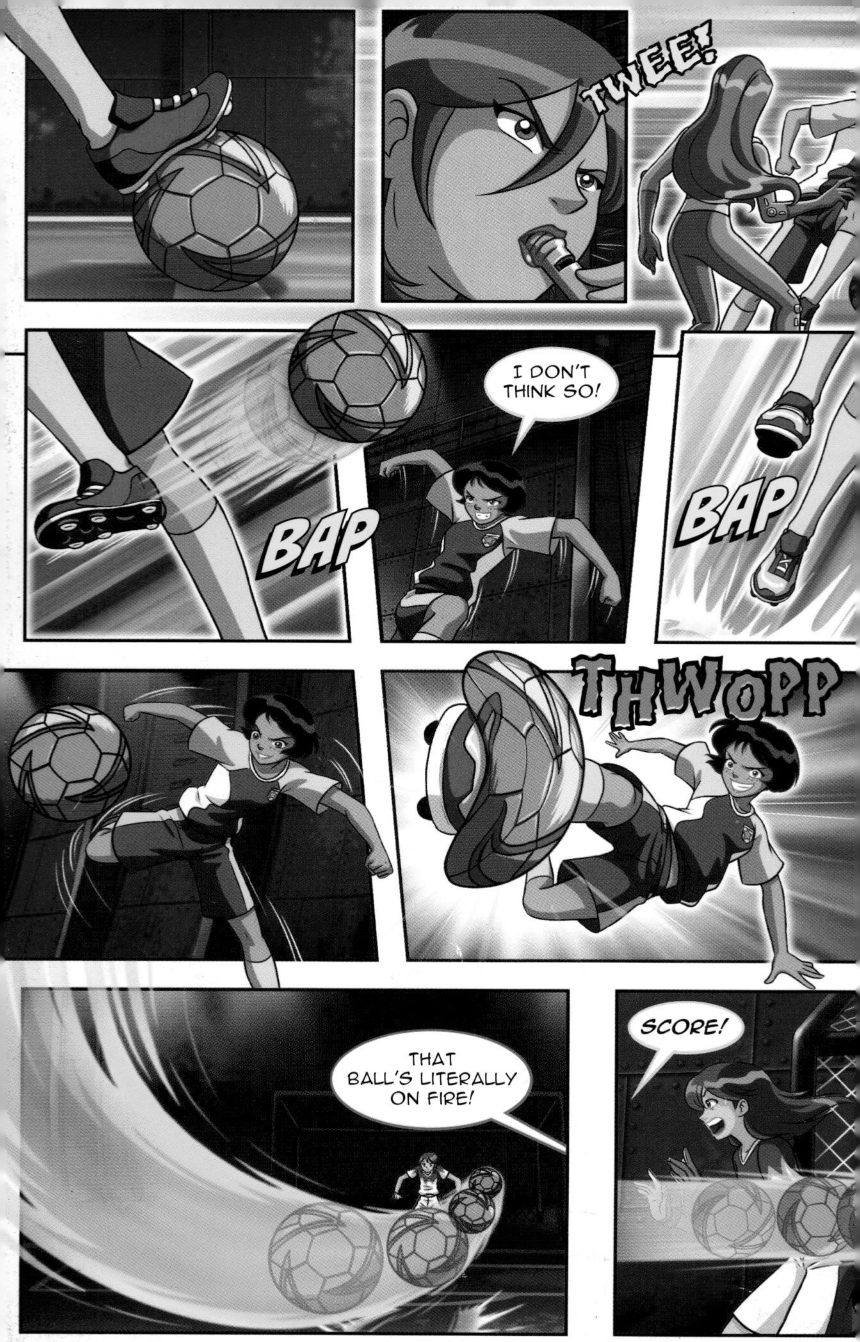
TWEE!
BAP
I DON'T THINK SO!
BAP
THWOPP
THAT BALL'S LITERALLY ON FIRE!
SCORE!

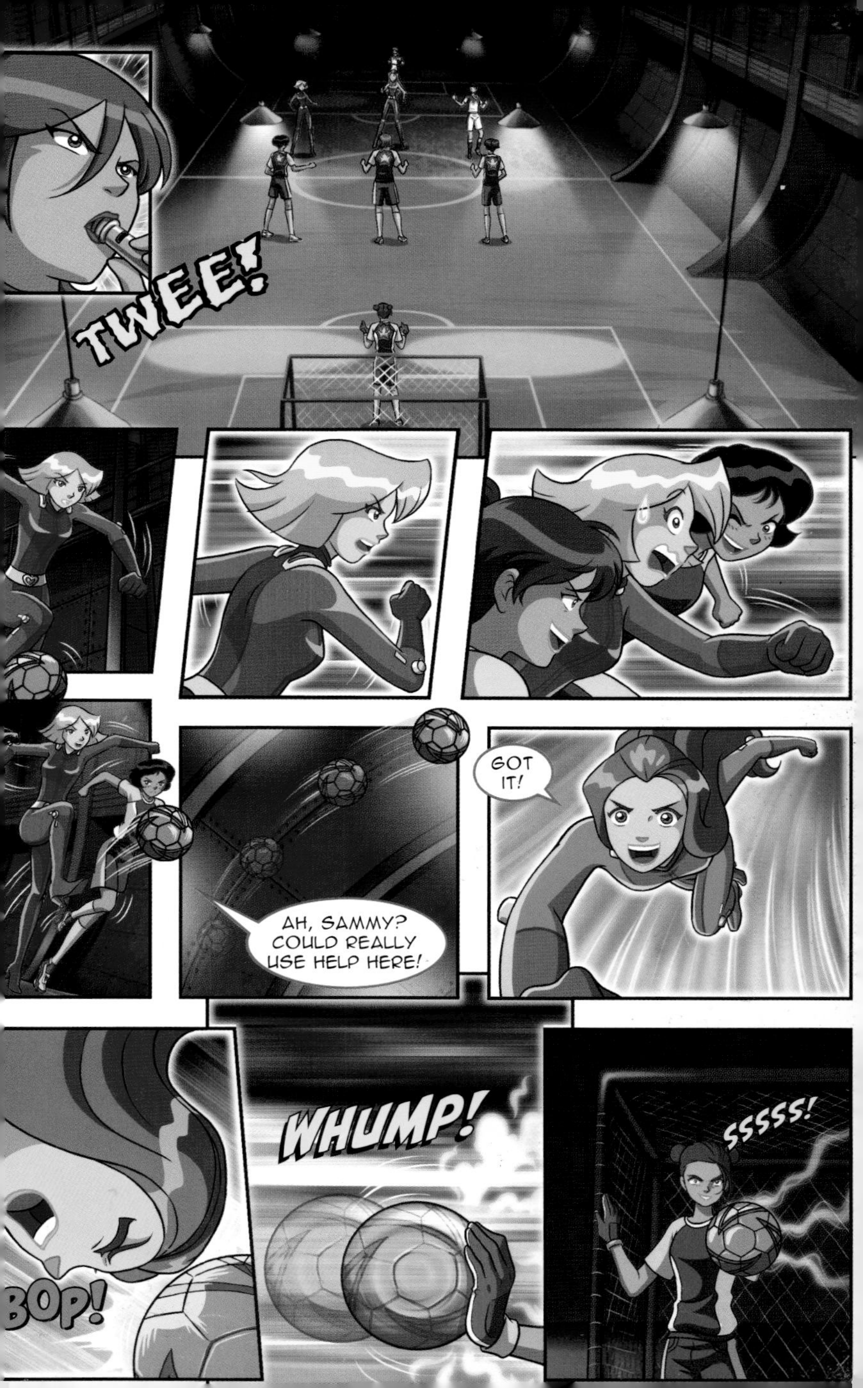
TWEE!
GOT IT!
AH, SAMMY? COULD REALLY USE HELP HERE!
BOP!
WHUMP!
SSSSS!

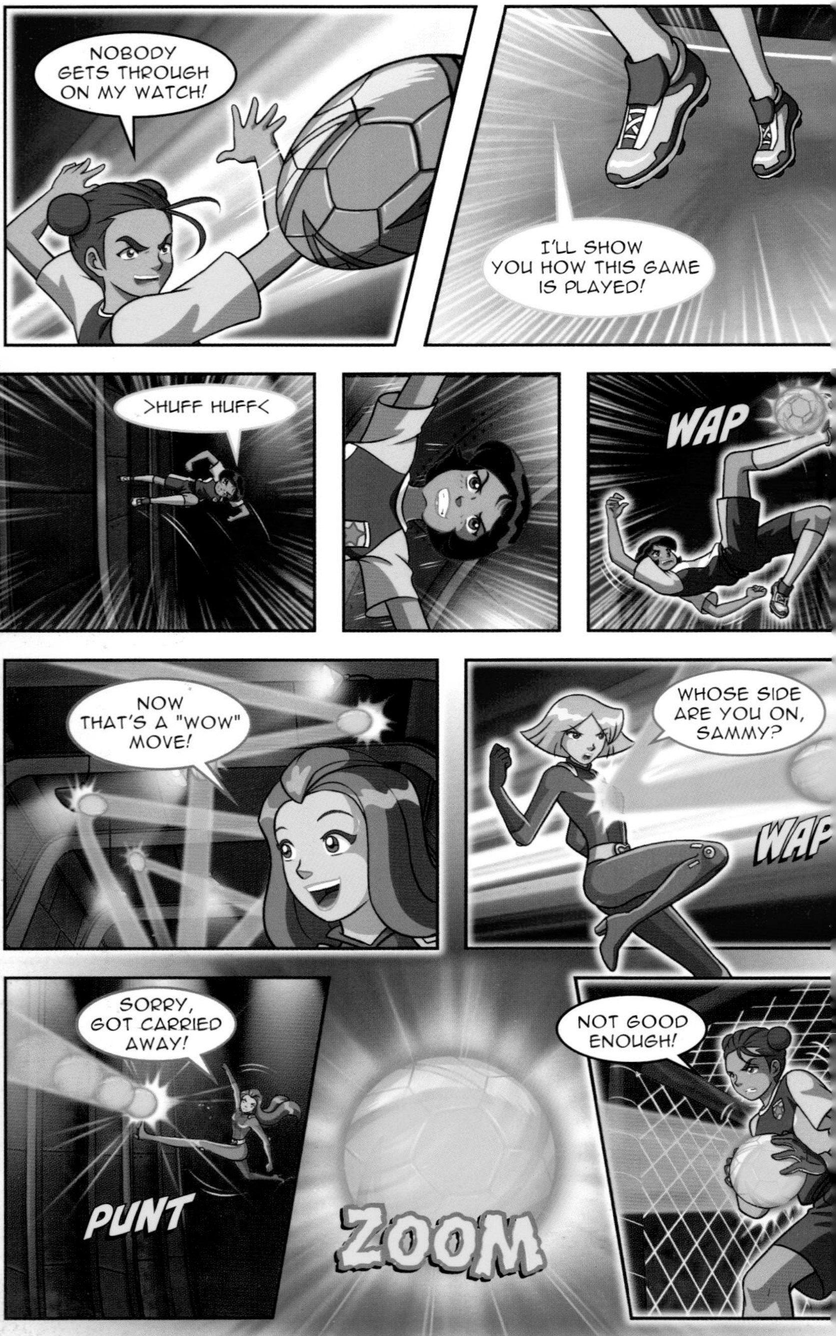
NOBODY GETS THROUGH ON MY WATCH!
I'LL SHOW YOU HOW THIS GAME IS PLAYED!
>HUFF HUFF<
WAP
NOW THAT'S A "WOW" MOVE!
WHOSE SIDE ARE YOU ON, SAMMY?
WAP
SORRY, GOT CARRIED AWAY!
PUNT
ZOOM
NOT GOOD ENOUGH!

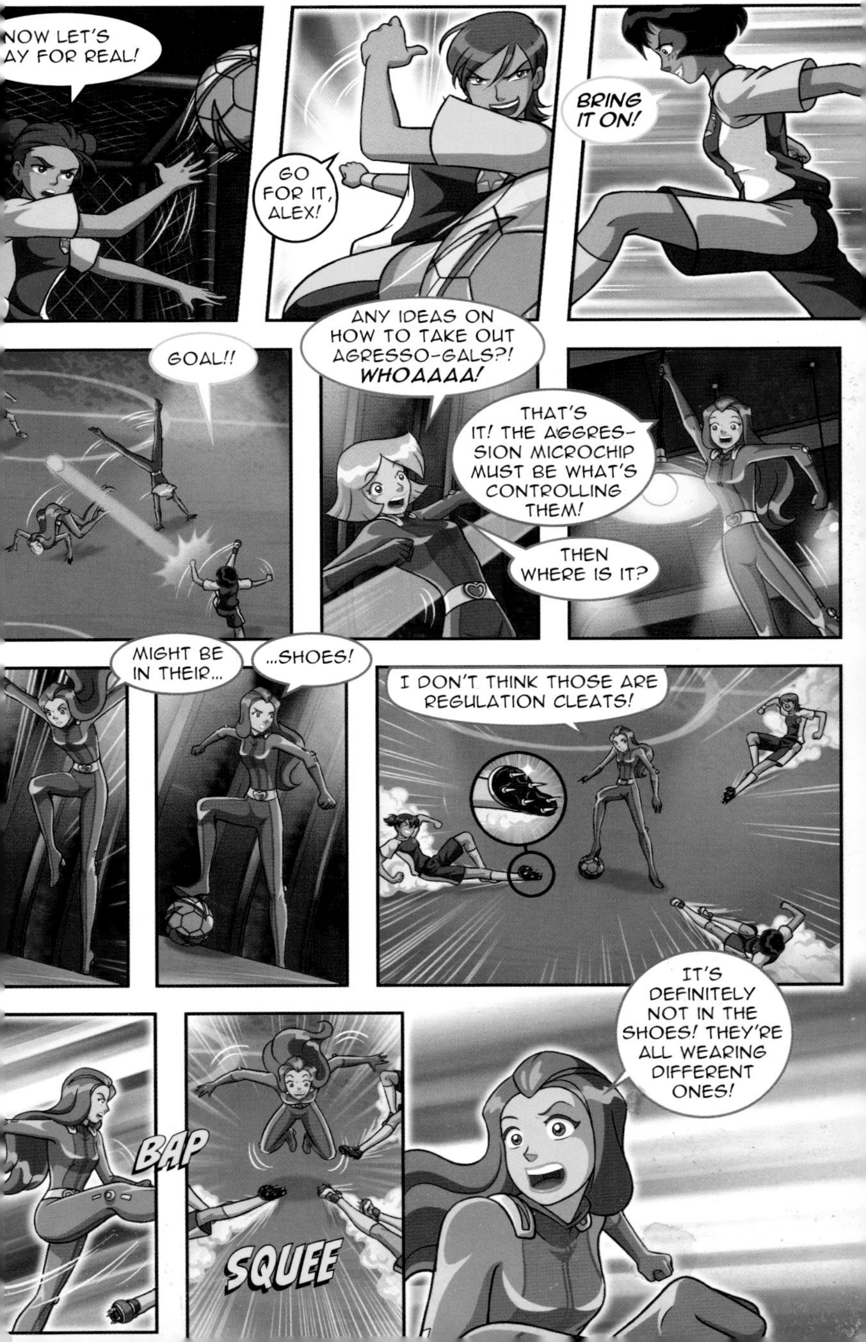
NOW LET'S
AY FOR REAL!
GO FOR IT, ALEX!
BRING IT ON!
GOAL!!
ANY IDEAS ON HOW TO TAKE OUT AGRESSO-GALS?! WHOAAAA!
THAT'S IT! THE AGGRES-SION MICROCHIP MUST BE WHAT'S CONTROLLING THEM!
THEN WHERE IS IT?
MIGHT BE IN THEIR...
...SHOES!
I DON'T THINK THOSE ARE REGULATION CLEATS!
BAP
SQUEE
IT'S DEFINITELY NOT IN THE SHOES! THEY'RE ALL WEARING DIFFERENT ONES!

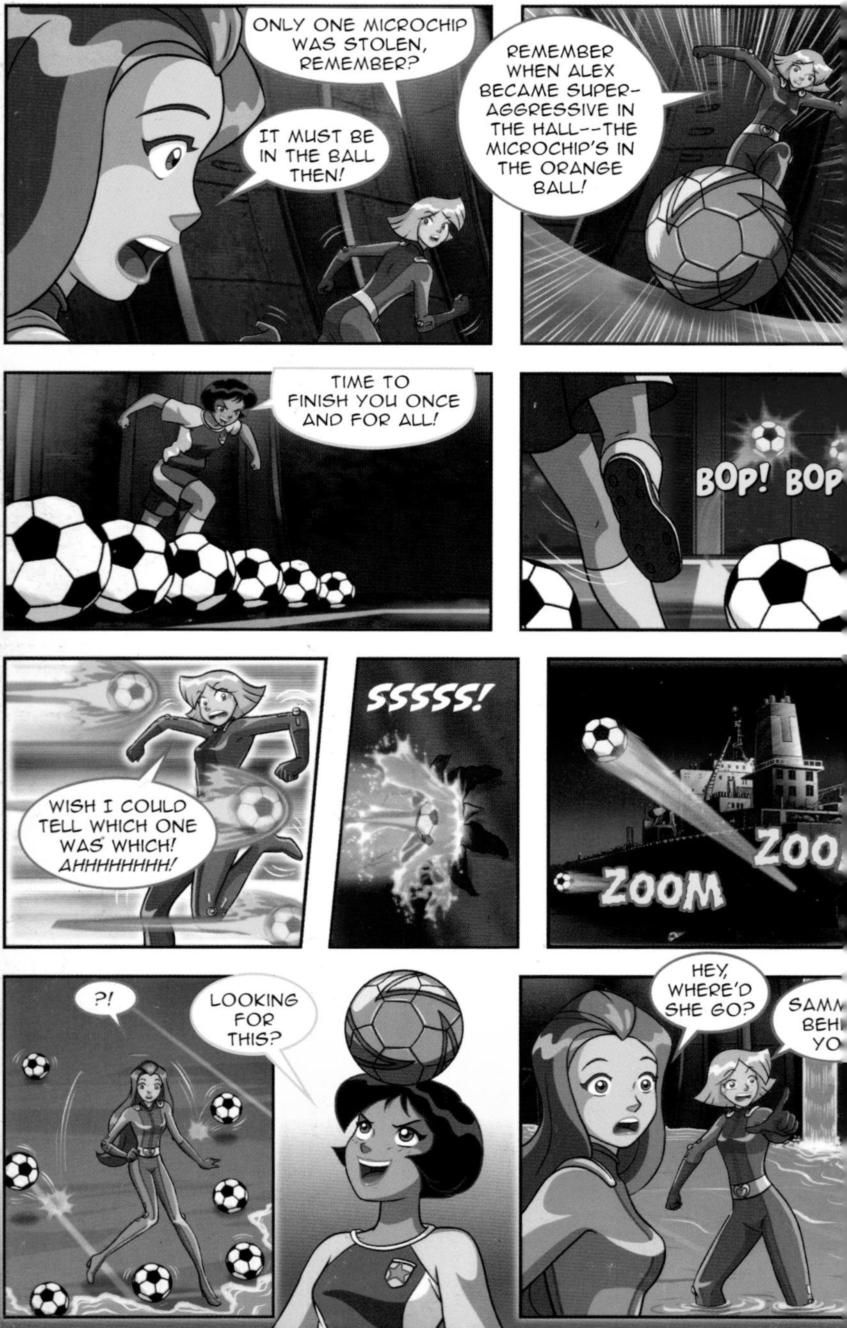
ONLY ONE MICROCHIP WAS STOLEN, REMEMBER?
IT MUST BE IN THE BALL THEN!
REMEMBER WHEN ALEX BECAME SUPER-AGGRESSIVE IN THE HALL--THE MICROCHIP'S IN THE ORANGE BALL!
TIME TO FINISH YOU ONCE AND FOR ALL!
BOP! BOP
WISH I COULD TELL WHICH ONE WAS WHICH! AHHHHHHHH!
SSSSS!
ZOOM
ZOO
?!
LOOKING FOR THIS?
HEY, WHERE'D SHE GO?

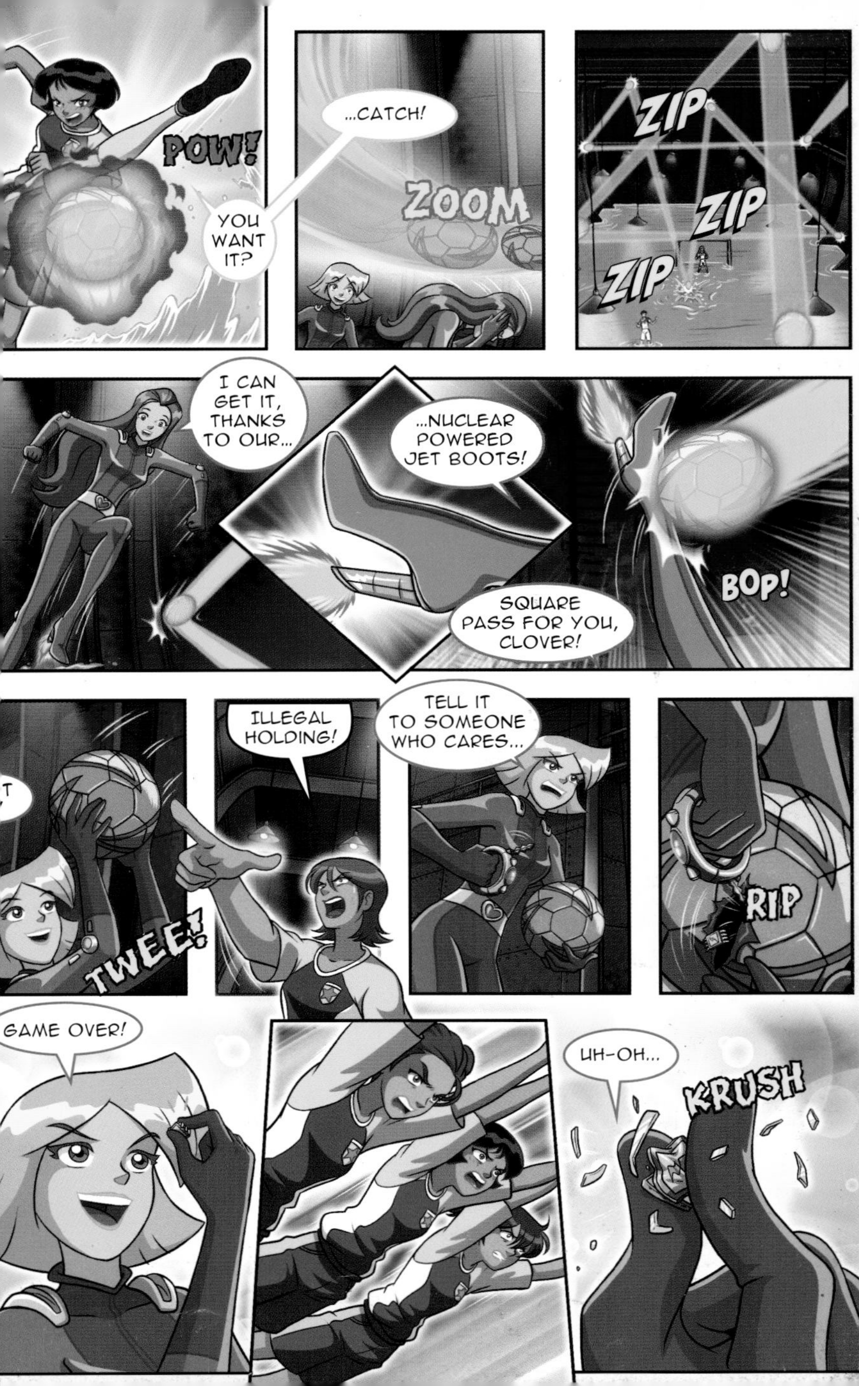
POW!
YOU WANT IT?
...CATCH!
ZOOM
ZIP
ZIP
ZIP
I CAN GET IT, THANKS TO OUR...
...NUCLEAR POWERED JET BOOTS!
SQUARE PASS FOR YOU, CLOVER!
BOP!
TWEE!
ILLEGAL HOLDING!
TELL IT TO SOMEONE WHO CARES...
RIP
GAME OVER!
UH-OH...
KRUSH

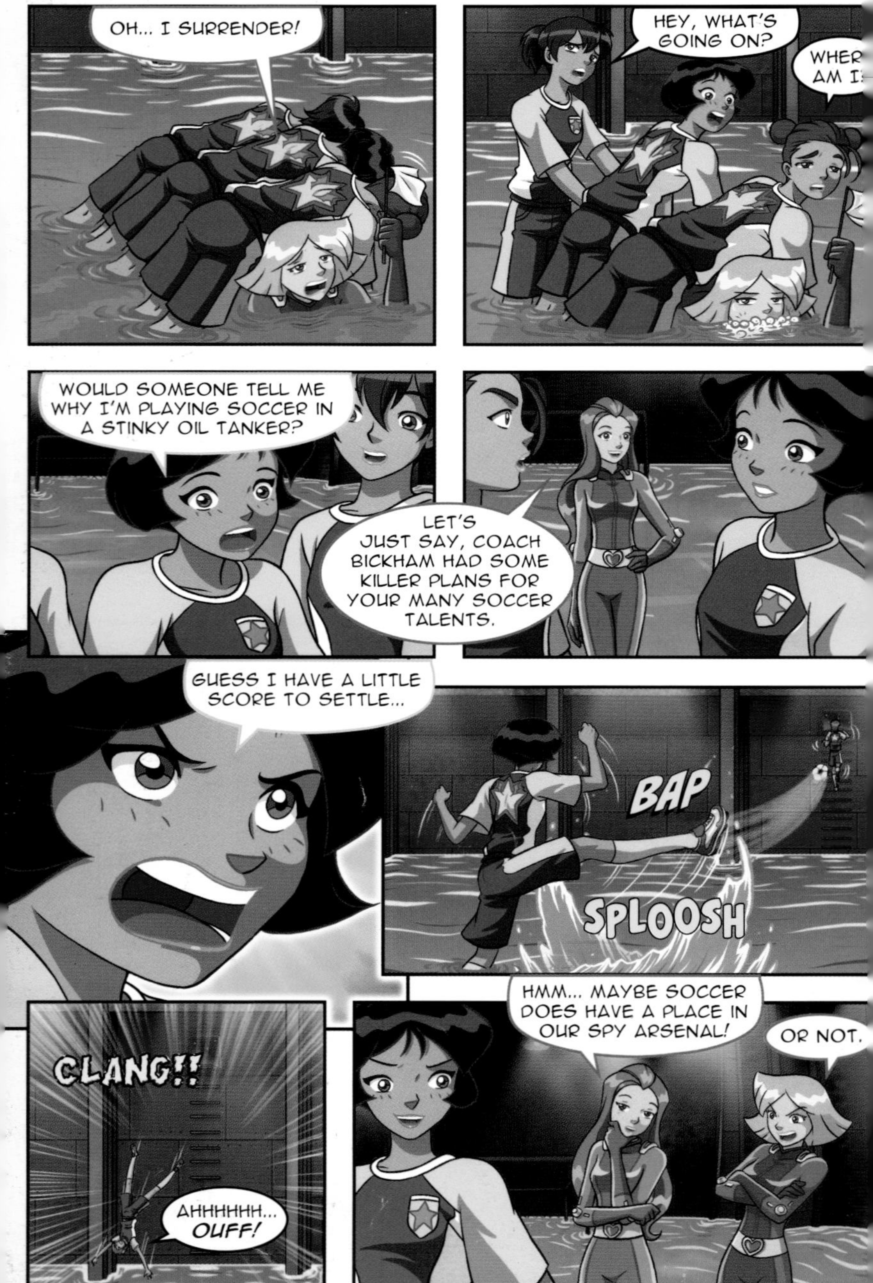
OH... I SURRENDER!
HEY, WHAT'S GOING ON?
WHER AM I
WOULD SOMEONE TELL ME WHY I'M PLAYING SOCCER IN A STINKY OIL TANKER?
LET'S JUST SAY, COACH BICKHAM HAD SOME KILLER PLANS FOR YOUR MANY SOCCER TALENTS.
GUESS I HAVE A LITTLE SCORE TO SETTLE...
BAP
SPLOOSH
CLANG!!
AHHHHHH... OUFF!
HMM... MAYBE SOCCER DOES HAVE A PLACE IN OUR SPY ARSENAL!
OR NOT.

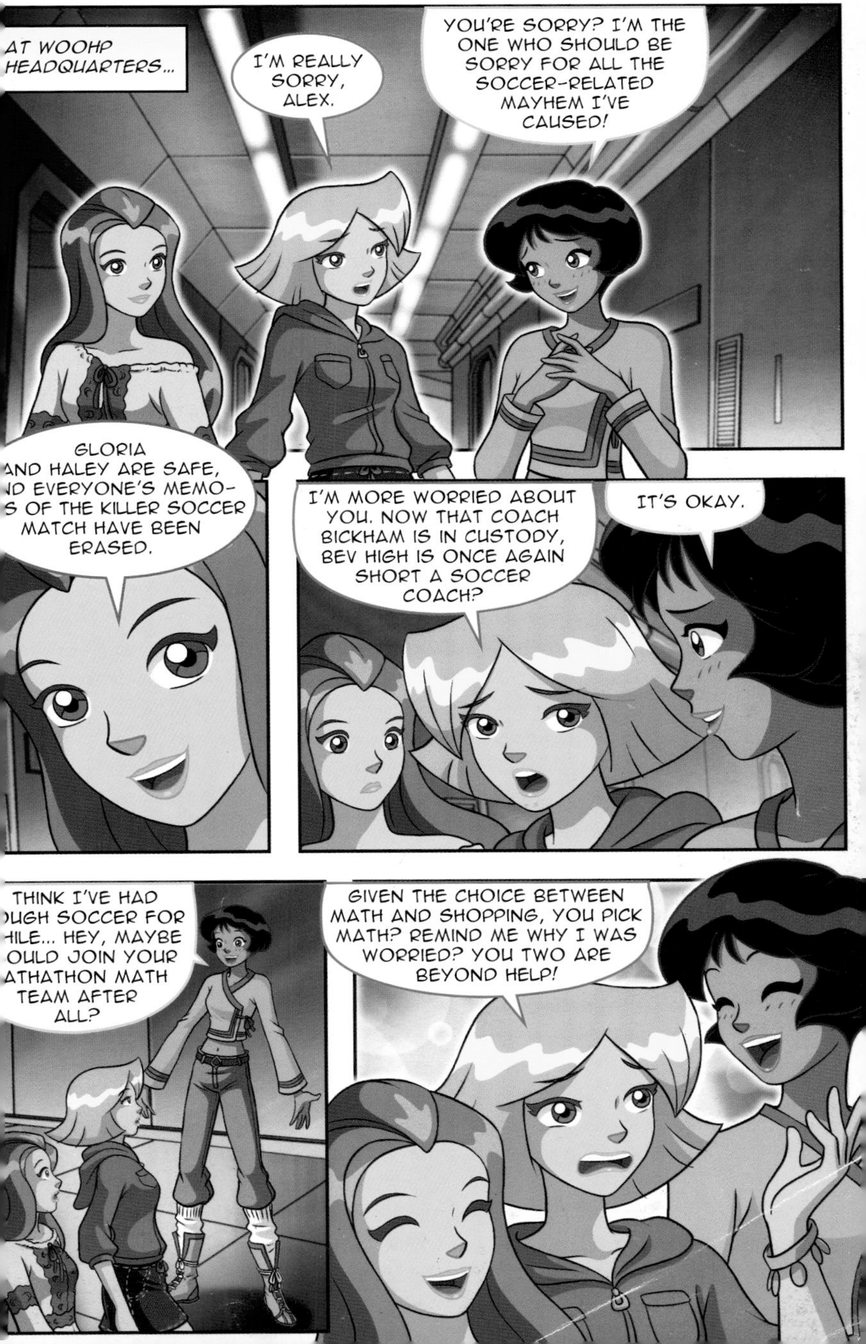
AT WOOHP HEADQUARTERS...
I'M REALLY SORRY, ALEX.
YOU'RE SORRY? I'M THE ONE WHO SHOULD BE SORRY FOR ALL THE SOCCER-RELATED MAYHEM I'VE CAUSED!
GLORIA AND HALEY ARE SAFE, ID EVERYONE'S MEMO- S OF THE KILLER SOCCER MATCH HAVE BEEN ERASED.
I'M MORE WORRIED ABOUT YOU. NOW THAT COACH BICKHAM IS IN CUSTODY, BEV HIGH IS ONCE AGAIN SHORT A SOCCER COACH?
IT'S OKAY.
THINK I'VE HAD OUGH SOCCER FOR HILE... HEY, MAYBE OULD JOIN YOUR ATHATHON MATH TEAM AFTER ALL?
GIVEN THE CHOICE BETWEEN MATH AND SHOPPING, YOU PICK MATH? REMIND ME WHY I WAS WORRIED? YOU TWO ARE BEYOND HELP!

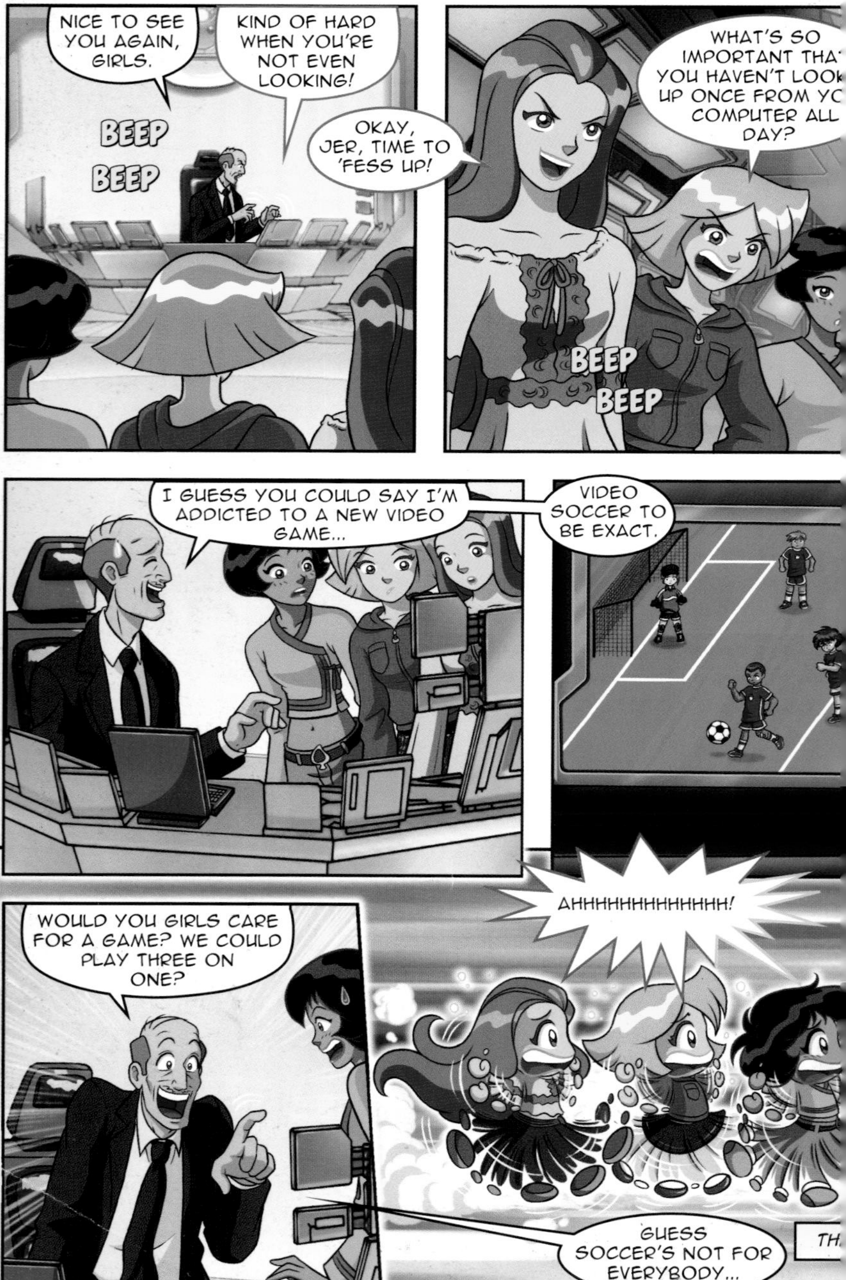
NICE TO SEE YOU AGAIN, GIRLS.
KIND OF HARD WHEN YOU'RE NOT EVEN LOOKING!
BEEP
BEEP
OKAY, JER, TIME TO 'FESS UP!
WHAT'S SO IMPORTANT THA YOU HAVEN'T LOOK UP ONCE FROM YO COMPUTER ALL DAY?
BEEP
BEEP
I GUESS YOU COULD SAY I'M ADDICTED TO A NEW VIDEO GAME...
VIDEO SOCCER TO BE EXACT.
WOULD YOU GIRLS CARE FOR A GAME? WE COULD PLAY THREE ON ONE?
AHHHHHHHHHHHHH!
GUESS SOCCER'S NOT FOR EVERYBODY...
TH

AL SNEEK PEEK AT TOTALLY SPIES GRAPHIC NOVEL #5 "MANI-MANIAC"

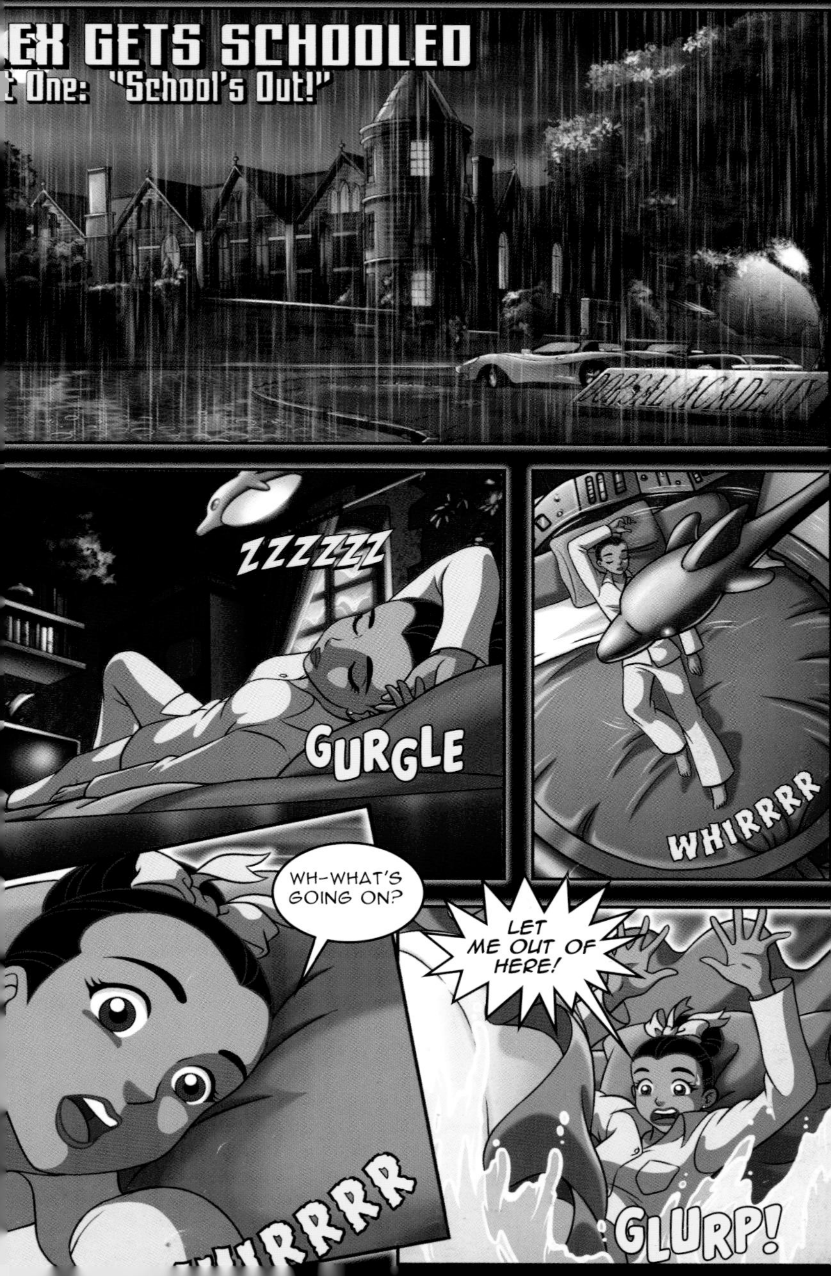
EX GETS SCHOOLED
t One: "School's Out!"
ZZZZZZ
GURGLE
WHIRRRR
WH-WHAT'S GOING ON?
LET ME OUT OF HERE!
WHIRRRR
GLURP!

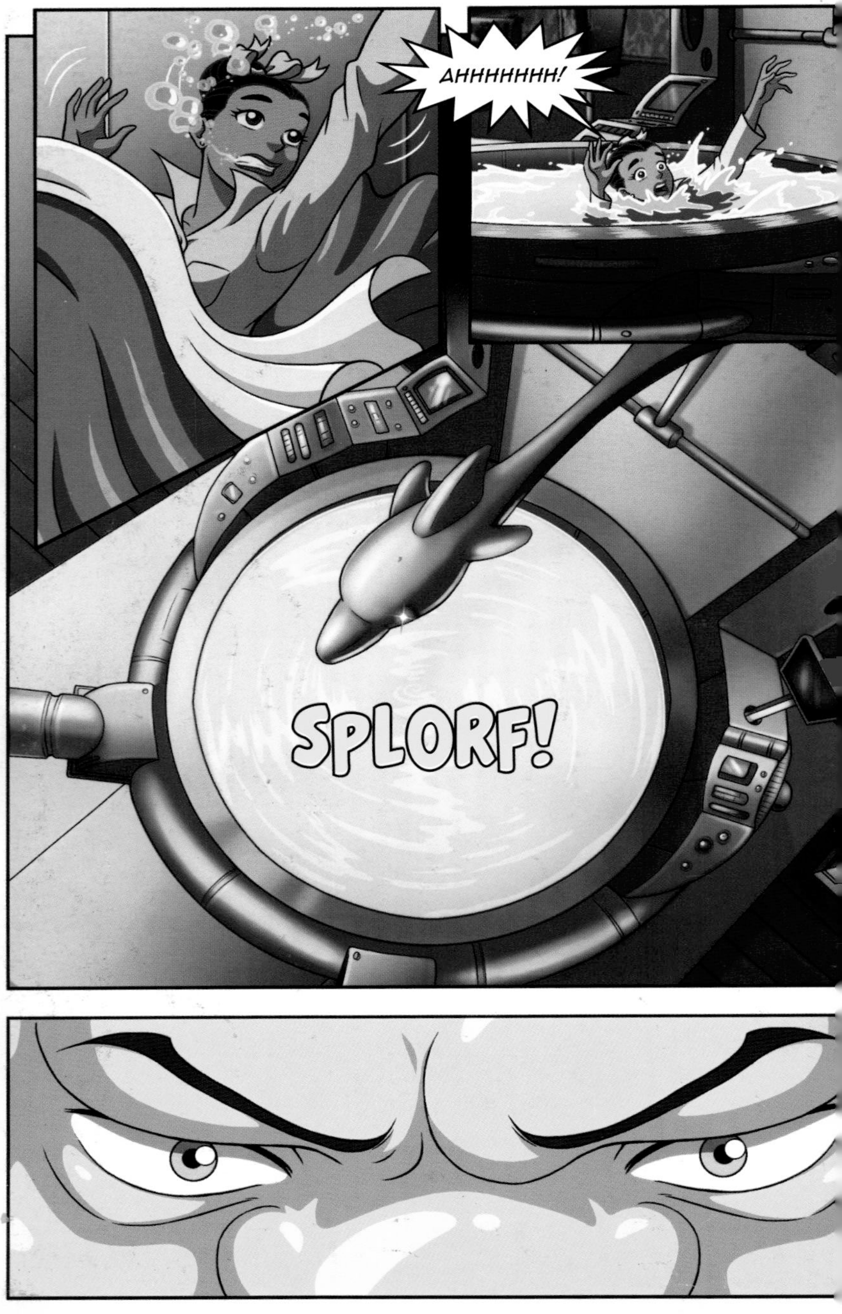
AHHHHHHH!
SPLORF!

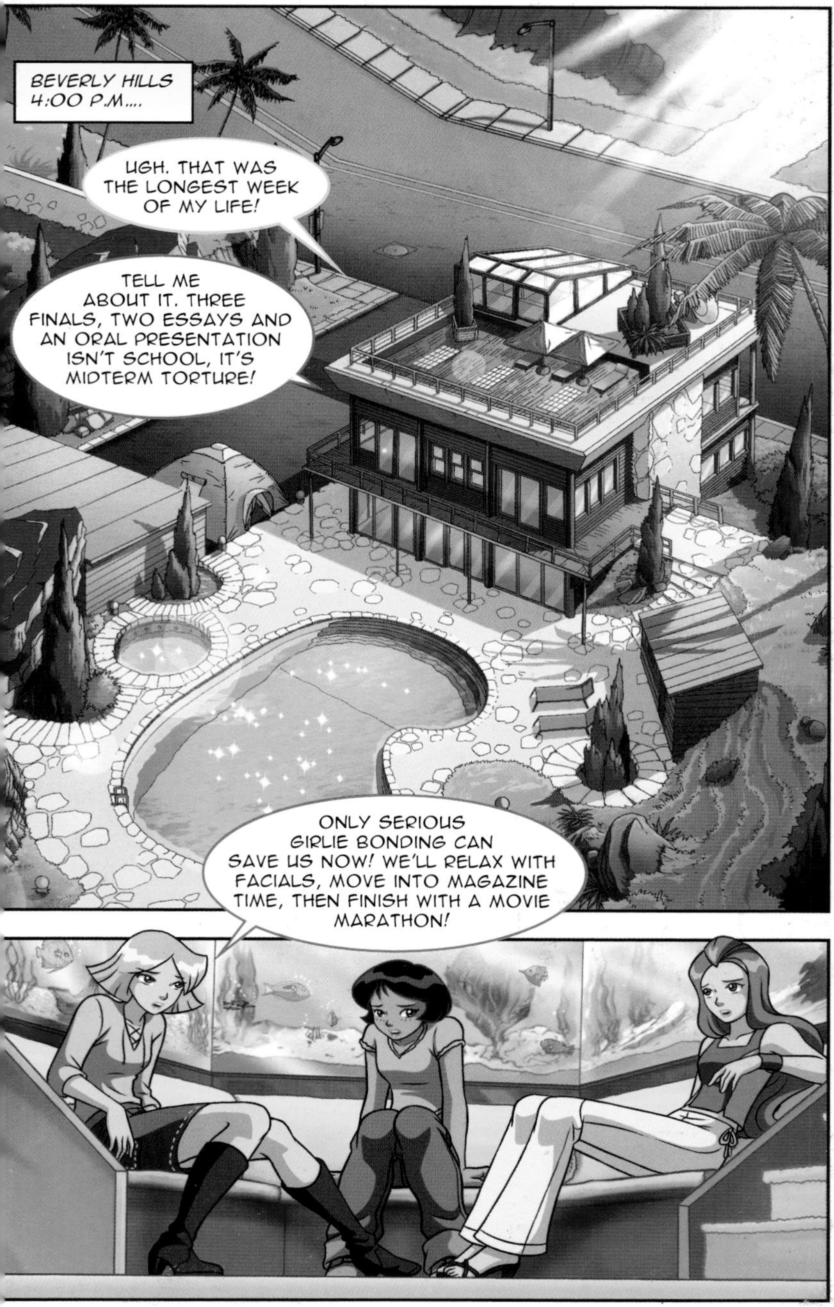
BEVERLY HILLS 4:00 P.M....
UGH. THAT WAS THE LONGEST WEEK OF MY LIFE!
TELL ME ABOUT IT. THREE FINALS, TWO ESSAYS AND AN ORAL PRESENTATION ISN'T SCHOOL, IT'S MIDTERM TORTURE!
ONLY SERIOUS GIRLIE BONDING CAN SAVE US NOW! WE'LL RELAX WITH FACIALS, MOVE INTO MAGAZINE TIME, THEN FINISH WITH A MOVIE MARATHON!

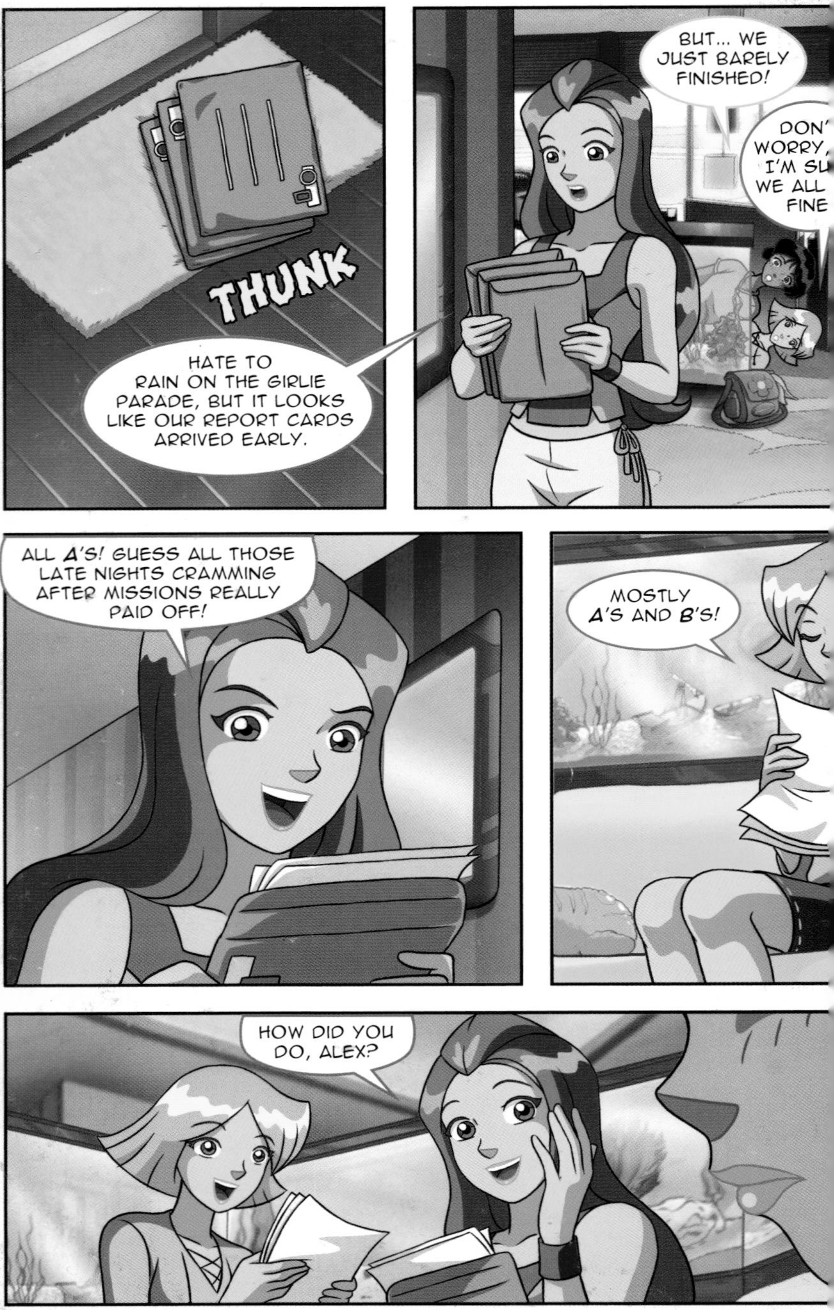
THUNK
HATE TO RAIN ON THE GIRLIE PARADE, BUT IT LOOKS LIKE OUR REPORT CARDS ARRIVED EARLY.
BUT... WE JUST BARELY FINISHED!
DON' WORRY, I'M SU WE ALL FINE
ALL A'S! GUESS ALL THOSE LATE NIGHTS CRAMMING AFTER MISSIONS REALLY PAID OFF!
MOSTLY A'S AND B'S!
HOW DID YOU DO, ALEX?

WATCH OUT FOR PAPERCUTZ

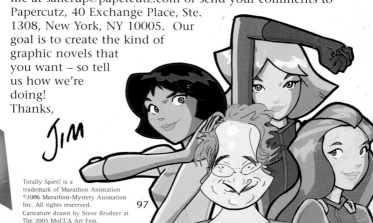

The publisher of graphic novels created just for YOU!

Hi, Papercutz people! It's me Jim Salicrup, the luckiest graphic novel editor in the world! Every day I get to work with the best writers, artists, letterers, and colorists to create comics for the best fans in the world – YOU!

As you may've noticed, we've added these Papercutz backpages — at no extra cost – to all of our ongoing graphic novel series. It's our way of keeping you up-to-date with all the excitement happening at Papercutz.

For example, we've got a great interview with Hardy Boys writer Scott Lobdell, an update on the new Nancy Drew movie, reports on Papercutz on Campus and in The New Book of Knowledge, and even a look at the very first Hardy Boys comicbook!

In fact, we're covering so much that we don't have any room left to tell you what's up in the world of Totally Spies! You'll just have to check www.papercutz.com or www.totallyspies.com for latest news regarding Alex, Sam, and Clover.

And don't forget – we always want to hear from you! Tell us what you think of our stories, our artwork, our characters, or anything at all regarding our graphic novels! Email me at salicrup@papercutz.com or send your comments to Papercutz, 40 Exchange Place, Ste. 1308, New York, NY 10005. Our goal is to create the kind of graphic novels that you want – so tell us how we're doing!

Thanks,

Jim

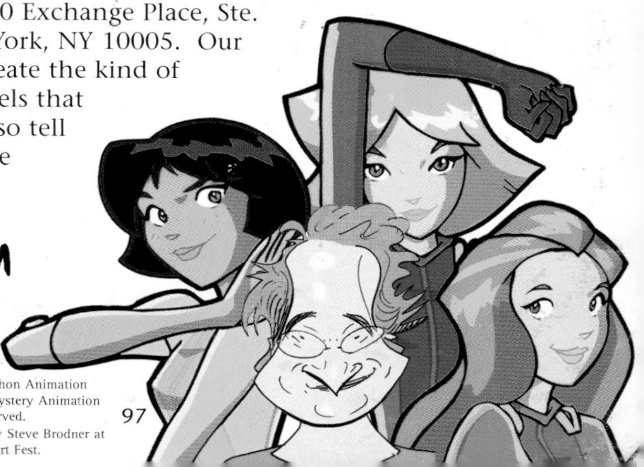

Caricature drawn by Steve Brodner at The 2005 MoCCA Art Fest.

PAPERCUTZ ON CAMPUS

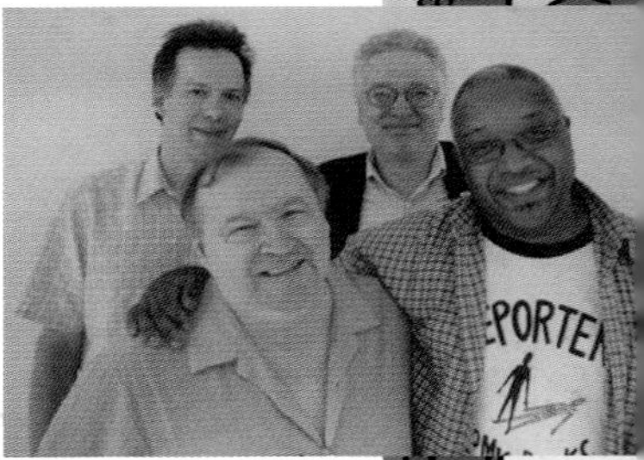

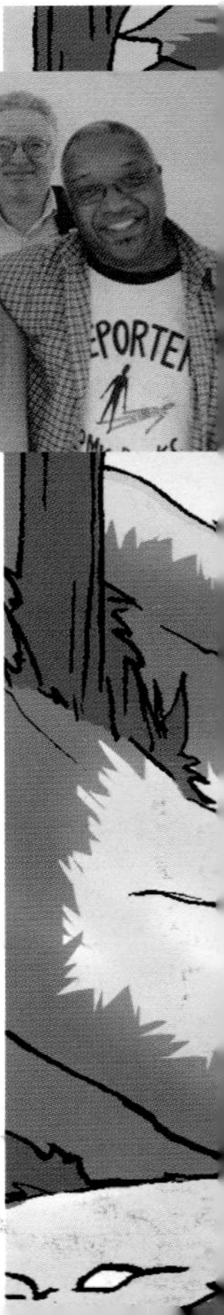

This may be hard to believe, but once upon a time comics were actually looked down upon by certain ill-informed individuals. We're delighted to report that those dark days are far behind us. These days comics and graphic novels are now strongly embraced by the academic community. Recently Papercutz Editor-in-Chief Jim Salicrup and Zorro writer Don McGregor were invited to join Pete Friedrich, editor of Roadstrips: A Graphic Journey Across America, on a panel hosted by Publishers Weekly Senior News Editor, Calvin Reid, all about graphic novels at the Columbia School of Journalism. The panel was presented before the one hundred students enrolled in the publishing course, which included graphic novels. The highly attentive audience had lots of great questions during the Q&A segment, and moderator Calvin Reid did an amazing job of keeping our long-winded Editor-in-Chief from going off on too many tangents. Don McGregor, whose Sabre graphic novel was one of the first to be offered to the American comics market directly in 1978, spoke enthusiastically, in his inimitable manner, about his experiences in the comics world. Jim Salicrup shared some of his experiences working with Don, especially how they approached taking the classic Zorro character and adapting it into the Papercutz graphic novel style. That style is to create the best possible graphic novels for audiences of all ages. In Zorro graphic novels #1-3, Don along with artist Sidney Lima does just that.

Both Jim and Don had a great time talking to the students, and signing copies of Zorro graphic novel #1, "Scars!" But when it was all over, Jim had to restrain himself from saying, "Class dismissed!"

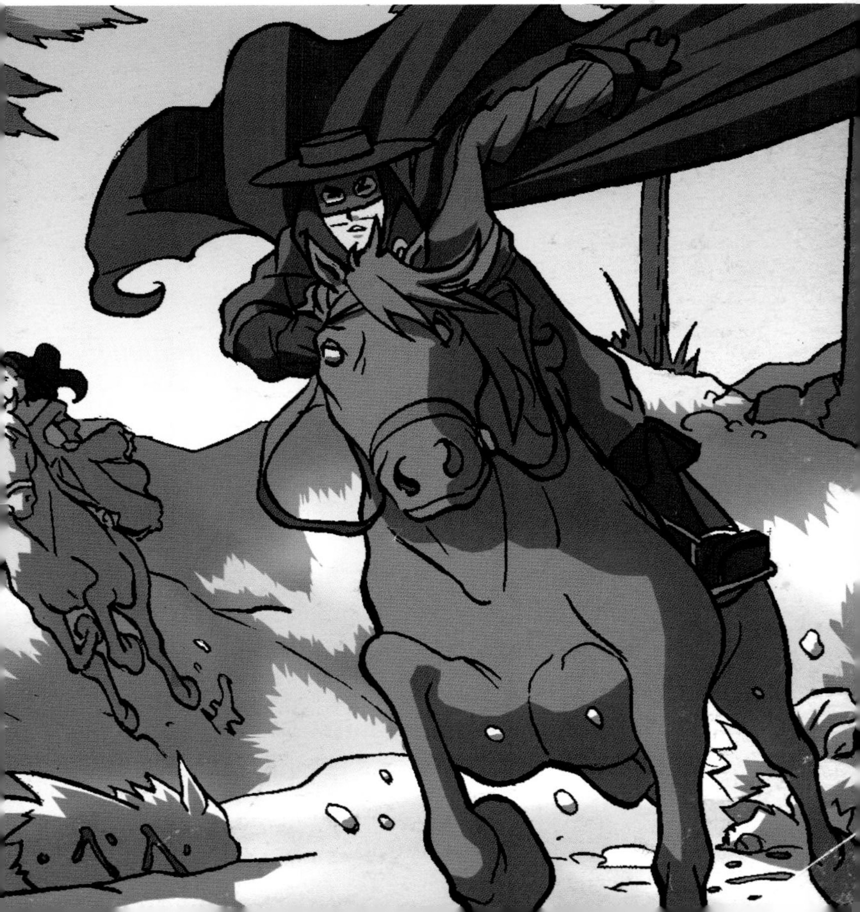

The Write Stuff

When Papercutz decided to publish the adventures of The Hardy Boys in all-new graphic novels, we never imagined we'd be able to land superstar writer Scott Lobdell, famed for his best-selling run on Marvel's The Uncanny X-Men, but somehow we did! We're thankful that Scott recently took time out of his busy movie and comics writing to answer a few questions for this interview...

The Hardy Boys ®Simon & Schuster

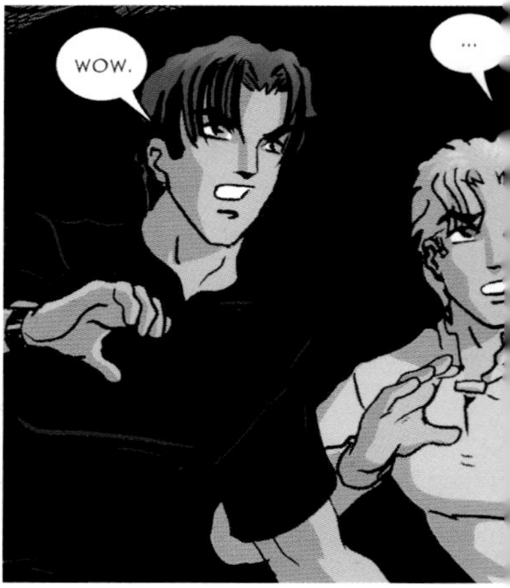
WOW.
...

Papercutz: Tell us, Scott, where are you from?

Scott: I come from a small town in upstate New York where I was raised with six brothers and sisters —quite a different experience from Joe and Frank's upbringing! I will tell you one thing, though, when you live in such a large family there isn't a lot of room for privacy so you come to appreciate your secrets because they are yours. Now, here I am, all these years later, writing the adventures of two of the world's most famous secret-busters.

Papercutz: How did you become a writer?

Scott: Years and years of rejection letters from magazines, comics, book publishers... but I kept trying. And maybe more importantly, I kept listening to the criticism and instructions from friends, family, and editors. I think, too often, beginning writers want only praise for their efforts and it is difficult to hear suggestions, or to hear that something is unclear or confusing in early drafts. I think by listening I was able to challenge myself to be a better writer. I used to say of comics "Either they are going to give up or I am! And I'm not!"

Papercutz: Did you read all the original Hardy Boys books by Franklin W. Dixon? Which is your favorite?

Scott: That is like asking me to pick out my favorite ice cream — or favorite snowflake! Every book is its own experience!

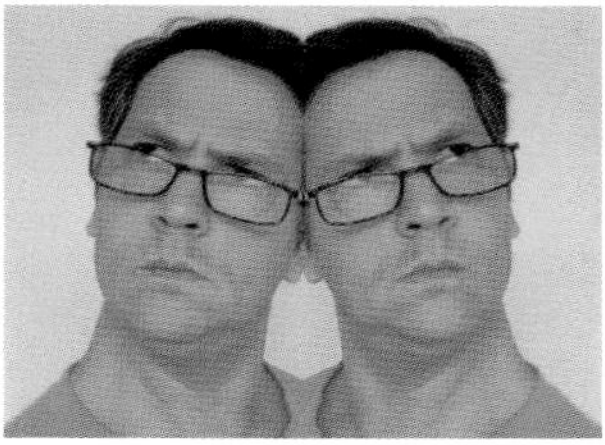

Scott agrees with Joe and Frank: when solving crimes, two heads are better than one!

Papercutz: How would you describe the Hardy Boys?

Scott: There have been a lot of famous detectives over the years, each interesting in their own way. But what I think is so compelling about Joe and Frank is their relationship. In some families there are brothers who haven't spoken for years — but here are the Hardy Boys who not only share their every adventure, but need to trust each other along every step of every case. They enjoy being together and they've always got each other's back. The only thing cooler than having a cool brother is being one.

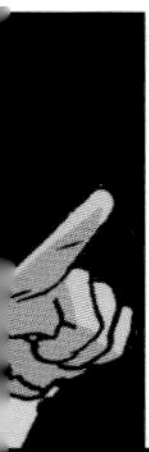

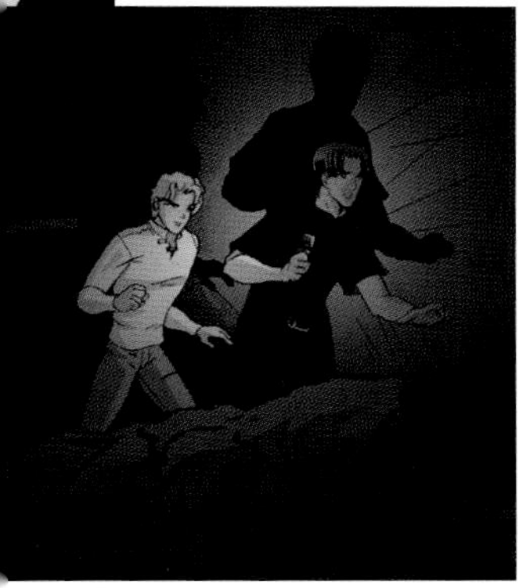

Papercutz: Where do you get your ideas?

Scott: Specifically, my Hardy Boys ideas seem to come from the headlines. *The Ocean of Osyria* and *Identity Theft* were both based on an all too real world problems. I often think, "If Joe and Frank lived in the here and now, what kind of problems would they be called on to solve as undercover brothers?"... And then I start writing.

Papercutz: How do you like working for Papercutz?
Scott: I have known Papercutz Editor-in-Chief Jim Salicrup for... a long time! Little known fact: Jim was the editor on my first published comicbook work, the historical "Last Charlie America" story for Marvel Comics' *What The — ?! #4*! So when he complains about my rarely broken deadlines, I like to point out he has no one to blame but himself! And publisher Terry Nantier puts up with a lot but always manages to be positive and supportive.

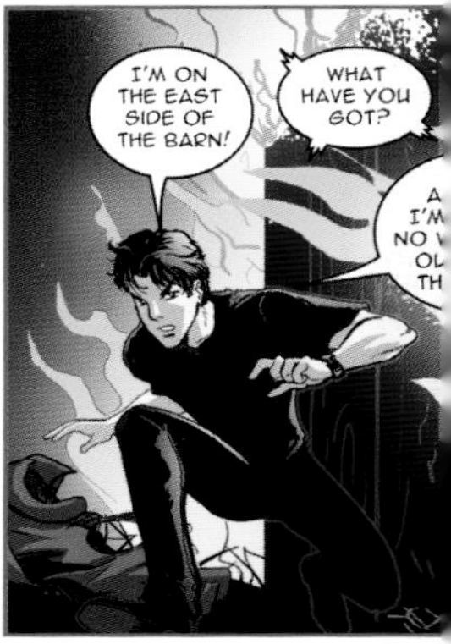
I'M ON THE EAST SIDE OF THE BARN!
WHAT HAVE YOU GOT?

Papercutz: How do you think Lea, Daniel, Sidney, and Paulo have handled your stories?
Scott: With that question, you've managed to stumble onto one of my favorite elements of writing this series of graphic novels. Unlike with most of my other comicbook writing, where I will write a plot for the artist and then wait for the penciled artwork before adding the dialogue, with The Hardy Boys I write a complete script – describing every scene with all the dialogue included. What is so fun about these books is that I don't even see them until they are published — so I get to experience all these talented artists and their storytelling techniques at the same time you do. Which makes me not only the writer of the Hardy Boys graphic novels... it also makes me a fan!

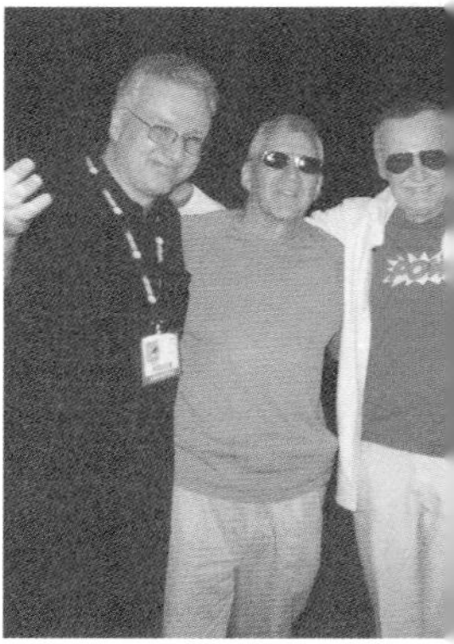
From left to right: Jim Salicrup, Gi
Champion, Stan Lee, and Scott Lo

Papercutz: What else do you write?
Scott: I am currently writing a horror movie for Rogue Pictures, a television episode of the NBC TV series, *Medium*, and an animated DVD for a guy named Ringo Starr who apparently used to be in a band from England a few years ago. (Also, if there is any justice, I'll get to work on my new favorite television show... *Jericho*!)

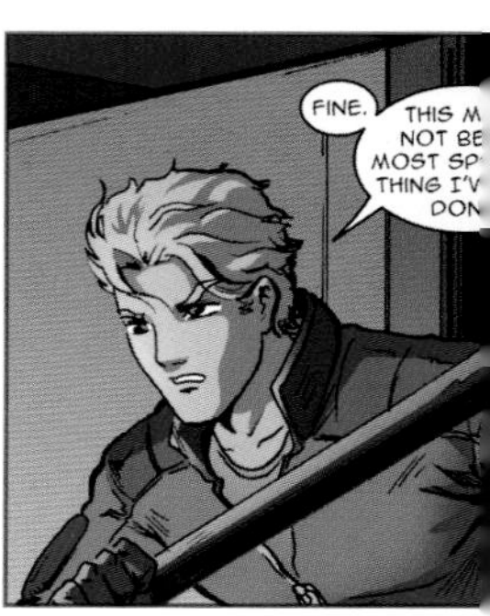
FINE.

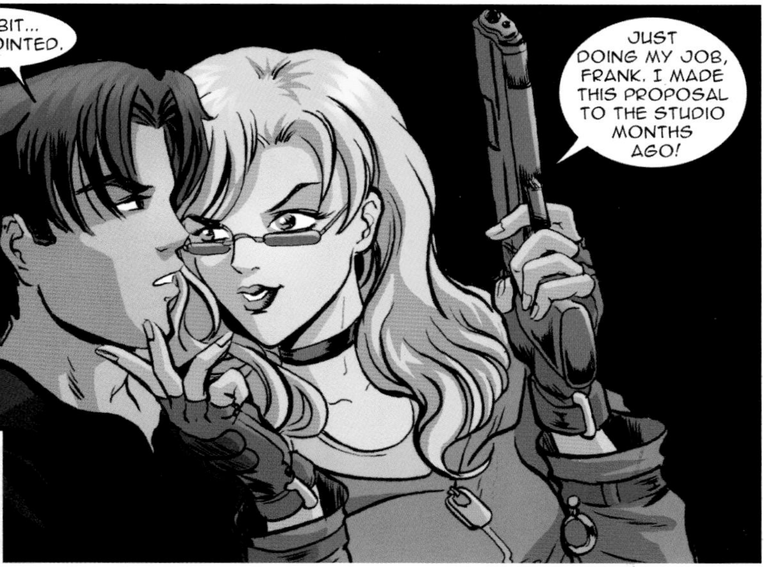
JUST DOING MY JOB, FRANK. I MADE THIS PROPOSAL TO THE STUDIO MONTHS AGO!

Papercutz: What can you tell us about future The Hardy Boys graphic novels?

Scott: I am very interested in seeing the brothers involved in cases that don't always come from A.T.A.C. I love this covert agency that uses the brothers to solve cases around the country — but I'd like to see Joe and Frank come across the occasional mystery in their free time.

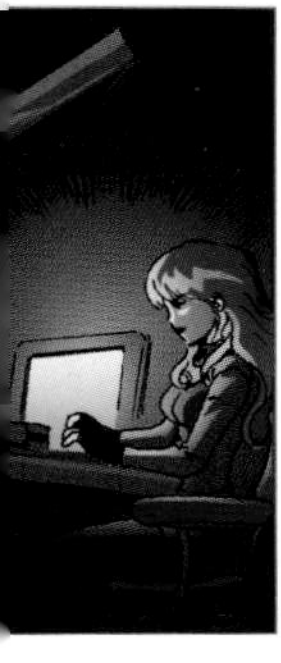

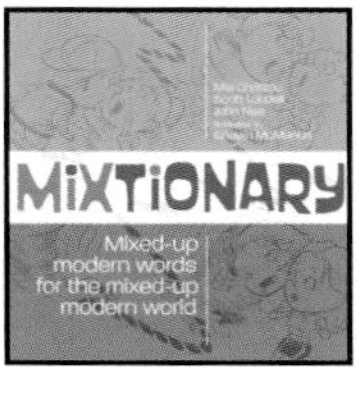
MiXTiONARY
Mixed-up modern words for the mixed-up modern world

Scott is one of the writers of Mixtionary.

The **Hardy Boys in Comics!**

Did you know that the all-new Hardy Boys graphic novels from Papercutz are not the first time Joe and Frank Hardy appeared in comics? It's actually the third series of Hardy Boys comics. We've done a little detective work ourselves and have come up with a bit of background information on the historic, very first series of Hardy Boys comics.

Way back in the 1940s and 1950s, one of the biggest comicbook publishers was Dell Comics. Known for their snappy motto, "Dell Comics are Good Comics," one of their top titles was called Four Color Comics, a reference to the four basic colors used in printing comicbooks. Surprisingly, the "Four Color Comics" title wasn't on most of its covers. According to the Official Overstreet Comic Book Price Guide, Dell published two series of Four Color Comics, the first lasting just 25 issues, and the second running for a record-breaking 1,354 issues. Yet it only was called Four Color Comics on #19 – 25 of the first series and on #1-99 and 101 of the second. Each issue featured a popular TV, movie, or comic strip character, and it was the name of the featured character that was displayed as the title on the covers. One issue could feature a western adventure based on the Gunsmoke TV series, another could adapt a John Wayne movie such as The Searchers, and yet another could spotlight comic-strip star, Mandrake, the Magician. In 1956, Four Color Comics #760 featured Walt Disney's The Hardy Boys.

"*Walt Disney's* The Hardy Boys"? That's correct. Back in 1955, the daily Disney TV series, The Mickey Mouse Club, featured a live-action four-part Hardy Boys adventure, "The Mystery of the Applegate Treasure" based on the classic Franklin W. Dixon series. The serial starred Tim Considine as Frank Hardy, Tommy Kirk as Joe Hardy, Russ Conway as Fenton Hardy, Carol Ann Campbell as Iola Morton, and Sarah Selby as Aunt Gertrude. Each episode was just fifteen minutes long, but it must've packed quite a punch. Just a couple of years later, the same cast were reunited for a fifteen-part Hardy Boys serial for The Mickey Mouse Club called "The Mystery of the Ghost Farm." The episodes have recently been released on DVD as part of the Walt Disney Treasures series.

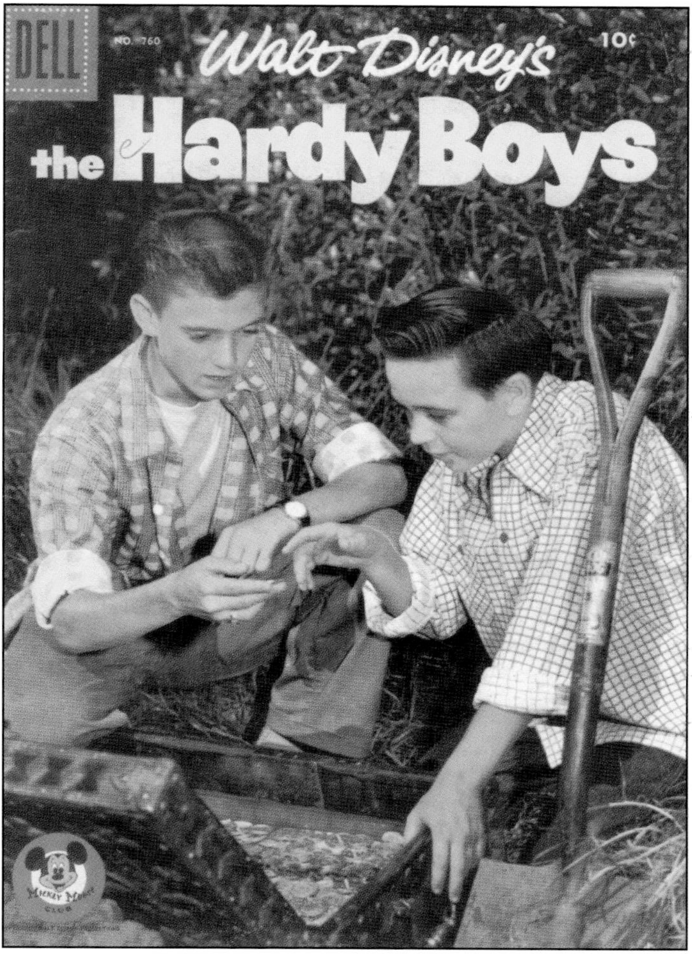
DELL
NO. 760
Walt Disney's
10¢
the Hardy Boys
Mickey Mouse
CLUB

The Hardy Boys ®Simon & Schuster

The very first Hardy Boys comicbook.

Papercutz Trivia Quiz

1) Who is the other Papercutz superstar who appeared on a Disney series in the 50s?
2) Which real-life Papercutz person appeared on Disney's The Mickey Mouse Club?
(Answers on next page)

Since Four Color Comics adapted so many Disney TV shows, it seemed only natural that they'd also include the TV version of The Hardy Boys. While the stars were just 15 and 14 years old at the time of their first Hardy Boys serial, and Tommy Kirk wasn't blond, the serial did capture the spirit of the classic books. The comic-book covers featured photos from the TV serial, and the interior artwork featured the actors' likenesses. The first comic nicely adapted "The Mystery of the Applegate Treasure," with suitably shadowy artwork providing the proper mysterious mood. Three more issues of Four Color Comics featured The Hardy Boys, #830 (August '57), #887 (January '58), and #964 (January '59). The Hardy Boys wouldn't appear in comics again until 1970 – but that's a story we'll save for the next installment of "The Hardy Boys in Comics!"

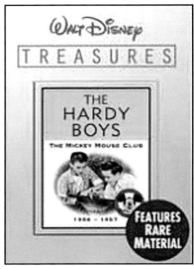

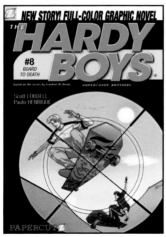

Walt Disney
TREASURES
THE HARDY BOYS
THE MICKEY MOUSE CLUB
FEATURES RARE MATERIAL
Hardy Boys DVD

NEW STORY! FULL-COLOR GRAPHIC NOVEL
THE HARDY BOYS
#8
BOARD TO DEATH
UNDERCOVER BROTHERS
Scott LOBDELL
Paulo HENRIQUE
PAPERCUTZ
Available now!

Answers:

1)The star of three Papercutz graphic novels, Zorro. He was played by Guy Williams in the Disney TV series, which debuted September, 1957.
2)Papercutz Editor-in-Chief Jim Salicrup appeared on an episode of the 90's revival of The Mickey Mouse Club, which also featured Britney Spears, Christina Aguilera, K.C. Chasez, Keri Russell, Ryan Gosling, and Justin Timberlake.

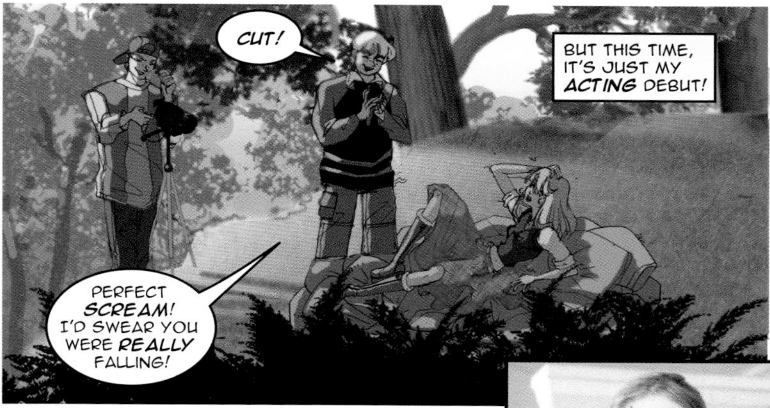
CUT!
BUT THIS TIME, IT'S JUST MY ACTING DEBUT!
PERFECT SCREAM! I'D SWEAR YOU WERE REALLY FALLING!

Nancy Drew®Simon & Schuster

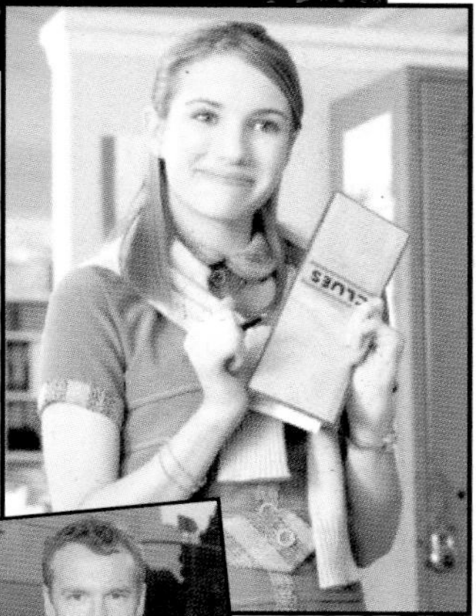

NANCY DREW MOVIE UPDATE – COMING SOONER!

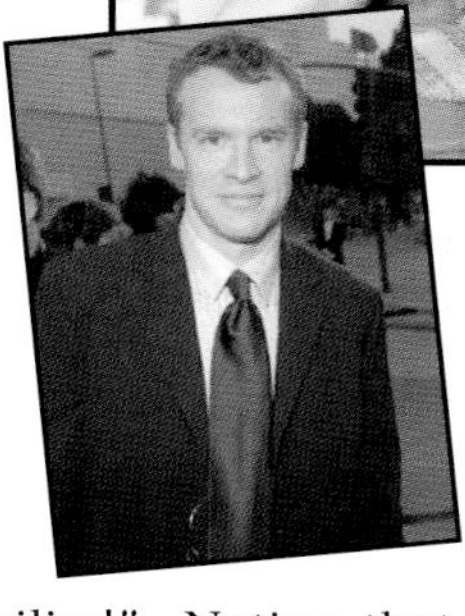

Great news, Nancy Drew fans! The release of the all-new Nancy Drew movie Warner Bros. has been moved from August 2007 to June 2007! That's right, the movie we've all been waiting for will soon be at your local multiplex starting the 15th of June 2007, starring Emma Roberts, of Nickelodeon's hit show *Unfabulous*, as our favorite Girl Detective.

Time Magazine, commenting on a Emma's similarity to a certain major movie star said, "Jeepers, she looks familiar!" Noting that Emma "shares the broad, screen-ready smile of her Aunt Julia (yes, that Julia)." The New York Daily News reported that Emma thought making the film "was a lot of hard work" but that she "liked the way it turned out." In the movie she has to "unravel a Hollywood mystery. Probably the most challenging thing was there was a lot of running around and a lot of stunts." The movie also stars Tate Donovan, as Nancy's lawyer dad, Carson Drew.

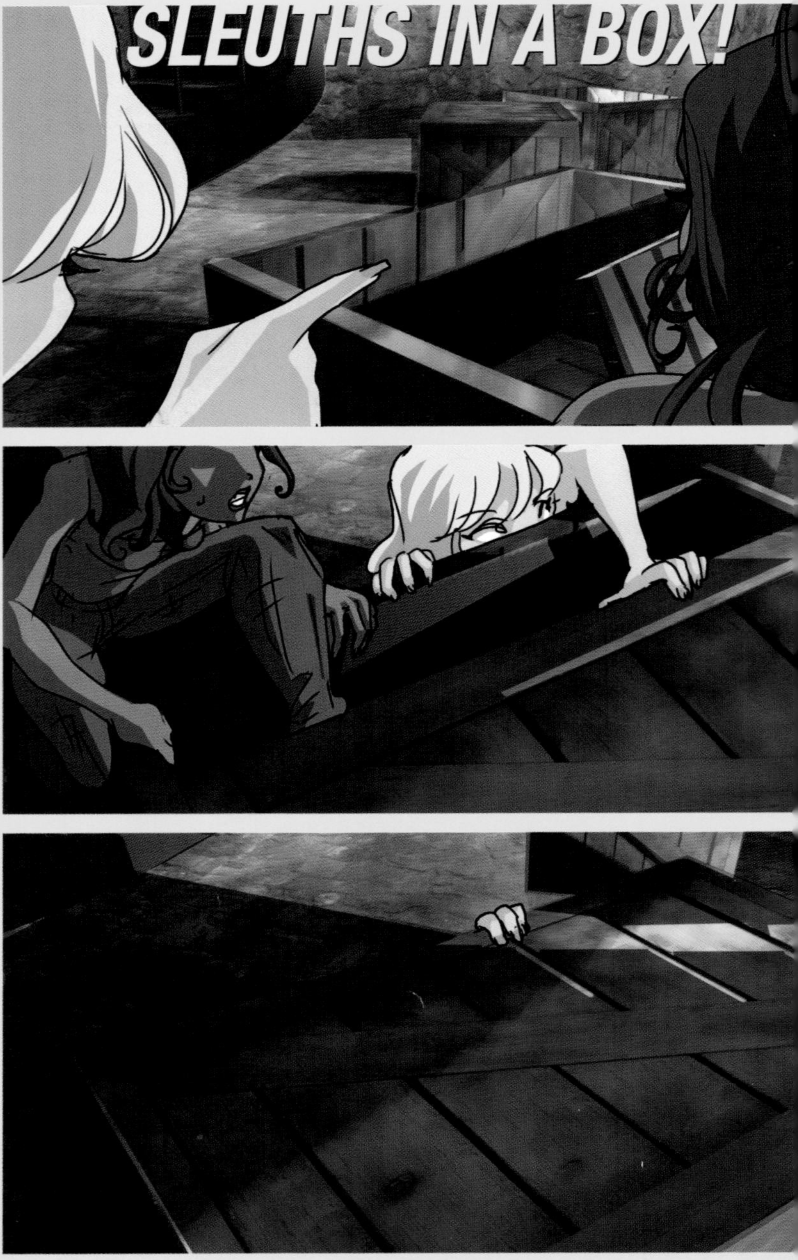
SLEUTHS IN A BOX!

Nancy Drew®Simon & Schuster

Nancy Drew in a box.

Back when Nancy Drew and her friend Kalpana were trying to escape from the bad guys in Nancy Drew graphic novel #4 "The Girl Who Wasn't There," they chose to get into a wooden box. It wasn't one of the Girl Detective's better ideas – they got bounced around pretty bad before getting re-captured.

What is a good idea, however, is collecting the first four volumes of Nancy Drew's Papercutz graphic novels in a box. It's such a good idea, that the first four Hardy Boys Papercutz graphic novels are also being collected in a boxed set. If you just started reading either series, these boxed sets are a great way to catch up on the early volumes at a great price. It's also a cool way to store your Nancy Drew and Hardy Boys graphic novels on your bookshelf.

NEW STORIES! FULL-COLOR GRAPHIC NOVELS
NANCY DREW
girl detective
INCLUDES FREE NANCY DREW COMPUTER GAME!
BASED ON THE SERIES BY CAROLYN KEENE
Stefan PETRUCHA • SHO MURASE
SPECIALLY PRICED BOX SET OF #1-4!
PAPERCUTZ
#1 #2 #3 #4

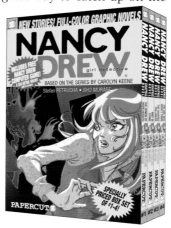

As a super special bonus, every Nancy Drew boxed set also features the Her Interactive Nancy Drew PC game "The Haunted Carousel." The game itself is sold separately for about $20.00, but comes free with the Nancy Drew boxed set. This has got to be one of the best deals ever! And since the Boxed Set also features Nancy Drew graphic novel #4, you get to see how Nancy and Kalpana finally do escape the bad guys!

NEW STORIES! FULL-COLOR GRAPHIC NOVELS
THE HARDY BOYS
SPECIALLY PRICED BOX SET OF #1-4!
UNDERCOVER BROTHERS
Scott LOBDELL • Lea HERNANDEZ
Daniel RENDON
based on the series by Franklin W. Dixon
PAPERCUTZ
#1 #2 #3 #4

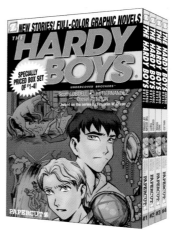

Even if you already have these great graphic novels, the Nancy Drew and The Hardy Boys Boxed Sets make a great holiday or birthday present for friends or family.

If you can't find these great Papercutz Boxed Sets at your favorite bookstores, or at Target or Sam's Clubs, just ask your favorite bookstore to order it for you. They'll be happy to do it.

TWO FOR THE BOOKS...

Everyone at Papercutz is still bustin' with pride that our very first Nancy Drew graphic novel, "The Demon of River Heights" won the 2006 Ben Franklin Award for Best Graphic Novel of the year. So you can just imagine how we felt when we saw The New Book of Knowledge 2006 Annual and it featured an article about the 75th Anniversary of Nancy Drew. The Young People's Book of the Year highlights events from 2005, and right there on page 259 is the beautiful cover of Nancy Drew graphic novel # 1 drawn by Sho Murase. The article is very well-written, giving a fact-filled history of everyone's favorite Girl Detective.

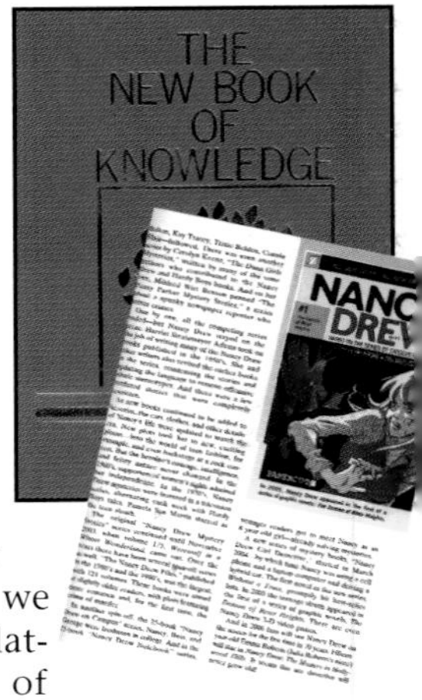
THE NEW BOOK OF KNOWLEDGE

For all of us at Papercutz, the publication of our first graphic novels was a major event. After all, we were launching our company as well. We're flattered that the editors of The New Book of Knowledge included the Nancy Drew graphic novel amongst all the amazing events of 2005. We're proud to be a small part of pop culture phenomenon that is Nancy Drew.

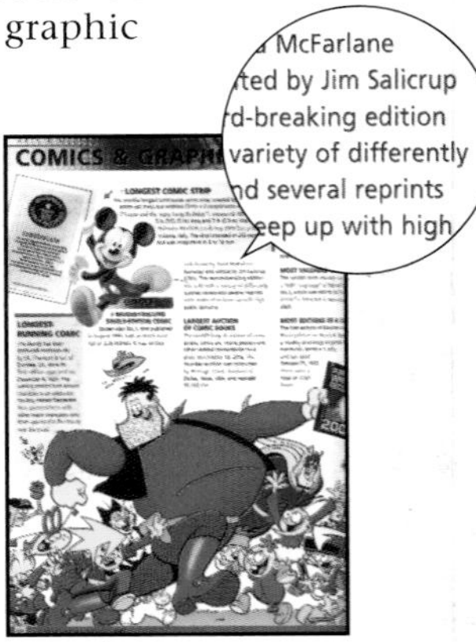

And if all of that wasn't enough to give us all swelled heads, you should've seen our Editor-in-Chief Jim Salicrup when Papercutz letterer Mark Lerer showed him the 2007 Guinness Book of World Records. Turns out that Spider-Man #1, the comic written and drawn by Todd McFarlane that Jim launched back when he was an editor at Marvel Comics is cited as the biggest-selling single-edition issue of comic ever published. While Jim is thrilled by the recognition, he vows to break that record at Papercutz. And at the rate things have been going for the graphic novel publisher for tweens, that may not be such an impossible goal!

A PAPERCUTZ™ MINI-MYSTERY?

Can you identify the boy being shot at on this page?

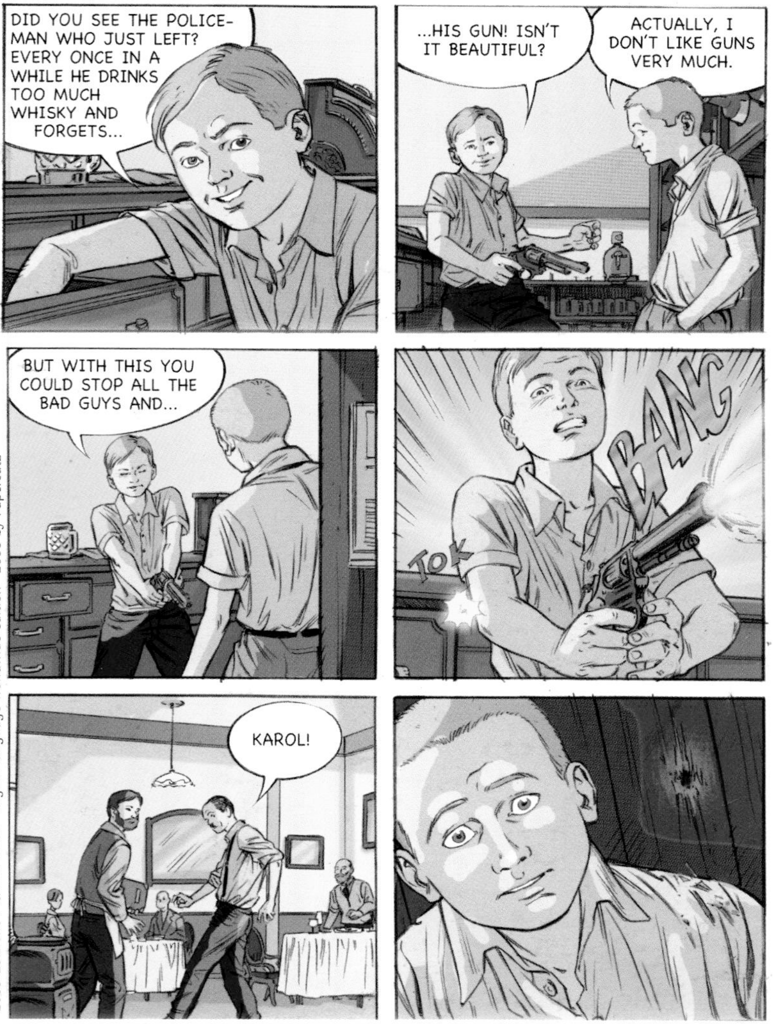

DID YOU SEE THE POLICEMAN WHO JUST LEFT? EVERY ONCE IN A WHILE HE DRINKS TOO MUCH WHISKY AND FORGETS...
...HIS GUN! ISN'T IT BEAUTIFUL?
ACTUALLY, I DON'T LIKE GUNS VERY MUCH.
BUT WITH THIS YOU COULD STOP ALL THE BAD GUYS AND...
BANG
TOK
KAROL!

Turn the page for the answer...

...it's young Karol Wojtyla, the boy who would become Pope John Paul II.

It's just a small part of the special Papercutz graphic novel The Life of John Paul II ...*In Comics!* It's an epic true tale of a young Polish boy and his amazing life. Here's a review that we just have to share with you...

"Once in a lifetime, someone extraordinary rises from the sea of humanity to lead by example.

"Pope John Paul II, Karol Wojtyla, was that man for our century. The leader of the Catholic Church, he rose from war torn Poland amidst propaganda, from a life of athletics to answer the greater call. Karol Wojtyla (1920-2005) gave himself fully to the Church, his savior Jesus, and to the service of those around him.

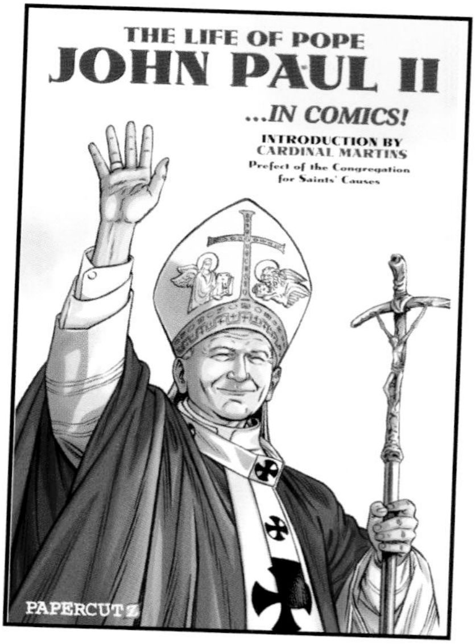
THE LIFE OF POPE
JOHN PAUL II
...IN COMICS!
INTRODUCTION BY
CARDINAL MARTINS
Prefect of the Congregation
for Saints' Causes
PAPERCUTZ

"Alessandro Mainardi and Werner Maresta and have combined their talents to tell the story of the Man who would be Pope, the man who reached out to the youth of the world, the man who reached out with an olive branch of ecumenism. The resulting 96 page graphic novel is outstanding. With such an active life, this could easily have been a thousand-pages long, but prayerfully chosen incidents portray the growth of young Karol from child, to actor, to priest, to bishop to Pope. Along the way, God's hand can be clearly seen in his life. As Pope, he traveled the world. As Pope, he reached out to any who hear. As Pope, he visited his native Poland to bring the gospel message and hope.

"The inspirational papacy he led is described from his own words and his faith and hope clearly shine through. I love the inclusion of scripture, and the thoughtful pacing of the story. Even after his passing, his influence will carry on.

"One of the many faith filled moments that captured me as I read this was the closing of his letters...OAMG, 'Omnium ad Maioram Dei Gloriam', all in the highest glory of God. I was filled with awe and a sense of admiration for Pope John Paul II.

"Through his example, the whole world was inspired. Just like you will be when you read this book.

"Look for this at your local bookstore or online at www.papercutz.com.

"I remain,
"A man of faith.
"Tim Lasiuta

"OAMG"

jgn